REBEL FIRE

By Andrew Lane

Sherlock Holmes: The Legend Begins

Death Cloud

Rebel Fire

ANDREW LANE

FARRAR STRAUS GIROUX
New York

SQUARE FISH

An Imprint of Macmillan Publishing Group, LLC

 First published in Great Britain under the title *Red Leech* by Macmillan Children's Books, 2011. Printed in the United States of America by LSC Communications US, LLC (Lakeside Classic), Harrisonburg, Virginia. For information, address Square Fish, 175 Fifth Avenue, New York, NY 10010.

Library of Congress Cataloging-in-Publication Data

Lane, Andrew.

[Red leech]

Rebel fire / Andrew Lane.

p. cm. — (Sherlock Holmes. The legend begins)

Summary: In 1868, teenaged Sherlock Holmes discovers that his American tutor is hunting a notorious killer who was supposedly killed by the United States government, but who is apparently alive and well in Surrey, England.

Includes bibliographical references.

ISBN 978-1-250-01033-9

[1. Mystery and detective stories. 2. Great Britain—History—Victoria, 1837–1901—Fiction.] I. Title.

PZ7.L231758Re 2011

[Fic]—dc22

2011000124

Originally published in the United States by Farrar Straus Giroux

First Square Fish Edition: October 2012

Square Fish logo designed by Filomena Tuosto

macteenbooks.com

4 6 8 10 9 7 5 3

AR: 6.2 / LEXILE: 920L

Dedicated to the three teachers who taught me how to write over the years—Sylvia Clark, Eve Wilson, and Iris Cannon—and also to the four writers whose work has acted as living tutorials for me—Stephen Gallagher, Tim Powers, Jonathan Carroll, and David Morrell.

And with grateful acknowledgement to: Marc and Cat Dimmock, for encouraging me; to Stella White, Michele Fry, Scott Fraser, A. Kinson, Chris Chalk, Susan Belcher, L. M. Cowan, L. Hay, Stuart Bentley, Mandy Nolan, D. J. Mann, and all the other people who wrote reviews of the first Young Sherlock book at exactly the time I needed to feel better about writing; and to Dominic Kingston and Joanne Owen at Macmillan U.K. for looking after me in such a great way. Thanks, everyone.

PROLOGUE

James Hillager thought he was hallucinating when he first saw the giant leech.

The Borneo jungle was so hot and so humid that walking through it was like being in a Turkish bath. His clothes were sopping wet, and there was so much water vapour in the atmosphere that the sweat wasn't even evaporating from his skin: it was just dripping from his fingers and his nose, or rolling down his body and collecting wherever his clothes touched his flesh. His boots were so filled with water that he could hear a squelching sound whenever he took a step. The leather was going to rot away within a few weeks if this kept up. He had never felt so miserable and uncomfortable in his life.

The heat was making his head swim, and it was that—and the fact that he was dehydrated and he hadn't eaten properly for days—which made him think he was hallucinating. He'd been hearing voices in the trees around him for some time now: whispering voices that were talking about him and laughing at him. Part of his mind was telling him that it was just the sound of the wind in the leaves, but another part wanted to yell back at them and tell them to shut up. And then maybe shoot them if they didn't obey.

He'd already seen animals that made his mind boggle. Maybe they were real; maybe they were hallucinations as well. He'd seen monkeys with huge, bulbous noses; frogs the size of his thumb that were bright orange, or red, or blue; a perfectly formed adult elephant no taller than his shoulder; and a piglike animal with dark hair and a long, pointed, flexible snout. How many of them were real, and how many a product of his fevered brain?

Beside him, Will Gimson stopped and bent over, hands on his knees, taking deep gulps of the steamy air. "Got to stop for a minute," he said breathlessly. "Finding it hard to move."

Hillager took the opportunity to mop his brow with a handkerchief that was probably wetter than his face. Maybe he was hallucinating because he was coming down with some kind of tropical fever. These Borneo forests were rife with strange diseases. He'd heard of men who'd been reported lost in the jungle for weeks wandering out with the flesh of their faces covered in pustules, or literally sliding off the bone.

He looked around nervously. Even the trees seemed to mock him. Their trunks were twisted and gnarled, and smaller plants and vines grew out of them like parasites. They grew so close together that he couldn't see the sky, and the only light that filtered down here was diffuse and shaded in green.

Despite the heat, he shivered. He wouldn't be in this terrible place if he didn't fear his employer even more.

"Let's call it a day," he urged. He really didn't want to spend any more time in this jungle. He just wanted to get back to the port, load up the crated animals they'd already picked up, and return to civilization. "It's not here. We've already collected enough animals to make him happy. Leave this one behind. He won't even notice."

"Oh, he'll notice all right," Gimson said grimly. "If we return with only one critter, this is the one he wants."

Hillager was about to argue the point when Gimson added: "Wait! I think I can see one!"

Hillager moved to join his colleague. The man was still bending over, but he was staring at the base of one of the trees.

"Look," he said, and pointed.

Hillager followed the direction of Gimson's finger. There, in a pool of water between two tree roots, was what looked like a bright red clot of blood the size of his hand. It glistened in the weak light of the sun.

"Are you sure?" he asked.

"That's what Duke said it would look like. That's *exactly* what he said it would look like."

"So what do we do?"

Instead of answering, Gimson reached out with his hand and took the thing between his finger and thumb. He picked it up. It drooped bonelessly. Hillager watched, fascinated.

"Yeh," Gimson said, turning it over and examining it closely. "Look—there's the mouth, or the sucker, or whatever you call it. Three teeth, set around the edge. And the other end's got a sucker as well. That's how it holds on—it attaches itself at both ends."

"And sucks your blood," Hillager said darkly.

"And sucks the blood of anything that passes by slowly enough that it can get a grip," Gimson explained. "Those tiny elephants, that tapir-thing with the pointy snout—anything."

The leech was changing shape as he watched, becoming thinner and longer. When Gimson had picked it up it had been nearly circular, but now it was more like a thick worm. His fingers were still clamped about a third of the way along from its head—if the bit with the mouth could actually be called a head.

"What does he do with them?" Hillager asked. "Why does he send people all this way to collect them?"

"He says he hears them calling out to him," Gimson replied. "And as to what he does when he gets them, you really don't want to know." He bent closer to the creature, examining it carefully. The creature waved blindly towards him, aware somehow that there was warm blood in the vicinity. "This one hasn't fed for a while."

"How can you tell?"

"It's looking for something to attach to."

"Should we leave it?" Hillager asked. "Look for another one tomorrow?" He hoped Gimson would say no, because he really didn't want to spend any more time in this jungle.

"This is the first one we've seen in a week," Gimson replied. "It could be longer before we see another. No, we need to take this one. We need to get it back home."

"Will it survive the journey?"

Gimson shrugged. "Probably, if we feed it before we start back."

"Okay." Hillager looked around. "What do you suggest? A monkey? One of those pig-things?"

Gimson didn't say anything.

Hillager turned back to find Gimson staring at him with a strange look on his face. Partly it was sympathy, but mostly it was distaste.

"I suggest," Gimson said, "that you roll up your sleeve."

"Are you *mad*?" Hillager whispered.

"No, I'm a tracker and guide," Gimson explained. "What exactly did you think *your* purpose on this expedition was? Now roll up your sleeve. This horror needs blood, and it needs it now."

Slowly, knowing what Duke's reaction would be if he found out that Hillager had let his leech die rather than feed it, Hillager began to roll up his sleeve.

ONE

"Have you ever thought about ants?" Amyus Crowe asked.

Sherlock shook his head. "Apart from the fact that they get all over jam sandwiches at picnics, I can't say I've ever given them much thought."

The two of them were out in the Surrey countryside. The heat of the sun weighed on the back of Sherlock's neck like a brick. An almost overpowering aroma of flowers and freshly mown hay seemed to hang in the air around him.

A bee buzzed past his ear and he flinched. Ants he was relatively ambivalent about, but bees still spooked him.

Crowe laughed. "What is it about the British and jam sandwiches?" he asked through the laughter. "I swear there's a nursery aspect to British eating habits that no other country has. Steamed puddings, jam sandwiches—with the crusts cut off, of course—and vegetables boiled so long they're just flavoured mush. Food you don't need teeth to eat."

Sherlock felt a stab of annoyance. "So what's so terrific about American food?" he asked, shifting his position on the dry stone wall he was sitting on. Ahead of him the ground sloped down to a river in the distance.

"Steaks," Crowe said simply. He was leaning on the wall, which came up to his chest. His square chin was resting on his folded arms, and his broad-brimmed hat shielded his eyes from the sun. He was wearing his usual white linen suit. "Big steaks, flame-grilled. *Properly* grilled so there's crisp bits around the edge, not just waved over a candle like the French do. An' not smothered in some kind of cream brandy sauce, also like the French do. It don't take the brains of an archbishop to cook and serve a steak properly, so why can't anybody outside the United States do it right?" He sighed, his bubbling good nature suddenly evaporating to expose an unexpected flat sadness.

"You miss America?" Sherlock said simply.

"I've been away for longer than a man should. An' I know Virginia misses her home as well."

Sherlock's mind was filled with a vision of Crowe's daughter, Virginia, riding her horse Sandia with her copper red hair flowing out behind her like a flame.

"When will you go back?" he asked, hoping it wouldn't be soon. He had grown accustomed to both Crowe and Virginia. He liked having them in his life since he'd been sent to live with his aunt and uncle.

"When my work here is done." A huge smile creased his lined, weather-beaten face as his mood changed. "An' when I consider that I have discharged my responsibility to your brother by teachin' you everythin' I know. Now, let's talk about ants."

Sherlock sighed, resigning himself to another of Crowe's impromptu lessons. The big American could take anything from around him, whether it was in the countryside, the town, or someone's house, and use it as the springboard for a question, a problem, or a logical conundrum. It was beginning to annoy Sherlock.

Crowe straightened up and looked around behind him. "I thought I'd seen some of the little critters," he said, walking over to a small pile of dry earth that was heaped up like a miniature hill in a patch of grass. Sherlock wasn't fooled. Crowe had probably spotted them on the way up and filed them away as fodder for his next training session.

Sherlock jumped down from the wall and walked across to where Crowe was standing. "An anthill," he said with little enthusiasm. Small black forms wandered aimlessly around the mound of earth.

"Indeed. The external sign that there's a whole bunch of little tunnels underneath which the little critters have patiently excavated. Somewhere under there you'll find thousands of tiny white eggs, all laid by a queen ant who spends her life underground, never seeing daylight."

Crowe bent down and gestured for Sherlock to join him. "Look at how the ants are movin'," he said. "What strikes you about it?"

Sherlock watched them for a moment. No two ants were heading in the same direction, and each one seemed to change direction at a moment's notice, for no visible reason. "They're moving randomly," he said. "Or they're reacting to something we can't see."

"More likely the first explanation," Crowe said. "It's called 'the drunkard's walk,' an' it's actually a good way of coverin' ground quickly if you're lookin' for somethin'. Most people searchin' an area will just walk in straight lines, crisscrossin' it, or divide the area up into a grid an' search each square separately. Those techniques will usually guarantee success eventually, but the chances of findin' whatever it is *quickly* are increased by usin' this random way of coverin' the ground. It's called the drunkard's walk," he added, " 'cause of the way a man walks when he's got a belly full of whisky—legs goin' in different directions to each other and head goin' in another direction entirely." He reached into his jacket pocket and removed something. "But back to the ants: once they find somethin' of interest, watch what they do."

He showed Sherlock the thing in his hand. It was a pottery jar with a waxed paper top held on with string. "Honey," he said before Sherlock could ask. "Bought it in the market." He pulled the string off and removed the waxed paper. "Sorry if this brings back bad memories."

"Don't worry," Sherlock said. He knelt beside Crowe. "Should I ask why you're wandering around with a jar of honey in your pocket?"

"A man never knows what might come in useful," Crowe said, smiling. "Or maybe I planned all this in advance. You choose."

Sherlock just smiled and shook his head.

"Honey is largely sugar, plus a whole load of other things," Crowe continued. "Ants love sugar. They take it back to the nest to feed the queen and the little grubs that hatch from the eggs."

Dipping his finger in the honey, which Sherlock noticed was runny in the heat of the morning sun, Crowe scooped up a huge shiny droplet and let it fall. It caught on a clump of grass and hung there for a few moments before strands of it sagged to the ground and lay in scrawled and glistening threads.

"Now let's see what the little critters do."

Sherlock watched as the ants continued in their random wanderings; some climbing up strands of grass and dangling upside down and others foraging amongst grains of dirt. After a while, one of them crossed a strand of honey. It stopped midway. For a moment Sherlock thought it was stuck, but it wandered along the strand, then wandered back, then dipped its head as though drinking.

"It's collecting as much as it can carry," Crowe said conversationally. "It'll head back for the nest now."

And indeed the ant did appear to retrace its steps, but rather than heading directly for the nest it continued to wander back and forth. It took a few minutes, and Sherlock almost lost it a couple of times as it crossed the path of other groups of ants, but eventually it reached the pile of dry earth and vanished into a hole in the side.

"So what now?" Sherlock asked.

"Look at the honey," Crowe said.

Ten, perhaps fifteen ants had discovered the honey by now, and they were all taking samples. Other ants kept joining the throng. As they joined, others broke away and headed vaguely in the direction of the nest.

"What do you notice?" Crowe asked.

Sherlock bent his head to look closer. "The ants appear to be taking a shorter and shorter time to get back to the nest," he said wonderingly.

After a few minutes there were two parallel lines of ants heading between the honey and the nest. The random wandering had been replaced with a purposeful direction.

"Good," Crowe said approvingly. "Now let's try a little experiment."

He reached into his pocket and took out a scrap of paper about the size of his palm. He laid it on the ground halfway between the nest and the honey. The ants crossed the paper back towards the nest as if they hadn't even noticed it.

"How are they communicating?" Sherlock asked. "How are the ants who have found the honey telling the ones in the nest where it is?"

"They're not," Crowe answered. "The fact that they are returnin' with honey is a signal that there's food out there, but they can't talk to each other, they can't read each other's minds, and they can't point with those little legs of theirs. There's something a lot cleverer goin' on. Let me show you."

Crowe reached down and deftly turned the scrap of paper ninety degrees. The ants already on the paper walked off the edge and then seemed lost, wandering aimlessly around, but Sherlock was fascinated to watch the ants who reached the paper walking across it until they reached halfway, then turning and heading at right angles to their previous path until they came to the edge and then walking off and starting to wander again.

"They're following a path," he breathed. "A path they can see but we can't. Somehow, the first few ants had laid that path down and the rest followed it, and when you turned the paper around they kept following the path, not knowing that it now leads somewhere else."

"That's right," Crowe said. "Best guess is that it's some kind of chemical. When the ant is carrying food, he leaves a trail of the chemical behind. Imagine it like a rag covered in something that smells strong, like aniseed, attached to one of their feet, and the other ants, like dogs, have a tendency to follow the aniseed trail. Because of the drunkard's-walk effect, the first ant will wander all over the place before he finds the nest. As more and more ants find the honey, some of them will take longer paths to the nest and some shorter ones. As more ants follow, the shorter paths get reinforced by the chemical because they work better and because the ants can get back quicker, and the longer paths, the wandering ones, fade away because they don't work as well. Eventually you end up with a nearly straight route. An' you can prove that by doin' what I did with the paper. The ants still follow the straight-line trail even though it now leads them away from the nest, not towards it, although eventually they'll correct themselves."

"Incredible," Sherlock said. "I never knew. It's not . . . intelligence . . . because it's instinctive and they're not communicating, but it *looks* like it's intelligent."

"Sometimes," Crowe pointed out, "a group is less intelligent than an individual. Look at people: one by one they can be clever, but put them into a mob an' a riot can start, 'specially if there's an incitin' incident. Other times a group exhibits cleverer behaviour than an individual, like here with the ants or with swarms of bees."

He straightened up, brushing dirt and grass from his linen trousers. "Instinct tells me," he said, "that it's nearly lunchtime. You reckon your aunt and uncle can make some space at the table for a wanderin' American?"

"I'm sure they can," Sherlock replied. "Although I'm not so sure about the housekeeper—Mrs. Eglantine."

"Leave her to me. I have bottomless reserves of charm which I can deploy at a moment's notice."

They wandered back across the fields and through coppices of trees, with Crowe pointing out clumps of edible mushrooms and other fungi to Sherlock as they went, reinforcing lessons that he'd taught the boy weeks before. By now, Sherlock was fairly sure that he could survive in the wild by eating what he could find without poisoning himself.

Within half an hour they were approaching Holmes Manor, a large and rather forbidding house set in a few acres of open ground. Sherlock could see the window of his own bedroom at the top of the house: a small, irregular room set beneath a sloping roof. It wasn't comfortable, and he never looked forward to going to bed at night.

A carriage was sitting outside the front door, its driver idly flicking his whip while the horse munched hay from a nose bag hung around its head.

"Visitors?" Crowe said.

"Uncle Sherrinford and Aunt Anna didn't mention anyone coming for lunch," Sherlock said, wondering who had been in the carriage.

"Well, we'll find out in a few minutes," Crowe pointed out. "It's a waste of mental energy to speculate on a question when the answer's goin' to be presented to you on a plate momentarily."

They reached the step leading up to the front door. Sherlock ran up to the door, which was half-open, while Crowe followed on sedately behind.

The hall was dark, with buttresses of dusty light crossing it from the sun shining through the high windows. The oil paintings lining the walls were nearly invisible in the gloom. The summer heat was an almost physical presence.

"I'll tell someone you're here," Sherlock said to Crowe.

"No need," Crowe murmured. "Someone already knows." He nodded his head towards the shadows under the stairs.

A figure stepped out, black dress and black hair offset only by the whiteness of the skin.

"Mr. Crowe," said the housekeeper. "I do not believe we were expecting you."

"People speak far and wide of the hospitality of the Holmes household," he said grandly, "and of the victuals it provides to passing travellers. And besides, how could I forgo the opportunity to see you again, Mrs. Eglantine?"

She sniffed, thin lips twitching under her sharp, thin nose. "I am sure that many women succumb to your colonial charms, Mr. Crowe," she said. "I am not one of those women."

"Mr. Crowe will be staying for lunch," Sherlock said firmly, though he felt a tremor in his heart as Mrs. Eglantine's needlelike gaze moved to him.

"That is up to your aunt and uncle," she said, "not to you."

"Then *I* will tell them," he said, "not *you*." He turned back to Crowe. "Wait here while I check," he said. When he turned back, Mrs. Eglantine had faded into the shadows and vanished.

"There's something odd about that woman," Crowe murmured. "She don't act like a servant. She acts like she's a member of the family sometimes. Like she's in charge."

"I don't know why my aunt and uncle let her get away with it," Sherlock said. "I wouldn't."

He walked across to the salon and glanced inside. Maids were bustling around the sideboards at one end of the room, preparing plates of cold meat, fish, cheese, rice, pickled vegetables, and breads that the family could come in and graze on, as was the normal way of taking lunch at Holmes Manor, but there was no sign of his aunt or uncle. Heading back into the hall, he paused for a moment before approaching the door to the library and knocking.

"Yes?" said a voice from inside, a voice that was used to practising the sermons and speeches that its owner spent most of his life writing: Sherlock's uncle, Sherrinford Holmes. "Come in!"

Sherlock opened the door. "Mr. Crowe is here," he said as the door swung open to reveal his uncle sitting at a desk. He was wearing a black suit of old-fashioned cut, and his impressively biblical beard covered his chest and pooled on the blotter in front of him. "I was wondering if it would be possible for him to stay for lunch."

"I would welcome the opportunity to talk to Mr. Crowe," Sherrinford Holmes said, but Sherlock's attention was distracted by the man standing over by the open French windows, his long frock coat and high collar silhouetted by the light.

"Mycroft!"

Sherlock's brother nodded gravely at the boy, but there

was a twinkle in his eye that his sober manner could not conceal. "Sherlock," he said. "You're looking well. The countryside obviously suits you."

"When did you arrive?"

"An hour ago. I came down from Waterloo and took a carriage from the station."

"How long are you staying?"

He shrugged, a slight movement of his massive frame. "I will not be staying the night, but I wanted to check on your progress. And I was hoping to see Mr. Crowe as well. I'm glad he's here."

"Your brother and I will conclude our business," Sherrinford said, "and we will see you in the dining room."

It was a clear dismissal, and Sherlock pulled the door closed. He could feel a smile stretching across his face. Mycroft was here! The day was suddenly even sunnier than it had been a few moments before.

"Did I hear your brother's voice?" Amyus Crowe rumbled from the other side of the hall.

"That's his carriage outside. He said he wanted to talk to you."

Crowe nodded soberly. "I wonder why," he said quietly.

"Uncle Sherrinford said you can stay for lunch. He said they'd meet us in the dining room."

"That seems like a plan to me," Crowe said in a louder voice, but there was a frown on his face that belied the lightness of his words.

Sherlock led the way into the dining room. Mrs. Eglantine was already there, standing by the wall in the shadow between two large windows. Sherlock hadn't seen her pass him in the hall. For a moment he wondered if she might be a ghost, able to pass through walls, but he quickly decided that was a stupid idea. Ghosts didn't exist.

Ignoring Mrs. Eglantine, he headed for the sideboard, grabbed a plate, and began to load it up with slices of meat and chunks of salmon. Crowe followed and began at the other end of the sideboard.

Sherlock's head was still spinning after the sudden reappearance of his elder brother. Mycroft lived and worked in London, capital city of the Empire. He was a civil servant, working for the government, and although he often made light of his position, saying that he was just a humble file clerk, Sherlock had believed for a while that Mycroft was a lot more important than he made out. When Sherlock had been at home with his mother and father before being sent away to live with his aunt and uncle, Mycroft had sometimes come down from London to stay for a few days, and Sherlock had noticed that every day a man would turn up in a carriage with a red box. He would give it only to Mycroft in person, and in return Mycroft would hand across an envelope containing, Sherlock presumed, letters and memoranda that he had written based on the contents of the previous day's box. Whatever he was, the government still needed to keep in touch with him every day.

Mouth full of food, he heard the door to the library open. Moments later, the tall, stooping figure of Sherrinford Holmes entered the dining room.

"Ah, *brōma theōn*," he proclaimed in Greek, gazing at the sideboard. Glancing in Sherlock's direction, he said: "You may use my library, my *psykhēs iatreion*, for your reunion with your brother." Turning to Crowe, he added: "And he specifically requested that you join the two of them."

Sherlock put down his plate and moved quickly towards the library. Crowe followed, his long legs covering the ground quickly despite his apparent slowness of gait.

Mycroft was standing in the same position over by the French windows. He smiled at Sherlock, then walked over and ruffled the boy's hair. The smile slipped from his face as he glanced at Crowe, but he shook hands with the American.

"First things first," he said. "After quite an exhaustive investigation by the police, we have found no trace of Baron Maupertuis. We believe he has fled the country for France. The good news is that we have not found any deaths of British soldiers, or anybody else, due to bee stings."

"It's debatable whether Maupertuis's plan would have worked," Crowe said soberly. "I suspect he was mentally unstable. But it was best we didn't take the chance."

"And the government is suitably grateful," Mycroft replied.

"Mycroft—what about Father?" Sherlock blurted.

Mycroft nodded. "His ship will be approaching India by now. I would expect him to disembark with his regiment within the week, but we will probably not get any word from him, or from anybody else, for a month or two—the speed of communication with that far continent being what it is. If I hear anything, I will tell you straightaway."

"And . . . Mother?"

"Her health is weak, as you know. She is stable for the moment, but she needs rest. I understand from her doctor that she sleeps for sixteen or seventeen hours a day." He sighed. "She needs time, Sherlock. Time and a lack of any mental or physical exertion."

"I understand." Sherlock paused, fighting a catch in his throat. "Then I am to stay here at Holmes Manor for the rest of the school holidays?"

"I am not sure," Mycroft said, "that Deepdene School for Boys is doing you much good."

"My Latin has improved," Sherlock responded quickly, then mentally cursed himself. He should be agreeing with his brother, not disagreeing.

"No doubt," Mycroft said drily, "but there are things a boy should be learning other than Latin."

"Greek?" Sherlock couldn't help asking.

Mycroft smiled despite himself. "I see that your rather pawky sense of humour has survived your time here. No, despite the obvious importance of Latin and Greek to the increasingly complicated world we live in, I rather think that you would respond better to a more personal and individual style of teaching. I am considering withdrawing you from Deepdene and arranging for you to be tutored here, at Holmes Manor."

"Not go back to the school?" Sherlock searched himself for some sign that he cared, but there was nothing. He had no friends there, and even his best memories were those of boredom rather than happiness. There was nothing for him at Deepdene.

"We need to look ahead to your matriculation," Mycroft continued. "Cambridge, of course. Or Oxford. I think you will have a better chance if we focus your learning a little more than Deepdene can manage." He smiled again. "You are a very individual boy, and you need to be treated that way. No promises, but I will let you know before the end of the holidays what arrangements have been put in place."

"Do I presume too much when I ask if I will have some small part to play in the youngster's teachin'?" Amyus Crowe rumbled.

"No," Mycroft said, lips twisting slightly, "you've obviously kept him on the straight and narrow so well to date."

"He's a Holmes," Crowe pointed out. "He can be guided, but he can't be forced. You were the same."

"Yes," Mycroft said simply. "I was, wasn't I?" Before Sherlock could check his sudden realization that Crowe had been Mycroft's teacher as well, Mycroft said: "Would you be good enough to allow Mr. Crowe and me to speak privately, Sherlock? We have some business to discuss."

"Will I . . . see you before you leave?"

"Of course. I won't be going until this evening. You can show me around the house, if you like."

"We could go for a walk in the grounds," Sherlock suggested.

Mycroft shuddered. "I think not," he said. "I do not believe I am properly dressed for rambling."

"It's just around the outside of the house!" Sherlock protested. "Not out in the woods!"

"If I cannot see a roof over my head and cannot feel floorboards or pavement beneath my feet, then it counts as rambling," Mycroft said firmly. "Now, Mr. Crowe—to business."

Reluctantly Sherlock left the library and closed the door behind him. Judging by the voices coming from the dining room, he thought his aunt had joined his uncle for lunch. He didn't feel like subjecting himself to the constant stream of chatter from his aunt, so he headed outside. He wandered around the side of the house, hands in pockets and kicking at the occasional stone. The sun was almost directly overhead, and Sherlock could feel a thin film of sweat forming on his forehead and between his shoulder blades.

The French windows to the library were ahead of him. The *open* French windows.

He could hear voices from inside the library.

A part of his mind was telling him that this was a private conversation from which he had been specifically excluded, but another part, a more seductive part, was saying that Mycroft and Amyus Crowe were discussing *him*.

He moved closer, along the stone balcony that ran beside the house.

"And they're sure?" Crowe was saying.

"You've worked for Pinkertons before," Mycroft replied. "Their intelligence sources are usually very accurate, even this far from the United States of America."

"But for him to have travelled *here* . . ."

"I presume America was too dangerous for him."

"It's a big country," Crowe pointed out.

"And much of it uncivilized," Mycroft countered.

Crowe wasn't convinced. "I would have expected him to head across the border to Mexico."

"But apparently he didn't." Mycroft's voice was firm. "Look at it this way—you were sent to England to hunt down Southern sympathizers from the War Between the States who had a price on their heads. What better reason for *him* to travel here than because *they* are here?"

"Logical," Crowe admitted. "Do you suspect a conspiracy?"

Mycroft hesitated for a moment. "'Conspiracy' is probably too strong a term as yet. I suspect they have all gravitated to this country because it is civilized, because people speak the same language, and because it is safe. But give it time, and a conspiracy could grow. So many dangerous men with nothing to do but talk to each other . . . we need to nip this in the bud."

Sherlock's head was spinning. What on earth were they talking about? He'd come into the conversation just too late to make sense of it.

"Oh, Sherlock," his brother called from inside the room, "you might as well join us, given that you're listening in."

TWO

Sherlock entered the library through the French windows with his head hung low. He felt hot and embarrassed and, strangely, angry; although he wasn't sure whether he was angry with Mycroft for catching him eavesdropping or with himself for being caught.

"How did you know I was there?" he asked.

"Firstly," Mycroft said without any trace of emotion, "I expected you to be there. You're a young man with an overdeveloped sense of curiosity, and recent events have shown that you have little regard for playing by the proper rules of society. Secondly, there is a slight breeze that blows in through the gap in the French windows. When you were standing outside, although you could not be seen, and your shadow wasn't cast in front of the windows, your body occluded the breeze. When it ceased for more than a few seconds I surmised that something was blocking it. The obvious candidate was you."

"Are you angry?" Sherlock asked.

"Not at all," Mycroft replied.

"What would have made your brother angry," Amyus Crowe said genially, "is if you had been careless enough to let the sun cast your shadow across the balcony in front of the windows."

"That," Mycroft agreed, "would have demonstrated a regrettable lack of knowledge of simple geometry, and also an inability to predict the unintended results of your own actions."

"You're teasing me," Sherlock accused.

"Only slightly," Mycroft conceded, "and with only the best of intentions." He paused. "How much did you hear of our conversation?"

Sherlock shrugged. "Something about a man who has come across from America to England, and you think he's a threat. Oh, and something about a family called the Pinkertons."

Mycroft glanced across the room at Crowe and raised an eyebrow. Crowe smiled slightly.

"They're not a family," he said, "although sometimes it feels like they are. The Pinkerton National Detective Agency is a company of detectives and bodyguards. It was formed by Allan Pinkerton in Chicago 'bout eighteen years ago, when he realized that the number of railroad companies in the States was growin' but they had no way of protectin' themselves against robbery, sabotage, an' union activity. Allan hires out his people like a kind of super police force."

"Entirely independent of government rules and regulations," Mycroft murmured. "You know, for a country that prides itself on its democratic founding principles, you do have a habit of creating unaccountable independent agencies."

"You called him 'Allan,'" Sherlock realized. "You *know* him?"

"Al Pinkerton an' I go back a long way," Crowe admitted. "I was with him seven years ago when he an' I snuck Abraham Lincoln through Baltimore on his way to his presidential inauguration. There was a plot by the Southern states to kill Lincoln in the town, but the Pinkertons had been hired to protect him an' we got him through alive. Since then I've been consulting for Al, on an' off. Never actually taken a salary, but he pays me a consultancy fee on odd occasions."

"President Lincoln?" Sherlock said, his brain racing. "But wasn't he—?"

"Oh, they caught up with him eventually." Crowe's face was as still and as heavy as a chunk of carved granite. "Three years after the Baltimore plot, someone took a shot at him in Washington. His horse bolted and his hat blew off. When they recovered his hat later, they found a bullet hole in it. Missed him by inches." He sighed. "An' then a year later, just three years ago, he was at the theatre in Washington, watchin' a play called *Our American Cousin*, when a man named John Wilkes Booth shot him in the back of the head, jumped onto the stage, an' escaped."

"You weren't there," Mycroft said softly. "You couldn't have done anything."

"I should have been there," Crowe said, just as softly. "So should have Al Pinkerton. In point of fact, the only bodyguard lookin' after the president that night was a drunken policeman named John Frederick Parker. He weren't even there when the President was shot. He was in the Star Tavern next door, drownin' himself in ale."

"I remember reading about it in Father's newspaper," Sherlock said, breaking the heavy silence that had descended in the room. "And I remember Father talking about it, but I never really understood *why* President Lincoln was killed."

"That's the trouble with schools these days," Mycroft muttered. "As far as they are concerned, English history stops about a hundred years ago and there's no such thing as world history." He glanced at Crowe, but the American seemed reluctant to continue. "You are aware of the War Between the States, I presume?" he asked Sherlock.

"Only from the reports in *The Times.*"

"Simply put, eleven states in the southern half of the United States of America declared their independence and formed the Confederate States of America." He snorted. "It's as if Dorset, Devon, and Hampshire suddenly decided that they wanted to form a different country, and declared independence from Great Britain."

"Or as if Ireland decided that it wanted to be independent of British rule," Crowe murmured.

"That's a different situation entirely," Mycroft snapped. Turning his attention back to Sherlock, he continued: "For a while, there were two American presidents—Abraham Lincoln in the North and Jefferson Davis in the South."

"Why did they want independence?" Sherlock asked.

"Why does anybody want independence?" Mycroft rejoined. "Because they don't like taking orders. And in this case there was a difference in political views. The Southern states supported the concept of slavery, whereas Lincoln had run his election campaign based on halting the spread of slavery."

"Not that simple," Crowe said.

"It never is," Mycroft agreed, "but it will do for the moment. The war began on April 12, 1861, and during the next four years 620,000 Americans died fighting one another—in some cases, brother against brother and father against son." He seemed to shiver, and for a moment the light in the room grew darker as a cloud passed across the sun. "Gradually," he continued, "the North, known as the Union of States, eroded the military power of the South, who were calling themselves the Confederacy of States. The most important Confederate general, Robert Lee, surrendered on the ninth of April 1865. It was as a direct result of hearing that news that John Wilkes Booth shot President Lincoln five days later. That was part of a larger plot—his confederates were supposed to kill the Secretary of State and the Vice President—but the second assassin failed in his task and the third lost his nerve and ran. The last Confederate general surrendered on June 23, 1865, and the last of their military forces—the crew of the CSS *Shenandoah*—surrendered on the sixth of November 1865." He smiled, remembering something.

"Ironically, they surrendered in Liverpool, England, having sailed across the Atlantic in an attempt to avoid having to surrender to the forces of the North. I was there, representing the British government. And that was the end of the War Between the States."

"Except that it wasn't," Crowe said. "There's still people in the South who want their independence. There's still people agitatin' for it."

"Which brings us to now," Mycroft said to Sherlock. "Booth's co-conspirators were caught and hanged in July 1865. Booth himself fled, and was allegedly captured and shot by Union soldiers twelve days later."

"'Allegedly'?" Sherlock questioned, picking up on the slight emphasis in Mycroft's words.

Mycroft glanced at Crowe. "During the past three years there have been repeated claims that Booth actually escaped his pursuers, and that it was another conspirator, one who looked like Booth, who was shot. It's said that Booth changed his name to John St. Helen and fled America, in fear of his life. He was an actor, in his personal life."

"And you think he's here now?" Sherlock said. "In England?"

Mycroft nodded. "I received a telegram from the Pinkerton Agency yesterday. Their agents had heard that a man named John St. Helen who met the description of John Wilkes Booth had embarked from Japan to Great Britain. They asked me to alert Mr. Crowe, who they knew was in the country." He glanced across at Crowe. "Allan Pinkerton believes that Booth arrived in England on board the CSS *Shenandoah* three years ago, stayed for a while, then moved abroad. Now they believe he's back."

"As I think I mentioned some time ago," Crowe said to Sherlock, "I was asked to come to this country to track down those people who had fled America because they committed the most horrific crimes durin' the War Between the States. Not killin's of soldiers by soldiers, but massacres of civilians, burnin's of towns, an' all manner of godless acts. Since I'm here, it makes sense for Allan Pinkerton to want me to investigate this man John St. Helen."

"Do you mind if I ask you," Sherlock said to Crowe, "what side you were on in the War Between the States? You told me you came from Albuquerque. I looked it up on a map of America, here in my uncle's library. Albuquerque is a town in the New Mexico territory, near Texas, which is a Southern state. Isn't it?"

"It is," Crowe acknowledged. "An' Texas was part of the Confederacy durin' the War. But just because I was born in Texas doesn't mean I automatically support anythin' they do. A man has the right to make his own decisions, based on a higher moral code." He grimaced inadvertently. "I find slavery . . . distasteful. I don't believe that one man is inferior to another man because of the colour of his skin. I may think that other things make a man inferior, includin' his ability to think rationally, but not somethin' as arbitrary as the colour of his skin."

"Of course, the Confederacy would argue," Mycroft said smoothly, "that the colour of a man's skin is an *indication* of his ability to think rationally."

"If you want to establish a man's intelligence, you talk to him," Crowe scoffed. "Skin colour ain't got a thing to do with it. Some of the most intelligent men I've ever talked to have been black, and some of the stupidest have been white."

"So you went to the Union?" Sherlock asked, eager to get back to Crowe's fascinating and unexpected history.

Crowe glanced at Mycroft, who shook his head slightly. "Let's just say I stayed in the Confederacy but I *worked* for the Union."

"A *spy*?" Sherlock breathed.

"An agent," Mycroft corrected quietly.

"Isn't that . . . unethical?"

"Let's not get into a discussion of ethics, otherwise we'll be here all day. Let's just accept that governments use agents all the time."

Something that Mycroft had said finally percolated through Sherlock's mind and sparked a response. "You said that the Pinkerton Agency asked you to tell Mr. Crowe about John St. Helen. That means"—he felt a wash of emotion flood across him—"that you didn't come here to see me. You came to see *him*."

"I came to see you both," Mycroft said gently. "One of

the defining characteristics of the adult world is that decisions are rarely made on the basis of one factor. Adults do things for several reasons at once. You need to understand that, Sherlock. Life is not a simple thing."

"It should be," Sherlock said rebelliously. "Things are either right or they are wrong."

Mycroft smiled. "Don't ever try for the diplomatic service," he said.

Crowe shifted from foot to foot. He seemed uneasy to Sherlock. "Where does this St. Helen fellow live?" he asked.

Mycroft took a piece of paper from his jacket pocket and consulted it. "He apparently has taken a house in Godalming, on the Guildford Road. The name of the house is"—he checked the paper again—"Shenandoah, which might be indicative or might just be a coincidence." He paused. "What do you intend doing?"

"Investigatin'," Crowe said. "That's why I'm here. Course, I'll have to be particular about how I go about it. A big American like me is likely to be spotted pretty quickly."

"Then be subtle," Mycroft warned, "and please do not try to take justice onto yourself. There are laws in this country, and I would hate to see you hanged for murder." He sniffed. "I dislike irony. I find it upsets my digestion."

"I could help," Sherlock said abruptly, surprising himself. The thought appeared to have gone straight from his brain to his mouth without engaging his reason.

The two men stared at him in surprise.

"Under no circumstances," Mycroft said sternly.

"Absolutely not," Crowe snapped, overlapping Mycroft's words.

"But I can just ride into Godalming and ask questions," Sherlock persisted. "Nobody will notice me. And haven't I shown that I can do that kind of thing with the Baron Maupertuis business?"

"That was different," Mycroft pointed out. "You became involved by accident, and most of the danger to you occurred while Mr. Crowe here was attempting to disentangle you." He paused, considering. "Father would never forgive me if I let any harm come to you, Sherlock," he said in a quieter voice.

Sherlock felt aggrieved at the description of his actions against Baron Maupertuis, which he felt ignored or distorted several important points, but he kept quiet. There was no point in starting an argument about things in the past when there was something more important on the table. "I wouldn't do anything to draw attention to myself," he protested. "And I can't see how it would be dangerous."

"If John St. Helen *is* John Wilkes Booth, then he's a confirmed killer and a fugitive," Crowe proclaimed, "who faces hangin' if he returns—or is returned—to the United States. He's like a cornered animal. If he thinks he's under threat, then he'll cover his tracks and vanish again, and I'd have to go after him. I'd hate to see you become one of the tracks that gets covered."

"There is something else," Mycroft murmured. He glanced at Crowe. "I don't know to what extent the Pinkerton Agency have kept you apprised of the situation, but there is a growing belief that Booth and his collaborators were a part of something bigger."

"Course they were," Crowe rumbled. "It was called the War Between the States."

"I meant," Mycroft said heavily, "that the idea behind the assassination of President Lincoln didn't come from them; that they were working under instructions, and that the guiding lights, if you like, are still at large. If Booth really is here in England then it's possible he's heading back to America, and if that is the case then one might well ask why? What is his aim?"

Crowe smiled. "If he's headin' back to America, then my job's a lot easier. All I have to do is raise the alarm and get him arrested when he steps off the boat."

"But wouldn't it be preferable to establish his intentions first? Stopping him doesn't necessarily stop the conspiracy."

"If there is a conspiracy," Crowe said, shaking his head.

Sherlock felt as if he was caught in the middle of a philosophical discussion. All he knew was that the informal tutor he'd got used to having in his life was faced with a problem that might call him back to his home country, or set him chasing this man all over the world. If Sherlock could do something to solve that problem, he would. He just wouldn't tell Mycroft about it.

"Can I go now?" he asked.

Mycroft waved a hand dismissively. "Go and ramble in the countryside, or whatever you do. We will talk for a while."

"Come to my cottage tomorrow mornin'," Crowe said, not even looking at Sherlock. "We'll continue then."

Sherlock slipped out while the two men were starting a conversation about the intricacies of extradition treaties between individual American states at the federal level and the British government.

Outside the sun was still a heavy presence in the sky. He could smell wood smoke and the distant malt odour of the breweries in Farnham.

Godalming couldn't be that far away, could it? There was a Guildford Road leading out of it, which indicated it was somewhere near Guildford, and Guildford was somewhere near Farnham.

Matthew Arnatt would know.

Matthew—or Matty, as he liked to be called—was a boy Sherlock had come to know pretty well over the past month or two. He lived alone, on a narrowboat, moving between towns on the canals, stealing food where he had to and avoiding the workhouse. He'd settled down in Farnham for longer than he usually stayed in a town, although neither he nor Sherlock had spoken about the reasons why.

If Sherlock was going to head across to Godalming to take a look at this house named Shenandoah, and the man who lived there who might or might not be an assassin named John Wilkes Booth, then he wanted Matty on his side. Matty had saved his life a couple of times already. Sherlock trusted him.

He walked around the back of the house past the kitchens, across to the stables. The horses that he and Matty had taken from Baron Maupertuis's manor house some weeks ago were both standing there, contentedly eating from a bag of hay. Sherlock hadn't quite known what to do with them after the Baron's colossal scheme fell apart, so he'd just asked the stable boys to look after them for him and slipped them a shilling. Nobody else seemed to notice that there were two extra horses hanging around the house. And, of course, he could go riding with Virginia. She was giving him lessons, and he was actually enjoying the fact that he could ride a horse properly.

Sherlock saddled up his horse and then, taking the reins of the other horse in his left hand, he trotted out into the open, leading the other horse after him. Having two horses rather than one to worry about made the ride slower, but he was still in Farnham within half an hour and heading for the spot on the river where Matty's narrowboat was moored.

Matty was sitting on top of the boat, staring out at the river. He jumped up when he saw Sherlock.

"You've got the horses," he said.

"I know," Sherlock said. "Your powers of observation are amazing."

"Shove off," Matty said calmly. "I *observe* that you want me to come with you someplace. If that's right, you don't want to be too sarcastic."

"Point taken," Sherlock replied. "Sorry. I can't help myself sometimes."

"So, what can I do for you?"

"I thought you might want to have a ride out to Godalming," Sherlock told him.

Matty squinted at Sherlock. "What would I want to do that for?"

"I'll tell you on the way," Sherlock replied.

The ride to Godalming took them up a gradual slope that went on for miles. The hill was actually the beginning of a ridge that led into the distance. It fell away to both sides, and the countryside spread out before them until it was lost in a haze of distant smoke.

Matty glanced over his shoulder at Sherlock. "We go along the Hog's Back for a while, then we come off downhill, through Gomshall. It'll take an hour or so. You okay to keep going, or do you want to rest for a moment?"

"Let's just admire the view for a minute or two," Sherlock said. "Let the horses get their breath back."

"The horses are fine," Matty pointed out. "You're not getting saddle-sore, are you?"

The rest of the ride was easier, taking them past fields and large areas of common ground where sheep and goats and pigs grazed side by side. As they came to the edges of Godalming they passed across a bridge over a narrow river lined with green reeds as tall as a man. Just over the bridge a road led off to the left.

"I think that's the Guildford Road," Matty said, pointing. "Which way do you want to go?"

"Let's head out of town for a while," Sherlock replied. "I've got a feeling the place I'm looking for is further out, more isolated."

They rode along, slower this time so Sherlock could check out the houses as they passed. Matty seemed content just to look around, without asking Sherlock what they were doing.

Many of the houses weren't named, or were smaller than Sherlock was expecting to find. After all, there was no point calling a place Shenandoah if it was a broken-down hovel, was there? A name, especially one that grand, implied something bigger, more substantial. A few of the houses had children playing outside, either with wooden tops and string or with leather balls. One or two of them waved as the boys trotted past.

Eventually they came to a house set apart from any other, not in its own grounds, but isolated by a bend in the road and a group of trees. From the road, Sherlock could see a wooden plate by the door. The word on it was long, and it might have begun with an "S." Or it might not. Purple-flowering wisteria vines curled up the side of the building, clinging to any gap or projection they could find.

"Is this it?" Matty asked. "Shall we go and knock?"

"No," Sherlock said. "Keep riding till we get past, then stop."

The front of the house was whitewashed, and there were open shutters on the windows. The garden was well maintained, he noticed as they went by. Someone was obviously living there.

Once past the house, the boys slowed to a stop.

"You're obviously looking the place over," Matty said, "and you don't want the bloke living there to know it. What's going on?"

"I'll tell you later," Sherlock promised. "I need to get closer to the front door. Any ideas?"

"Walk up the path and knock?"

"Funny." He glanced around. Nothing immediately suggested itself. "Can you ride back to those kids we saw playing with the ball?" He delved into his pocket and brought out a handful of coins. "Give them a few pennies and ask if we can borrow the ball for a while. Tell them we'll bring it back."

Matty looked at him strangely. "We came a long way to play ball games."

"Just do it—please."

Matty sighed and took the coins, then trotted off, glancing back over his shoulder and making an audible "tch" noise.

Sherlock dismounted and waited patiently, tying up his horse and then moving closer to the edge of the trees and looking at the house. Nobody was moving. Was it Shenandoah, or something else, like Summerisle or Strangeways?

After what seemed an age, Matty returned. He was holding the ball under one arm.

"We were done," he said, stopping. "This ball is flat."

"Doesn't matter. Let's wander back down the road, throwing the ball to each other. When we get to the house, whoever has the ball throws it but deliberately misses, and gets it as close to the front door as they can."

"So the other one can run and fetch it. Yeh, okay."

"So that *I* can run and fetch it. I need to see what it says on that sign, and you can't read, remember? Not properly, anyway."

They wandered back down the road, throwing the ball back and forth. Once or twice Matty would drop it to the ground and kick it up in the air towards Sherlock.

When they got to the point on the road nearest the house, where a path led off towards the front door, Matty manoeuvred himself around so that he was at the other side of the road. He brought the ball behind his shoulder and threw it high, over Sherlock's head. It sailed into the garden and bounced once, floppily, before rolling towards the front door.

Sherlock made a dumbshow of irritation, throwing his hands wide and shrugging, then turned around and scooted up the path towards the front door. Without making it obvious, as he reached the ball and bent down to retrieve it he glanced up at the sign beside the door.

Shenandoah.

It was the right house. Now all he had to do was decide on his next step. Did he want to stay and watch it for a while, so he could describe the occupant to Mycroft and Amyus Crowe, or did he dare sneak in and look around, if the occupant wasn't home?

The decision was taken away from him as the door was flung wide open and a man appeared out of the darkness. He was thin, with a narrow, pointed beard shot through with grey hairs, but the thing that made Sherlock freeze in shock was the left side of his face. He'd been burned at some stage, badly burned; the skin of his face was red and lumpy, and his eye was just a dark hole, with no eyeball showing.

"You yapping little cur," he snarled. He grabbed Sherlock's hair and dragged him inside the house before he could make a sound.

THREE

Sherlock's scalp felt like it was on fire. He grabbed at the man's arm and let himself be pulled along, trying to lessen the agony of his entire body weight hanging off a handful of hair. He half expected chunks to tear out at the roots, leaving bleeding areas of raw flesh exposed to the air.

"I was just getting my ball back!" he cried.

The man ignored him. He was muttering a stream of profanities and accusations to himself as he pulled Sherlock along.

The hall of the house was light, with the sun shining through a skylight high above. It had an empty, half-furnished feel to it. The man's footsteps echoed on the tiled floor.

He pushed open a door with his left hand and dragged Sherlock inside. It was a reception room: comfortable chintz-covered chairs with antimacassars on top to stop the hair oil of any gentleman from staining the cloth, and some occasional tables sitting around with nothing on them but lace doilies. It had an unlived-in feel—a house, not a home.

Oh, and there was a body on the floor. Sherlock only just caught sight of a pair of boots and the lower half of a body, facing downward against the carpet, as he was pulled past and thrown into a chair.

He quickly reached up to check his hair, feeling for warm blood or raw flesh, or even just for some looseness in his scalp where it might be peeling away from the skull beneath, but it all felt normal. Except for the pain. That didn't feel normal at all.

"Please!" he cried, still trying to pretend that he was an innocent victim, just passing by, "let me go. My ma and pa will be worried about me! They just live down the road!"

The man wouldn't meet Sherlock's gaze. Instead, his head kept jerking back and forth like a bird's, going from window to door, door to window, back and forth.

Sherlock took a moment to look properly at the man. All he had really caught in the doorway was the ruined flesh on the left-hand side of the man's face, but now he let his gaze roam up and down the man's body, trying to spot something that might help.

The man's suit was good cloth, that much Sherlock was sure of. It was black, and quite fine, and the way the jacket and the trousers hung made Sherlock think that it had been made by a tailor who knew what he was doing. It didn't look like a wool sack with sleeves, which some of the jackets worn around Farnham did. But there was something odd about the cut, something . . . almost foreign. Sherlock found a part of his mind wondering whether you could identify which tailor had made a suit just by the stitching and the cut; or, at the very least, whether the tailor followed a particular style—German, or English, or American.

The man was thin, and his wrist bones and Adam's apple stood out prominently. From the right side his face was classically handsome, with a prominent moustache and goatee beard, but from the left side it was a wreck. The skin was red and shiny and cratered like the surface of the moon. The beard on that side was sparse and sickly, poking through the skin like the charred remains of a forest fire, and the eye socket was just a red-scarred hole in his face.

"Mister—" Sherlock started, but the man cut him off with an abrupt gesture.

"Quiet!" he commanded. His voice was piercing, but there was a whining tone in it that made Sherlock's flesh creep. "Quiet, you little whoreson whelp!"

His voice was tinged with an accent that wasn't English. It sounded more like the way Amyus and Virginia Crowe spoke, but it wasn't quite the same. Perhaps slightly more cultured. And he spoke as if he expected to be listened to. He *projected*, as if he were on a stage, performing. Sherlock had seen some interminable Shakespeare plays performed in the open air at his mother and father's manor house in Reigate, and if it wasn't for the twitching of his head Sherlock would have put this man down as an actor from the way he stood and the way he spoke.

"How long have we got?" the man asked abruptly. "How long till they're back?"

"I don't—" Sherlock started to say, but the man stepped towards him and belted him across the face with the back of his hand. Stars and galaxies burst apart in Sherlock's head. Shocked, he tasted blood.

"Don't lie to me, boy. I can smell a lie on the wind. How long have we got?"

"Maybe an hour . . ." Sherlock replied. He wasn't sure what the man wanted, but he was sure the man wasn't stable. The best thing to do was just to play along.

"Smoke . . ." the man said out of nowhere. His head was raised, and he was sniffing. "I can smell smoke." Abruptly he looked at Sherlock. "We need to get away. Back to the Orient. It's safe there. Too many people looking for me here. Too many eyes. Too many ears."

"I could check out back, see if the coast is clear," Sherlock offered.

"The coast!" The man's eyes seemed to light up. "We get a boat. A ship. We can sail to Hong Kong. Hide out there till it's safe."

"Safe from *what*?" Sherlock asked, but the man just glared at him.

"Don't pretend you're not in on it. You're *all* in on it. Every last mother's son."

Remembering the discussion back at Holmes Manor, Sherlock tried to work out whether this man had it in him to assassinate anyone, let alone the president of the

United States of America. He was obviously unstable, on the edge of a nervous collapse, but he *was* American, and maybe whatever he'd been through had driven him to the edge of madness. Sherlock had enough information now to take back to Amyus Crowe and to his brother—the problem was, would he ever be able to get away?

The man's head suddenly jerked around, as if it were attached to a string that someone had pulled from outside. "Smoke!" he cried. He dashed out of the room abruptly, leaving Sherlock alone.

Apart from the body.

For a moment, Sherlock considered making a run for it. If he moved fast he might be able to get past his captor, even if the man was standing outside in the hall, and get to the front door. Or he could head in the other direction, to the reception-room window, and get out into the garden that way. Matty would still be waiting for him, and they could escape together on the horses.

But there was a body with him in the room, and he had to check to see whether the person was dead or wounded. He knew he couldn't just leave him there. That would haunt him for the rest of his life.

He left the chair and crouched beside the body, checking for the return of his captor. It was a man with muttonchop whiskers. His head was turned to one side, and his eyes were closed, but Sherlock was relieved to hear him breathing heavily through his mouth. The hair on the back of his head was matted with blood that had partially clotted into a thick, glutinous mass. He'd obviously been struck from behind and fallen. He was lucky to be alive.

Sherlock thought for a moment. The man who had dragged him into the house was obviously mentally deranged. Was the man on the floor here some kind of keeper? A guard? And the lunatic had somehow managed to knock him out and was now looking for some way to escape from the house?

Sherlock dragged the unconscious man into a more comfortable position, one where his breathing wouldn't be obstructed by the angle of his head. He couldn't help noticing that the man's clothes were cut in a similar style, and from a similar cloth, to those of his captor. They probably came from the same place.

A noise from out in the hall alerted him. He just managed to get back to the chair before his captor re-entered the room. His forehead gleamed with beads of sweat, but the glossy red ruin of the left side of his face was as dry as bone.

"There's a ship a-waiting to take me to China!" he declared, but his eye was open so wide that the white of the eyeball was visible all the way around, like a frightened horse, and Sherlock knew that he was hallucinating the existence of the ship in the same way he appeared to be hallucinating the smoke that he kept smelling. The smoke from the fire that, Sherlock assumed, had caused that terrible scarring.

"You go ahead," Sherlock said, as calmly as he could. "I'll follow on." He was hoping that his confident, level tone of voice might persuade the man to just turn around and go, but it had the opposite effect. The man brought his hand up in front of him, and with a chill of horror Sherlock saw that the hand was holding a silvery gun with an immensely long barrel and a revolving drum just above the handle.

"Leave no trace behind!" the man declared, and pointed the gun at Sherlock's forehead.

Sherlock rolled sideways off the chair as the gun exploded with smoke and noise, and the antimacassar where Sherlock's head had been resting turned into a burst mess of torn fabric and horsehair stuffing. He came up underneath an occasional table and heaved it towards the man with the gun. The man fired again, wildly, and the lead ball tore long splinters out of the table's surface, knocking it spinning away from the two of them.

He aimed at Sherlock again. This time the lead ball screamed over Sherlock's head and hit the window, shattering the glass.

Sherlock ran for the door to the hall. A fourth shot caught the door frame, knocking chunks of wood out of it as Sherlock passed.

The route down the hallway to the front door was too far. By the time he was struggling to throw the door open, the man would be in the hall and firing at him again, and he would be trapped. Instead, he turned and headed up the stairs.

The man appeared at the bottom of the stairs just as Sherlock reached the upstairs hall. He was in the process of reloading the gun. Obviously not completely mad, Sherlock thought as he sprinted along the first-floor landing. The head of an elk that had been mounted on a shield-shaped board suddenly jerked sideways as the gun went *bang!* downstairs; a hole appeared where one of the glass eyes had been. It wasn't enough that the poor thing had been shot once; it had to endure the indignity of being shot again, and this time it couldn't even run!

The landing ended with a choice of two doors. Sherlock could hear footsteps on the staircase. He considered, trying to remember the layout of the house as he'd seen it from outside. There had been wisteria growing up to one window, on this side. Was it the left or the right?

He chose the right, more on a whim than anything else. If he left it any longer, trying to work out which door to go through, he'd be dead anyway. He had a fifty-fifty chance.

The door opened under the pressure of his hand. He slipped through the gap and quickly closed the door again. If the man with the gun had to check both bedrooms, that might give Sherlock a few minutes' grace before he was discovered.

There was a bed in the room, unmade, as if the occupant had just stumbled out of it and got dressed without worrying about tidiness, and no maid had come to straighten the room out. Sherlock assumed that the only people in the house were the man with the gun and his captor/guard. If they were up to no good, hiding from some undefined peril, then a maid would be a risk. Best for the men to keep isolated, avoiding arousing any interest. And that meant they were probably doing all the cooking and cleaning themselves.

And that, Sherlock suddenly thought, probably meant there was a third man at least, if the madman needed constant supervision.

Wary of noises outside, or the sudden movement of the door, Sherlock crept across to the window. As he passed the bed, he noticed a black Gladstone bag on the floor beside it. The top of the bag gaped open, and inside Sherlock could see the gleam of glass and metal. Intrigued, he moved closer and looked in.

A series of vials containing a colourless fluid were strapped into individual compartments on one side of the bag. A collection of medical instruments, scalpels and suchlike, had been thrown willy-nilly into the bottom. And separate from both of them was a long, flat box that Sherlock recognized. He'd seen boxes like that before, belonging to the doctors who had treated his sister during her periods of illness. They usually contained hypodermic syringes: hollow cylinders of glass ending in plungers and tipped with sharp needles, used for injecting drugs into the bloodstream. For a moment he wasn't in that bedroom anymore, he was in his own home, watching through a gap in the door as the doctors and nurses bustled around his sister's bed. Needles and syringes fascinated him: the light glinting on them, their grotesque functionality, the way they blurred the boundary between the inside of the body and the outside. The way they made things better. The way they stopped the screams.

He shivered. No time for memories. He had a madman with a gun just a few seconds behind him.

For a moment he thought the window was bolted, or nailed shut. It wouldn't move as he tugged it upward. It *had* to, he told himself. If this room had medical equipment scattered around then it wasn't the madman's bedroom, and there would be no point in sealing the window.

The madman's window, he felt sure, would have bars on it.

He threw all his strength into tugging at the window till, with a squeal of wood on wood, it slid upward. Blessedly cool air washed across his face. He squirmed out onto the windowsill and looked around. No sign of Matty in the garden or on the road. No sign of anyone.

He looked down. The wisteria grew all the way down to the flower beds beneath. He could climb down easily.

And then what? If the madman entered the bedroom while he was halfway down, then he was a sitting duck. The man could just shoot him in the head and watch him fall.

He glanced upward. The wisteria went all the way up

to the roof, as far as he could tell, its tendrils infiltrating the mortar between the bricks of the wall, and there was a balcony, or a sill of some kind, running all the way around the edge. If—when—the madman came into the bedroom and across to the open window, then his immediate reaction would be to look downward. If Sherlock was climbing upward, he might evade capture. At the very least, he would buy himself a few more seconds.

He stood on the windowsill and grabbed hold of the wisteria vines to one side with his right hand, using his left to slide the window carefully shut. His retreat was blocked off, but it might gain him a few additional moments of safety.

He extended his right leg out to the side and felt gingerly with his foot for a point where two vines crossed and the junction would take his weight. After what seemed like forever he found something that gave a little under pressure but would support him.

Nervously, he let the vines take his weight and scrabbled around with his left foot for another point of purchase. When he found one, he boosted himself up and reached with his left hand for another vine to grip. Instead it found a gap between two bricks. He jammed his fingers in and it took his weight. Laboriously, one step after another, he hauled himself up until the window was below him and he was climbing towards the roof.

Brick dust fell past him and stung his eyes. He shook his head, eyes closed, to dislodge it. More dust and small bits of rubble pit-patted against his head and shoulders.

The wisteria lurched suddenly beneath him. His weight was pulling it out of the wall, dragging the tendrils from where they had infiltrated through gaps and nooks and crannies and were gripping the brickwork. He could feel his centre of gravity pulling away from the wall. He glanced down and felt immediately sick when the ground seemed to eddy back and forth beneath him as he swayed. The vines in his right hand became loose, and he quickly scrabbled further up, looking for a firmer handhold. His fingers closed around a thick stem that appeared to be anchored in place, and he pushed upward with his right foot. His left hand closed around a flat tile on the edge of the roof. Thankfully, he rested for a moment, getting his breath back.

From beneath him he heard the grinding sound of the window being slid up.

He froze, pulling himself as close to the wall as he dared.

Sherlock sensed, rather than saw, a dark figure craning out of the window and scanning the ground beneath. He held his breath, desperate not to make a single noise that might give him away.

More brick dust rained down. He felt the vine he was holding in his right hand begin to pull loose from the wall. He'd been holding onto it for too long—he should have transferred his weight off by now, but he didn't dare.

More brick dust blew into his eyes, making him blink. His nostrils tickled. He wanted to sneeze, but he wrinkled his nose, clamping his nostrils shut.

The figure below him swung back and forth, its gaze scanning the ground like the beam of light from a lighthouse. Beyond, in the garden at the side of the house, Sherlock could see several wooden crates piled up. There were gaps between the slats and he thought he saw something moving behind them, but then his attention was forced back as the figure below turned around and looked upward.

At him.

"You insolent, cowardly cur!" he screamed, and fired the gun again.

The lead ball buzzed past Sherlock's ear like an enraged hornet. He felt the heat of its passage singe his hair. Desperately he dragged himself up to the flat ledge on the roof, pulling his legs after him as the lunatic shot again.

Silence for a moment as he caught his breath. Sliding towards the edge, Sherlock glanced over.

The window was empty. The lunatic was coming up the stairs to get him.

Sherlock looked around desperately. The ledge he was on was just a few feet wide. The roof proper began then, tiled and rising up at a steep slant to a peak. Dormer windows punctuated the ledge every ten feet or so—presumably second-floor bedrooms or storage rooms.

He had to find a way out, and quickly.

He knew he could never make it back down the wisteria vine, so he sprinted along the ledge to the first window. It was either locked or stuck in place. He moved to the next one, but it was the same. The third window was open a crack, but the wood had warped and it would not go up any further.

He made a move for the fourth window, but he suddenly realized that the madman with the gun was standing on the corner of the ledge where it went around the back of the house. He had obviously found a way out before Sherlock found a way in.

He pointed the long barrel of the gun at the centre of Sherlock's chest.

"Down, down to Hell," he screamed, spittle flying out of his mouth, "and say I send thee thither!"

Sherlock waited for the lead ball to hit him and send him plummeting off the roof. He wondered for a moment if the ball would kill him before the fall did. It would be the last experiment of his life.

Another man stepped around the corner of the roof, a burly man with pale hair and broken veins in his nose and cheeks. He grabbed the madman in a neck lock with his left arm while his right hand jabbed the needle of a syringe into the man's shoulder. He pressed the plunger, sending whatever drug was in the syringe coursing into the madman's bloodstream.

The madman sagged in his arms, the gun clattering onto the ledge. He was still trying to talk, but his words were slurred. His eyes fluttered for a few moments, and then he was still.

The newcomer pulled the syringe from the lunatic's shoulder. Clear fluid dripped out and the man slumped to the ledge. Straightening up, he gazed levelly at Sherlock.

"What're you doing here, boy?"

"I was just looking for my ball in the garden," Sherlock replied, trying to sound younger and more vulnerable than he was, "when this bloke grabbed me and pulled me into the house." He couldn't help noticing that when the man had straightened up, he had brought the revolver up with him and was keeping it held with the barrel along his leg.

"And what did this gentleman want to do to you, once he got you inside the house?"

"I don't know. I swear I don't."

The newcomer was silent for a few moments, thinking. The long barrel of the revolver tapped against his trousers.

"Get in the house," he said eventually. The barrel of the gun swung casually up to cover Sherlock. "And take him with you," he added, nodding towards the unconscious madman. "Drag him round the corner. There's an open window there. Just slide him inside."

"But—"

"Don't argue, boy. Just do what your betters tell you."

Sherlock glanced from his face to the gun and back again. This man wasn't twitchy, or edgy, or mad. He was perfectly sane, but just as likely to shoot.

Sherlock moved forward and took the madman by his shoulders. The newcomer stepped back to give him space. Sherlock dragged the unconscious body around the corner and along to the open window, aware all the time of the nearness of the edge of the ledge. One misstep and he would fall.

The man's body was heavy and difficult to manoeuvre, and Sherlock felt sweat springing out across his entire body as he wrestled with it. Eventually he managed to get it halfway in the bedroom window. Climbing over it with difficulty, he pulled it in after him.

And all the time, the man with the gun watched.

A pair of arms suddenly appeared over Sherlock's shoulder and took hold of the unconscious body.

"I'll take him from here," said a high-pitched voice.

Sherlock turned his head, surprised. A fourth man was standing close to him. This man was short and portly and bald. He was also missing part of his right ear.

Sherlock stepped back and let the newcomer pull the body along the floor, out into the corridor and along to a different bedroom. This one had a key sticking out of the lock. Inside, while the newcomer was hoisting the unconscious body onto the bed, Sherlock noticed that this room did actually have bars on the windows. This was the madman's room.

The third man—the burly one with the blond hair—was standing in the doorway. He still had the gun.

"How's Gilfillan?" he asked.

"Nasty head wound," the small, bald man replied, still arranging the madman on the bed. "He'll have one hell of a headache when he wakes up, but I think he'll be okay." He sniggered. "He's got a thick skull. You'd have to hit him a lot harder to cause any significant damage."

"I might just do that," the burly man snarled. "Damn fool, letting Booth get the drop on him like that. He could've derailed the entire plan. The last thing we need is Booth running wild across the countryside, especially in his current state."

Booth! Sherlock tried not to react, but inside he felt a warm glow of satisfaction. The man *was* John Wilkes Booth, not John St. Helen.

The burly man was still talking. He gestured at Sherlock with his gun. "And now, because of him, we're saddled with a witness."

The bald man stopped what he was doing and looked up at Sherlock for the first time. "What are we going to do with him, Ives?"

The burly man—Ives—shrugged. "I don't see we've got much of a choice," he said.

The bald man was suddenly nervous. "Look, he's just a kid. Can't we just, you know, let him go?" He turned towards Sherlock. "You ain't seen anything, have you, kid?"

Sherlock tried to look terrified. It wasn't hard. "Honest, guv," he said, putting as much sincerity into his voice as he could muster, "I'll forget all about it. I promise I will."

Ives ignored him. "What's the verdict on Booth?"

"The sedative worked a treat. He'll be out for a few hours."

Ives nodded. "That gives me enough time, then."

"Enough time to do what?"

Ives raised the long-barrelled revolver and pointed it directly at Sherlock. "To kill the kid and dump his body. Rule number one, remember—never leave anyone behind who's seen your face."

FOUR

Sherlock felt a shudder run through him. They were going to dispose of him, just throw him away like a sack of potato peelings! He glanced back and forth between the two men, looking for a way to escape, but Ives was standing in the doorway and the small, bald man was between Sherlock and the barred window.

"Please, mister, I ain't seen nothing," he whined, trying to buy himself some time.

"Don't come the innocent with me, son," Ives growled. He moved back into the corridor and gestured to Sherlock to follow him. "This way, and be quick about it." He glanced over at the short, bald man—who Sherlock assumed had some kind of medical training, as he seemed to be the one Ives deferred to when it came to injuries and insanity. "Berle, you secure Booth good and proper, and then you look to getting Gilfillan up and moving. I want to clear out of this place. There's too many people already who've spotted something odd. I guarantee our friend here didn't sneak around because he was looking for some lost ball, but because of some kind of dare, or because he wanted to see what we were doing."

Sherlock moved out into the hall. He glanced back at

Berle, who wouldn't meet his gaze. "Please, mister, don't let him hurt me," Sherlock said in the best whine he could manage, but Berle turned away, back to the unconscious John Wilkes Booth. "Sorry, kid," he murmured, "but there's too much at stake here. If Ives says you got to die, then you got to die. I ain't going to get involved."

Berle hesitated for a moment, looking at something on the dresser.

"What about this thing?" he asked Ives.

"What thing?"

Berle reached out and picked up a jar. It was made of glass, and the top was covered with a piece of muslin cloth held on with string. From where he stood Sherlock could see that tiny holes had been pricked into the muslin with a sharp knife. It was the kind of thing a kid would do to keep a caterpillar or beetle alive—cover the top of the jar so that the creature couldn't escape but punch some airholes in the top so that it could still breathe—but he couldn't see any insects or other creatures inside. The only thing in the jar was a mass of glistening red stuff, like a piece of liver or a massive clot of blood.

Ives glanced at it dismissively. "We take it with us," he said. "The boss wants it. He wants it almost as bad as he wants Booth, here."

Berle shook the jar dubiously. "You sure it's still alive?"

"It had better be. The boss ain't a man known for his

patience when it comes to being let down, an' this thing's come all the way from Borneo." His face fell into concerned lines. "I once heard that a servant of his dropped a pitcher of iced mint julep on the veranda one time. Duke just looked at him, not sayin' anythin'. The servant started to shake, an' he backed away down the garden to where it ended in a riverbank, shakin' all the time and cryin', an' he walked backwards into the river an' just disappeared, out of sight. Like he was hypnotized. Never seen again. Duke once said there are alligators in that river, but I don't know if he's tellin' the truth."

Berle looked dubious. "I would've thought Duke would use one of those two things he has on leashes. Ain't they supposed to be his killers?"

"Maybe he just wanted to make a point. Maybe those things weren't hungry." Ives shook his head. "It don't matter. That thing's comin' with us, all the way home."

He pushed Sherlock down the corridor towards the stairs with the barrel of the gun.

"What are you going to do to me?" Sherlock asked.

"Can't shoot you," Ives mused. "Not unless you give me no choice. If a kid's body is found with a ball in it then there'll be some kind of investigation, and the house with four foreigners in it is going to be the first place the police look. Could inject you with an overdose of one of Berle's drugs, I suppose, but that's a waste. We might need those drugs, the rate Booth's getting through them.

No, I think I'll just suffocate you with a rag in your mouth. That way there's no obvious sign of violence. There's a quarry a few miles away. I'll put you in the cart, cover you up with some sacking, and drive you out there. There's plenty of holes in the ground I can throw you into. If you're ever found, the authorities'll assume you just fell in and hit your head."

"Is it really so important?" Sherlock asked.

"Is what so important?"

"Whatever you're doing here? Is it really so important that you need to kill me to make sure nobody ever finds out?"

Ives laughed. "Oh, people'll find out all right. The world will find out in time, but that's a time of our choosing."

Sherlock was at the top of the stairs by now, and Ives gestured to him to head down, towards the first floor. Reluctantly Sherlock obeyed. He knew he had to make a break for it sometime, but if he tried now Ives would shoot him and find some other way of disposing his body so that it would never be found. Apart from causing Ives some momentary inconvenience, Sherlock was pretty sure that running now would achieve nothing. Maybe he'd get a chance when they got out into the open air.

Heading down the stairs, he felt something underneath the sole of his shoe; something lying on the carpet runner. Before he could see what it was, Ives had pushed him onward. Sherlock turned, curious, just in time to see a length of string suddenly pull tight across the stairs, from banister to panelled wall. It was the string, lying on the carpet, that he had stepped on.

Ives's foot caught under the string as he was going down to the next step. His body kept on moving while his foot stayed where it was, trapped. His eyes widened comically as he fell forward. His hands scrabbled for the wall and the banister, his right hand banging the revolver against the panelling of the wall before he dropped it. Sherlock stepped to one side as Ives fell past him. The man hit the stairs with his shoulder and rolled in an ungainly way, over and over, until he hit the first floor and lay sprawled across the landing.

Sherlock glanced over the edge of the banister from where he stood halfway up the stairs. Beneath him, in the shadows of the first floor, he saw Matty, his pale face staring up at him, his hand holding one end of a piece of string. Sherlock traced the string up to the banister and across the stairs to where a nail had been roughly pushed into the gap between the skirting board and the wall. The string was tied to the head of the nail.

"You were lucky the nail didn't pull out when his weight was pulling on the string," Sherlock observed calmly, although his heart was beating fast and heavy in his chest.

"No," Matty corrected, "*you* were lucky it didn't pull out. It made no difference to me. He didn't know I was here."

Sherlock descended to the first-floor landing and bent to check on Ives. The man was unconscious, with a nasty red mark on his forehead. Sherlock picked up the gun. No point taking any chances.

Matty joined him. "What is it about you and other people's houses?" he asked.

"What do you mean?"

"I mean I have to keep getting you out of trouble." He glanced up the stairs. "What's going on up there? I saw the cove with the burned face pull you into the house, and then I saw two other coves pitch up in a wagon. Next thing I know, there's three of you out on the roof. I saw guns, so I thought I'd better come in and get you." He shook his head. "For a kid with a big brain you spend a lot of time a prisoner. Can't you just talk your way out of trouble?"

"I think," Sherlock said, "that it's the talking that gets me *into* trouble, sometimes." He paused. "Where did you get the string from?"

"In me pocket, of course," Matty replied. "You never know when you might need string."

"Come on," Sherlock said. "Let's get out of here."

"There's another bloke downstairs," Matty pointed out, "but he's knocked out. At least, he was when I came up. We'd better be careful in case he's awake by now."

The two of them crept down the stairs to the ground floor and past the reception room where the man whom

Sherlock had first seen unconscious and bleeding—Gilfillan, Ives had called him—was now lying on the sofa and snoring. Sneaking by, they headed out of the front door, out of the garden and down the road to where Matty had hitched the horses.

"Did you find out what you needed to know?" Matty asked as they mounted the horses.

"I think so," Sherlock said. "There's four men in the house, and they're all American. At least, three of them are—I never heard the other one speak. One of the men is disturbed in the head, and one of them is a doctor looking after him. The other two I guess are guarding him, making sure he doesn't escape. They must have left one man in charge when the other two went out—maybe to get food or something—and the disturbed man, whose name is John Wilkes Booth, knocked him out. He assumed I was part of some kind of plot against him, which is why he pulled me into the house."

"But what are they doing here in England in the first place?" Matty asked.

"I don't know, but there's something going on. This isn't just a rest home for mad assassins.

"Mad *assassins*?"

"I'll tell you all about it when we get to Holmes Manor."

The ride back to Farnham took over an hour, and Sherlock's spirits fell with every mile they travelled. How was he going to explain to Mycroft and to Amyus Crowe that his quiet little investigation had ended with the four men in the house alerted that someone knew they were up to no good? If he'd thought about it properly, he would never have gone near the house.

Mycroft's carriage was still outside Holmes Manor when they got there.

"Well," Matty said after they'd put the horses in the stables, "good luck."

"What do you mean, good luck? Aren't you coming in with me?"

"Are you joking? Mr. Crowe scares me, and your brother terrifies me. I'm going back to the narrowboat. Tell me all about it tomorrow." And with that he turned and walked off.

Taking a deep breath, Sherlock entered the hall, crossed to the library, and knocked on the door.

"Come in," his brother's voice boomed.

Mycroft and Amyus Crowe were sitting together at a long reading desk over to one side of the library. A huge pile of books was sitting in front of them—histories, geographies, philosophies, and three very large atlases which had been opened to show a map of what looked to Sherlock like the Americas.

Mycroft looked Sherlock up and down critically.

"You have been assaulted," he said, "and not by someone your own age."

"Or from this country," Amyus Crowe rumbled.

"In fact," Mycroft said, glancing at Sherlock's shoes, "there were two assailants. One of them was mentally deficient in some way."

"And both men were armed with pistols," Crowe added.

"How do you know these things?" Sherlock asked, amazed.

"A trifling matter," Mycroft said, waving his hand airily. "Explaining it would waste time. More important is, where did you go and why were you attacked?"

Reluctantly Sherlock told them both everything that had happened, ending with the realization that he still had Ives's pistol tucked into the back of his trousers. He pulled it out and put it on the desk in front of the two men.

"Colt Army model," Crowe observed mildly, ".44 calibre, six rounds. Fourteen inches from hammer to the end of the barrel. Replaced the Colt Dragoon as the preferred weapon of the U.S. Army. Accurate up to around a hundred yards." His fist slammed down on the table, making the gun jump. "What in the name of God and all his angels did you think you were doin', goin' to that house?" he shouted. "You've alerted Booth an' his handlers to the fact someone's on to them! They'll clear out like greased lightnin'."

Sherlock bit the inside of his lip, trying to stop himself responding. "I just wanted to take a look," he said eventually. "I thought I could help."

"You've not helped; you've actively hindered," Crowe

exploded. "This is a business for grownups. You ain't got the skills or the knowledge to do it properly."

Part of Sherlock's mind—a dispassionate, detached part—noticed that Amyus Crowe's accent became thicker when he was angry, but the greater part was cringing at the knowledge that he had let down two of the three men whose opinion mattered most to him in the world. He opened his mouth to say "Sorry," but his mouth was dry and he couldn't get the word out.

The expression on Mycroft's face was of disappointment rather than anger. "Go to your room, Sherlock," he said. "We will call for you when"—he glanced at Crowe—"we can be more assured of a calmer discussion. Now go."

Feeling his cheeks burning with shame, Sherlock turned around and walked out of the library.

The hall was stifling in the afternoon heat. He stopped for a moment, head hanging, letting the feelings drain away from him and waiting until he felt he could face the long climb up to his room. His head hurt.

"No longer the favoured child?" said a voice from the shadows.

Sherlock glanced up as Mrs. Eglantine glided out from the cubbyhole beneath the stairs. She was smiling nastily. Her black crinoline dress moved stiffly around her, and the sound of it brushing against the floor was like someone whispering in a distant room.

"How is it that you manage to survive in this house, being so rude to everyone?" he asked mildly, knowing that he had nothing to lose. Things were already as bad as they were going to get that day. "I would have fired you years ago, if I was in charge."

She seemed surprised by his reaction. The smile slipped from her face. "You have no power here," she snapped. "*I* have the power in this house."

"Only until Uncle Sherrinford dies," Sherlock pointed out. "Neither he nor Aunt Anna has any children, so possession of the house will pass to my father's side of the family. And then you need to step *very* carefully, Mrs. Eglantine."

Before she could say anything in response, he headed up the stairs to his room. Looking down from the first-floor landing, he could still see her standing there.

He lay down on his bed, flung an arm across his eyes, and let the whirl of thoughts in his head take him over. What had he been thinking? Mycroft and Crowe had both warned him off from helping. What exactly was it that he had been trying to prove?

He must have drifted into a doze after a while, because the light in the room seemed to suddenly change, and he had pins and needles in his arm from where it was awkwardly crossing his face. He got up and slowly went downstairs; more to find food than for any other reason. He was suddenly ravenous.

The maids were setting the table for dinner. Mycroft was just emerging from the library. There was no sign of Amyus Crowe.

Mycroft nodded at Sherlock. "Feeling better?" he asked.

"Not really. I did something stupid."

"Not for the first time, and probably not for the last time. Just make sure you learn a lesson from this. Making a mistake is excusable the first time. After that it becomes tedious."

One of the maids emerged from the dining room with a small gong in a frame. Without looking at Mycroft or Sherlock she banged the gong once, loudly, and then retreated back into the dining room.

"Shall we?" Mycroft asked.

Within a few moments they had been joined by Sherrinford and Anna Holmes. Mycroft spent most of dinner discussing the accuracy of the Latin translation of the Greek translation of the Hebrew and Aramaic books of the Old Testament. Aunt Anna spent most of the time talking to Sherrinford and Mycroft, oblivious of the fact that they were already talking to each other, although from some sense of gallantry Mycroft would turn around every so often and answer one of the questions that passed by in her continuous monologue. Sherlock spent his time eating, and avoiding the stare of Mrs. Eglantine, who glared at him from a position by the windows.

After dinner, Sherrinford and Anna escorted Mycroft to the front steps to say goodbye.

"Your Greek is fluent, and your Latin is particularly well constructed," Sherrinford said, apparently the highest praise he could think of. "And I have enjoyed our discourse. Your knowledge of the Old Testament is lacking, but you have made some surprising deductions already, based on what I have told you. I will need to think long and hard about what you have suggested concerning the early days of the Church. Please visit us again soon."

Aunt Anna surprised everyone by stepping forward and placing a hand on Mycroft's arm. "You are always welcome here," she said. "I . . . regret . . . the animosity that has split the family. I wish it could be otherwise."

"Your kindness is a force that could overcome all adversities," Mycroft replied gently. "And the charity you have shown by looking after young Sherlock is a humbling example to us all. Consider the rift more than repaired, but eradicated." He cast a glance into the shadows of the hall, where Sherlock thought he could just make out a figure, dressed in black, watching them. Mycroft lowered his voice. "But while a particular person still has influence within this house, I suspect I will never feel quite as accepted as you would wish me to feel."

Anna looked away. Sherlock thought he could see the gleam of tears in her eyes. "We are where we are," she said cryptically. "And we do what we do."

Mycroft stepped back. "I will take my leave of you," he said, "with many thanks. Might I presume upon your good natures one last time, and ask that Sherlock accompany me to the station? The carriage can bring him back afterwards."

"Of course," Sherrinford said, waving a hand airily.

As the carriage took them out of the grounds of the manor and onto the road, Sherlock looked back. There were three figures on the steps now—his aunt, his uncle, and Mrs. Eglantine. And either by accident or design, Mrs. Eglantine was standing on the highest step, towering over her employers.

"You still want to talk about what happened today," Sherlock guessed as the carriage bounced over potholes and stones.

"Of course. We will be stopping at Mr. Crowe's cottage. There is still much to discuss."

The carriage rattled through the landscape.

Sherlock could still feel an ache in his scalp where the scarred lunatic had grabbed him by the hair and dragged him into the house. He reached up and surreptitiously tugged at a lock, just to check that it wasn't going to come out. The sudden pain made tears spring out in his eyes, but the hair stayed where it was. Thank God.

Within ten minutes the carriage was slowing down, and Sherlock could see the loaflike shape of a thatched roof rising above a clump of bushes.

"Come," said Mycroft as the carriage stopped outside a gate in a dry stone wall. "Mr. Crowe is expecting us."

The cottage door was open. Mycroft knocked and then entered without waiting for an answer.

Amyus Crowe was sitting in a chair by the hearth, his massive form dwarfing the wooden frame. He was smoking a cigar. "Mr. Holmes," he said equably, nodding.

"Mr. Crowe," Mycroft responded. "Thank you for seeing us."

"Please, sit yourselves down."

Mycroft chose the only other comfortable chair in the room. Sherlock sat on a stool near the cold, empty fireplace and looked around. Amyus Crowe's cottage was as untidy as he remembered. A pile of letters was fastened to the wooden mantelpiece with a knife, and a lone slipper on the floor beside the fireplace contained a bunch of cigars, sticking upward in various directions. And there was a map of the local area attached to a wall with drawing pins. Circles and lines had been drawn on it in some apparently random pattern. Some of the lines continued off onto the plaster of the wall.

Sherlock wondered where Crowe's daughter, Virginia, was. There was no sign of her in the cottage, and given her headstrong attitude he wouldn't expect her to stay in her room meekly while the men talked. Maybe she was out riding around the countryside, as she seemed to do a lot of the time. He hadn't seen her horse, Sandia, outside the cottage.

He smiled. Virginia hated being inside. In some ways she was more like an animal than a person.

"Might I offer you a glass of sherry?" Crowe asked. "Can't stand the stuff myself—tastes like something's crawled into the barrel an' died—but I keep a bottle for visitors."

"Thank you, but no," Mycroft replied smoothly. "Sherlock does not drink, and I prefer a brandy at this time of day." He glanced over at Sherlock. "America has still not managed to develop a national drink," he said. "The French have wine and brandy, the Italians *grappa*, the Germans wheat beer, the Scots whisky, and the English ale, but our transatlantic cousins are still in the process of working out their own identity."

It sounded to Sherlock as if Mycroft wasn't really talking about drinks at all, but trying to make some other, much more subtle point, but for the life of him he couldn't work out what it was.

"The Mexicans have a drink they distil from a cactus," Crowe said good-humouredly. "Tequila, they call it. Maybe we could adopt that."

"What's a cactus?" Sherlock asked.

"It's a fleshy plant with a thick skin an' covered with spikes," Crowe responded. "It grows in the heat an' the sand of the hot, arid lands in Texas an' New Mexico an' California. The thick skin keeps the water from evaporatin' away, an' the spikes stop cows an' horses an' suchlike from eatin' it for the water content. Either the cactus is evidence of a Designer who makes things differently for different environments, so they can best survive, or it's evidence that there's some force that pushes livin' organisms to change and develop so as to best survive in whatever place they find themselves, as Mr. Charles Darwin contends. You pay your money and you make your choice."

"Back to the subject at hand, what have you been able to discover?" Mycroft asked.

Crowe shrugged. "I found the house. It's empty. Looks like the occupants cleared out in a hurry. I talked to a farmworker along the road who saw them leave. He said there were four of them. One looked like he was asleep, one had his head all bandaged up, an' the other two were scowlin' like they'd got a long an' unpleasant journey ahead of them."

"The birds have flown." Mycroft considered for a moment. "Is there any more evidence that the sleeping man was John Wilkes Booth?"

Crowe shrugged. "Save what your brother told us, nothin'. It's instructive that his face was scarred by an old fire. The last thing that was heard of John Wilkes Booth was when he was involved in a shootout in a barn in Virginia with the Army. They'd tracked him down an' ordered him to surrender, but he opened fire. The Army fired back, an' somewhere along the line the barn caught fire. Prob'ly an oil lamp got knocked over. Anyhow, when the fire had died down the Army recovered a body from the wreckage. It was so badly burned they couldn't identify it properly, but they assumed it was Booth. Looks now like Booth escaped but some accomplice got caught in the fire an' couldn't get out in time." He paused. "Booth was always highly strung. Seems now that the enormity of what he did an' the subsequent escape an' the fire have caused his mind to snap. What's interestin' to me is that he's obviously under the care an' protection of an organization of some kind, an' they obviously have a need for him. He ain't goin' to lead anyone anymore, not from what the lad here has said, so what else can he do for them?"

"He's a figurehead," Mycroft pointed out. "Probably the most famous Confederate apart from General Lee and Jefferson Davis. If there's even a stub of Confederate supporters left in America, and if they have even the slightest flicker of interest in overturning the new presidency and installing one more sympathetic to their own beliefs, then John Wilkes Booth would be an ideal man for them to use as a rallying point. All they have to do is wheel him out at a few secret rallies and make a point about how he had the courage to try to bring down the Union with a few well-aimed bullets, and they could whip up a crowd into a frenzy."

"That's what I was afraid of," Crowe said, nodding. "Don't matter if he's of unsound mind—they just have to dope him up enough so he can stand still on a stage, an' they can make all kinds of speeches around him." He paused for a moment. "What's the position of the British government on all of this?"

"I can't speak for the British government," Mycroft said judiciously, "but I am aware that the Foreign Office is in favour of the current regime, and would not like to see the Confederacy resurgent. Slavery is an abhorrent practice, and it needs to be stamped out. The first thing a Confederate president would do is to reverse the advances made by President Lincoln and his successor. That will not do."

Crowe sighed. "They're goin' to head back to the United States, aren't they?"

Mycroft nodded.

"Then I have to follow 'em."

"We could send a telegram," Mycroft offered. "It would beat them across the Atlantic."

Crowe shook his head. "We don't know which ship they'll be on."

"We can check the manifests," Mycroft said. "Granted they'll be travelling under false names, but we can look for four men travelling together, one of whom is obviously sick."

"They won't be travelling together." Crowe sounded certain. "They'll book tickets separately, and possibly engage the services of a nurse to look after Booth. No, we'll be tryin' to track down four individuals whose descriptions are vague an' whose names are unknown." He suddenly hit the arm of his chair with a balled fist, making Sherlock jump. "I'm a tracker. I have to track 'em. Simple as that. I'll assume they're headin' for New York an' start there."

"I could help," Sherlock said, surprising himself. "I'm the only one who's seen them. I could go to the docks and see who boards the ships."

"We don't know where they're embarkin' from," Crowe pointed out.

"It could be Southampton, or Liverpool, or even Queenstown," Mycroft added gently. "One boy can't cover three ports, no matter how clever he is."

"But . . ." Sherlock started to say, and then trailed off. What he wanted to say was that Crowe couldn't leave England, because Sherlock was only just beginning to understand the lessons that Crowe was teaching him, and if he *was* going to leave then he couldn't take his daughter, Virginia, with him. Sherlock was developing feelings for her that he didn't quite understand and he wanted to see where those feelings were going to lead him, even though they scared him. But he knew that neither of those arguments would hold any water when set against some vague but obviously important conspiracy directed against the government of an entire country.

But it looked as though his life was about to be turned upside down.

Again.

FIVE

Mycroft and Crowe started discussing ship timetables and ports of embarkation and disembarkation. Sherlock got bored very quickly. His mind kept attacking the problem, trying to find something that would mean Amyus and Virginia Crowe wouldn't have to leave England.

"You still don't know what the men look like," he pointed out after a few minutes. "You can track them, but how will you know when you've found them? As long as they keep the man with the burn scars out of sight, they'll just be three men. There's nothing particularly distinctive about them, apart from their accents, and I'm assuming that once you get to a dock with a ship heading for America there's going to be a lot of American accents around."

"You can tell me the details of what they look like," Crowe responded. "I've already trained you in lookin' for the small details that distinguish one face from another—the outline of the ears, the hairline, an' the shape of the eyes. We might even be able to come up with a couple of sketches based on your descriptions. Virginia's a dab hand with a pencil."

"I'm not sure that will be enough," Mycroft mused.

"The recollections of one witness, even one as observant as my brother, can often be mistaken, and affected by stress. It's something I have long been interested in—the way the human mind can invent details and convince itself that they are true. I suspect there are many innocent men incarcerated in British prisons based on the uncertain recollections of one person. Once you have been told that you are looking for a man with a beard, suddenly all you can see is men with beards. No, whatever Sherlock remembers needs to be taken with a pinch of salt."

Sherlock was about to protest that he had a perfect recollection of all four men, but something held him back. He sensed that the argument was beginning to swing back in his favour, with Mycroft and Crowe realizing that the problem was bigger than they had thought, and he didn't want to do anything to disrupt them.

But at the same time that his heart was trying to stop Amyus and Virginia Crowe from leaving, his head was telling him that this was important. Both Mycroft and Crowe were looking as serious as he had ever seen them. He wasn't sure that he completely understood the potential ramifications of what was going on—how could four men, one of them certifiably insane, affect the politics of an entire nation?—but he could tell that what was at stake here dwarfed his petty problems. If he could help, he should, regardless of the cost to himself.

It was a strangely grownup thought, and he didn't like the implications.

"Matty's seen them as well," he said suddenly, his words only momentarily behind his thoughts.

"What do you mean?" Mycroft asked, turning his head.

"I mean that Matty saw the man who pulled me into the house—the man who might be John Wilkes Booth—and then later, when he rescued me, he saw at least two of the other three men. One of them was unconscious—neither of us got a good look at him. If you want a description but you're worried about the reliability of my memory, then why not get Matty over here? Between the two of us you could probably get a good description, especially if you ask us separately rather than together. That way neither of us will inadvertently affect what the other is saying."

"The boy has a point," Crowe rumbled. "Two heads are better than one. Mayhap I could send Virginia to pick the boy up. She knows where his narrowboat is moored." He nodded to himself. "A sketch based on both their memories would be far closer to the truth than one based on the memory of either one alone."

Mycroft gazed levelly at Sherlock. "I understand that you don't want Mr. Crowe or his daughter to go," he said quietly. "And yet you provided a suggestion that made it more likely they *would* go. You are thinking like a man, not a boy. I'm proud of you, Sherlock. And Father would be as well."

Sherlock turned away so that Mycroft would not see the sudden glistening of his eyes.

Oblivious to the exchange between the two brothers, Crowe had levered himself up out of the tight chair and lumbered towards the door of the cottage. "Ginny!" he yelled, opening the door. "I have need of you!" He stood there for a moment until he was sure that she was on her way, then he came back and stood beside the chair.

Virginia Crowe appeared in the doorway. She glanced at Sherlock and smiled. As usual, he was struck by the sheer amount of colour about her—the redness of her hair, the brown tan on her skin, the smattering of freckles across her cheeks and nose, and the violet shade of her eyes. She made other girls look like black-and-white drawings.

"Yes, Father?"

"Got an errand for you. I need you to ride over an' fetch the Arnatt boy from his boat. Tell him I need to ask him a few questions about today. Tell him he ain't in trouble, but I need his help."

She nodded. "You want me to bring him back on Sandia?"

"Quicker that way. The horse can take both your weights. He's a small lad."

"But scrappy," Sherlock added in Matty's defence.

"Of that I have no doubt," Crowe said. He looked over at Virginia. "Be fast, now."

She glanced again at Sherlock, looking as if she wanted to say something, maybe ask him if he wanted to go with her, but instead she turned and left. Within a few moments Sherlock heard the high whinny of Virginia's horse welcoming her, the jangle of reins, and the diminishing sound of hoofs on hard earth.

Crowe and Mycroft got back to discussing ways of getting across the Atlantic Ocean faster than the four Americans. It all seemed to depend on which ship they took and which port they sailed from. Some ships were faster than others. Sherlock picked up from the discussion that some of the newer ships didn't rely only on wind and sails to take them across the sea but supplemented that with powerful steam engines driving massive wheels, like those of a water mill, which had wooden paddles spaced around their circumference. The motion of the paddles against the water, powered by the steam engines, would push against the water and move the ship forward even if there wasn't any wind. Was there anywhere the steam engine could not go, any problem it could not solve? What would come next, he wondered—carts and carriages driven by steam filling the roads and taking men from London to Liverpool in a few hours? And perhaps even further—could man one day reach the *moon* using steam-driven craft?

Shaking his head to dislodge these incredible thoughts, he returned to listening to Mycroft and Amyus Crowe discussing politics, travel, and revolution.

The talk went on, and Sherlock found himself fading in and out of it. The politics was above his head, although every now and then Crowe would bring it down to earth with an example of the number of people who died at a particular place or time, or how a particular town had been razed to the ground to make a point.

Eventually, he heard the rapid drumbeat of approaching hoofs. He went to the door, ready to welcome Virginia and Matty.

Outside, in the early evening light, he could see Sandia, Virginia's horse, approaching. The mass on its back had to be Virginia and Matty, and for a moment Sherlock found himself jealous of Matty's closeness to her. Only for a moment, though.

As Sandia got closer the dark mass on his back resolved into one figure rather than two. It was Virginia, and she pulled Sandia to a halt just beside Sherlock. Her eyes were wild, and her hair had been pulled by the wind into a tangled mass.

"Where's Matty?" Sherlock asked.

She jumped down from the horse's back and pushed past him, running into the cottage. Sherlock followed.

"They've taken Matty!" she cried.

"What do you mean?" Mycroft said, rising from the table.

"I got to the narrowboat, and I got him to come with me," she said in a rush. "We were both on the back of Sandia. We got to just down the road, and there was a tree across it, blocking the way. It wasn't there when I went out, I swear. I thought about jumping it, but with Matty on Sandia's back with me I wasn't sure we could make it, so I stopped so Matty and I could shift the tree.

Two men ran out of the woods at us. They must have been hiding in the bushes. One of them hit Matty around the head. It must've knocked him out, because he didn't fight anymore. The other man came for me. He tried to grab my hair, but I bit his hand. He pulled away, and I ran for Sandia. I jumped on his back and rode away. When I looked back, the two of them were carrying Matty away." Her face was white and shocked. "I left him there!" she cried, as if she'd just realized what had happened. "I should have stayed and rescued him, or gone back for him."

"If you'd done that, likely as not you'd have been taken too," Crowe pointed out. He moved across the cottage with surprising speed for such a large man and pulled her to him in a rough embrace. "Thank the Lord you're safe."

"But Matty!" Sherlock cried.

"We'll get him back," Mycroft promised, levering his bulk up from his chair. "It's obvious that—"

Before he could complete the sentence there was a crashing of glass, and something heavy flew through the air from the shattered window and thudded against the floor. Crowe ran for the door and threw it open. From outside, Sherlock could hear hoofs thudding into the earth as someone raced away on horseback. Crowe cursed volubly. There were words in there that Sherlock had never even heard before, although he could guess at their meaning.

Sherlock bent to pick up the object that had been thrown in through the window. It was a large stone, about the size of two clenched fists held together. A length of string was tied around it, fastening a torn piece of paper to the stone's surface.

Mycroft took the stone from Sherlock's hands and put it on the table. Deftly, he took a knife from the table and sliced through the string. "Best to preserve the knots," he said to Sherlock without turning his head. "They may tell us something about the man who tied them. Sailors, for instance, have a whole set of peculiar knots they use that have not found their way into the knowledge of the general populace. If you have a few days to yourself I really would commend to you a study of knots."

Sliding the string to one side, presumably for later analysis, he unwrapped the paper from the stone and smoothed it out on the table.

"It's a warning," he said to Crowe. " 'We have your boy. Cease from your persecution of us. Do not attempt to follow us. If you leave us alone, he will be returned to you in three months—unharmed. If you do not leave us alone, he will still be returned—in pieces, and over a period of some weeks. You have been warned.' "

Crowe was holding Virginia in his arms. "They obviously assume Matty is my son," he said, "probably because they saw him and Ginny on the same horse. They'll realize their mistake soon enough when they hear him speak."

"Not necessarily," Mycroft pointed out. "They don't know how long you've been here in England. In fact, they probably don't even know you're American. I think young Matthew will be safe enough for the moment. Now, what can we tell from the note?"

"Forget the note—we should go after them!" Sherlock cried.

"The boy is right," Crowe rumbled. "There's a time for analysis and a time for action. This is the latter." He pushed Virginia away gently. "You stay here. I'm going after them."

"And so am I," Sherlock said forcefully. When Crowe opened his mouth to argue, he added, "Matty's my friend, and I got him into this. And besides, two of us can cover more ground."

Crowe glanced over at Mycroft, who must have nodded imperceptibly, because he said, "Okay, young 'un, mount up. We ride now."

Crowe headed for the door and Sherlock followed.

Outside, Crowe had already saddled one horse and was preparing a second for Sherlock. By the time Sherlock had mounted, Crowe was already galloping away.

Sherlock pressed his heels into his horse's flanks, and the horse began to gallop in pursuit.

The sun was heading towards the horizon, veiled by wispy clouds so that Sherlock could see it as a ball of red light. Crowe and his horse were racing ahead of him. He struggled to keep up. The thudding of his horse's hoofs on the road transmitted itself up his spine, a constant vibration that made it hard to take a full breath.

How did Crowe know in which direction to go? he wondered. Presumably he'd made some quick calculation about the most likely road out of Farnham, if the men were heading to the coast. Southampton would be the obvious place for departure if they were going to America. But Crowe might have been wrong—the men might have been intending to embark at Liverpool, travelling up by train from London, which meant they would be leaving Farnham in an entirely different direction. For the first time, Sherlock realized that logical thought could only go so far, and that it produced a single answer only rarely. More often than not, logical thinking produced several possible answers, and you had to find another way to choose between them. You could call it intuition, or guesswork, but it wasn't logic.

Cottages and houses flashed past too quickly to recognize. In the distance Sherlock could see a stone building on a hill: Farnham Castle, perhaps? The wind whistled past his ears, freezing them despite the heat from the day which had been absorbed by the earth and was coming back up from the ground. He thought he could hear the echo of his horse's hoofs, but there was nothing for the sound to echo off. He glanced over his shoulder and was amazed to see Virginia behind him, pressed close to Sandia's neck. She flashed a grin at him. He grinned back.

He should have known that there was no way she would have been kept away from the action. She really was unlike any other girl he'd ever met.

The three of them rode through a tiny hamlet of cottages clustered together. People scattered out of their path. Sherlock could hear raised voices behind them as they rode away. Ahead of them the road was empty until it curved out of sight. How long would Crowe keep riding before he acknowledged that they had gone in the wrong direction?

Virginia caught up with Sherlock. She glanced sideways, eyes almost glowing. Sherlock suspected she was enjoying herself, despite the urgency of their mission. She loved to ride, and this was a chance to ride like she'd never ridden before.

Ahead, past Amyus Crowe's bulky body and wide white hat, which was somehow managing to stay on his head despite the speed at which the man was riding, Sherlock suddenly caught sight of a carriage. It was rocking back and forth as it pelted along the road, the wheels on one side leaving the road for a few moments before bouncing back as it went around a curve. Above it, Sherlock thought he could see the slender line of a whip flicking forward as the driver thrashed the horses to greater and greater efforts. Was Matty in the carriage? The driver was obviously making every effort he could to race along the road. If it wasn't the Americans inside, then it was a huge coincidence that someone else was so desperate to leave Farnham that they were willing to risk their lives doing it.

Sherlock pressed his horse to race faster, and she complied. The gap between Sherlock and Crowe narrowed, and he could see the carriage better. It was a four-wheeler, pulled by a team of two horses, and the springs were bouncing up and down as the wheels hit ruts, holes, and bumps in the road.

Virginia drew alongside Sherlock's left shoulder. He glanced across at her again. Her teeth were bared in what looked like a grin but which Sherlock suspected was more like a snarl.

Sherlock glanced right, at Virginia's father. His gaze was fixed on the carriage ahead, and there was such volcanic force in his eyes that Sherlock was momentarily scared. He'd always thought of Crowe as being a gentleman to whom logic and the gathering of facts were more important than anything else, but Virginia had told him that Crowe had been a hunter of men back in America, and often hadn't brought them back alive. Looking at Crowe now, Sherlock could believe it. No force on earth could stop a man with that look in his eyes.

Crowe's horse was foaming at the mouth, he was pushing it so hard. Tiny flecks of foam were caught by the wind and carried backwards, into the distance.

The road veered right, and the carriage ahead took the curve without slackening speed. The two wheels on the outside of the curve left the road and the carriage itself looked as if it was going to topple over and be dragged along the ground by the horses, but the men inside must have thrown their weight towards the left because it suddenly lurched sideways, and the wheels dropped to the ground.

Sherlock, Crowe, and Virginia took the curve as well, their horses leaning sideways so that their hoofs could get a purchase on the road. Ahead of them, as they straightened out, Sherlock suddenly caught sight of a cart heading towards the careering carriage, loaded with bundles of freshly cut hay. The driver was frantically gesturing to the carriage to get out of the way, but he must have known that it was too late, because he swerved his cart off the road and into a ditch. The carriage thundered past, missing the back end of the cart by a few inches. Moments later, Sherlock, Crowe, and Virginia galloped past as well. Sherlock glanced sideways, to check that the driver was all right. He was standing up in the front of the cart, gesturing at them in rage. And then they were past and he was receding into the distance behind them like a fragment of memory.

Movement at the side of the carriage caught Sherlock's attention. A man was leaning out, holding a stick of some kind. Sherlock thought it was one of the men from the house in Godalming but he couldn't be sure. The man pointed the stick backwards along the road, towards the three riders, and flame suddenly blossomed at the end of it. He was holding a rifle!

Sherlock couldn't tell where the bullet went. The carriage was bouncing so much as it tore through the evening that the gunman could have no way of accurately aiming the rifle, but that didn't mean he couldn't hit one of them, or one of the horses, at random.

The man fired again, and this time Sherlock thought he could hear the sound of the bullet as it passed him by: a furious buzzing sound, like an angry wasp.

Crowe urged his horse to greater efforts, and for a moment he seemed to draw closer to the carriage. He was gripping the reins with one hand while the other was pulling at his belt. He withdrew a pistol, which he pointed at the man leaning out of the carriage. He fired, the recoil knocking his hand back and twisting his body in the saddle. The man with the rifle pulled himself back inside the carriage. Sherlock couldn't tell whether he was injured or just cautious.

They were racing along the side of a river now. Silvery light reflected from the surface of the water.

The man with the rifle appeared again, leaning out of the same side that he had before, but this time he was facing forward. He pointed the rifle ahead, and pulled the trigger. Again, flame burst like an exotic flower in the dusk. For a confused moment Sherlock thought he was shooting at the horses that were pulling the carriage, but he was firing over their heads! Sherlock realized immediately that he was trying to terrify them into galloping even faster than they already were, and it seemed to work.

The gap between the carriage and the pursuing horses quickly widened as the carriage raced ahead. They couldn't keep that speed up for long—the horses would quickly exhaust themselves—but he obviously had something else in mind.

The gunman disappeared inside the carriage again, but only for a moment. The door suddenly sprang open and the man dived out. He'd timed his dive perfectly, and hit the mass of reeds and vegetation that lined the riverbank. He vanished from sight, but Sherlock could track his path by the long ripped gap that appeared in the reeds as they slowed his progress.

Crowe slowed his horse for a moment, uncertain what to do, then urged it on, heading after the carriage rather than for the man, but Sherlock watched as the man emerged from the reeds. He was soaking wet, and there were gashes across his face from where the reeds had cut his skin.

He held a rifle in his hands. He raised it as Crowe raced ahead, took careful aim along the long barrel, and fired.

At the same moment the fire blossomed out of the barrel, Crowe threw his arms up to his face and fell backwards, out of the saddle. He hit the road, right shoulder first, and rolled over and over in the dirt until he lay still, like a dusty log. His horse rode on, but without Crowe urging it on it slowed to a canter, then to a trot, then to a halt. It stood there, apparently watching the carriage as it receded into the distance and wondering what all the rush had been about.

Virginia screamed, "Father!" as she pulled her horse to a skidding halt and threw herself out of the saddle. She pelted along the road towards him, regardless of the man with the rifle who was watching her approach.

And raising his rifle.

All this had happened within the space of a scattered handful of seconds. Sherlock dug his heels into his horse's flanks. The horse surged forward.

"Down!" he shouted.

Virginia glanced back over her shoulder, saw him bearing down on her, and dived. As she rolled over, Sherlock pulled up on the reins. His horse jumped over her, seeming to sail through the air regardless of gravity.

The horse's front hoofs hit the ground hard, and it stumbled, just as the gunman fired again. Sherlock didn't even hear the shot. He was flung from the saddle and over the horse's head. His mind was filled with the enormity of the ground as it rose up towards him. Time seemed to stretch out, and he found that he was wondering whether he would crack his skull or break both legs first. Something made him curl into a ball, tucking his head onto his chest and wrapping his arms around it while bringing his knees up to his stomach. He hit the ground and rolled, feeling stones bite into his flesh beneath his ribs, back, and legs. The world flashed around him, over and over; dark, light, dark. He lost track of where he was.

After an eternity he came to a stop. Raising his head cautiously, he tried to work out where he had ended up. Everything was blurred, and he felt like part of him was still rolling over and over even though the feel of the stones beneath his hands and knees told him that he was stationary. His stomach clenched, and he had to stop himself throwing up. He could feel the rough burn of scratches across his whole body.

In the distance, the carriage in which Matty was being held prisoner was vanishing into a cloud of dust.

A shadow fell across Sherlock. He looked up. The man with the rifle was standing over him. He wasn't sure, but it looked like it might have been the man who'd been knocked out by the lunatic, John Wilkes Booth. The other men had called him Gilfillan. His head was bandaged, and his eyes were full of vicious hatred.

"What is it with you kids?" he asked, raising the rifle. "I swear we've had more trouble from you in the past day than from the whole Union Army since the end of the war!"

"Give my friend back," Sherlock snarled, climbing to his feet.

"Tough talk from someone who ain't goin' to be alive in a minute's time," the man said, smiling grimly. "We took the kid to stop you an' that guy in the white hat from comin' after us, but ah guess that didn't work out the way we expected. So I'll just kill you all now, and cable ahead to tell Ives to kill him, 'cause we don't need him anymore." He took his finger off the trigger and showed the back of the hand to Sherlock. There was blood on it, and what looked like a set of teeth marks in the soft flesh between the base of the thumb and the first finger. "That girl bit me!" he protested disbelievingly.

"Yeh," Sherlock said, "I imagine you hear that a lot," and he whipped his hand around from behind his back, releasing the stones that he'd picked up from the ground. They flew through the air in blurs, hitting Gilfillan on his cheek, his forehead, and his left eye. He threw up his hands to his face, dropping the rifle. It bounced once, twice on the ground. Sherlock rushed forward to grab it, but the man kicked it out of the way. His hand caught in Sherlock's hair and he twisted. Sherlock cried out in a mixture of anger and pain, and lashed out with his foot. His boot connected with Gilfillan's shin, and the grip on his hair suddenly released. Sherlock sprang back, looking for the rifle. He caught sight of it at the same time as the American, and they both dived for it. Sherlock got there first, fingers clutching at the stock and body rolling out of the way as the man cursed.

They both stood there for a moment, breathing heavily. The man wiped the back of his hand across his mouth.

"You ain't got the gumption," he said. "I'm goin' to come for that gun an' I'm goin' to wrap it around your throat an' choke the life from your scrawny body!"

He moved forward, and Sherlock raised the rifle menacingly.

"Don't . . ." he said.

The man kept coming, a grimace stretching across his face and his dirty hands reaching forward for Sherlock.

SIX

Knowing that he had no choice, Sherlock pointed the rifle at the man's chest and pulled the trigger, bracing himself for the resulting recoil.

Nothing happened. The rifle failed to fire.

Gilfillan grinned triumphantly. "Grit in the mechanism," he said. "Got to treat them old rifles right. Smallest thing can stop 'em from firin'." He reached into a trouser pocket and pulled out something small and dark. He flicked his hand, and suddenly there was a blade in it, a wickedly curved blade. "Not like a knife. Knives work under most circumstances, I find. Slower than a rifle, but a lot more fun."

He stepped forward and slashed the knife sideways, aiming for Sherlock's eyes. The boy stumbled back, feeling the cold breeze following in the wake of the blade as it brushed his eyelashes. The low rays of the sun, reflected from the sharp point at the end of the blade, traced a red line across Sherlock's vision that persisted even when the knife had gone.

Gilfillan stepped forward, jerking the knife upward, trying to get it into Sherlock's stomach, but Sherlock blocked it with the stock of the rifle. The impact knocked him backwards, but Gilfillan held his wrist and swore.

"That's it," he snarled. "I ain't goin' to treat you like an equal anymore. I'm goin' to slaughter you like cattle."

He reached out and grabbed Sherlock by the ear before the boy could get away, pulling him closer even as he raised the knife towards Sherlock's throat. Instinctively, Sherlock brought the rifle up between them, trying to block the blade, but as the barrel passed his face he had a sudden inspiration and he jabbed it straight upward into Gilfillan's right eye.

The American screamed and staggered backwards, clutching at his face. Blood streamed from between his fingers. Sherlock expected him to fall to the ground, incapacitated, but his intact eye fixed on Sherlock and he screamed again, a sound of pure rage that echoed through the woods and sent pigeons flying from the trees. Lurching forward, he held the knife extended, reaching out for Sherlock. Still holding the rifle, Sherlock swung it at the American's head. It connected with the bandage, an impact that echoed all the way down the stock, through Sherlock's hands, and up into his shoulders. The American fell like a carelessly thrown sack of corn, gracelessly and shapelessly to the ground.

Sherlock watched him for a few moments, half expecting him to climb back to his feet and try again, but he just lay there, unmoving apart from the laboured rise and fall of his chest. His right eye, from what Sherlock could see of it, was a crater of red flesh, while blood seeped through the bandage on his head, which was rising up as the flesh beneath it swelled even as Sherlock watched.

The man was like some supernatural force, impervious to pain and injuries that would fell a normal man. Sherlock felt his breath burning in his chest as he waited for Gilfillan to struggle to his feet again. Were all Americans like this? he wondered. Something to do with that frontier spirit that he had heard about? Part of him wanted to step forward and bring the rifle down several more times on the man's head, making certain that he would never move again, but Sherlock wasn't entirely sure whether that part of his brain was worried about Gilfillan regaining consciousness or whether he just wanted revenge for what the man had done to Amyus Crowe and tried to do to him. After a while he lowered the rifle. He wasn't a murderer. Not a deliberate murderer, anyway.

When he was quite sure that Gilfillan wasn't going to move for a while, he backed away, still watching, until he could hear Amyus Crowe's horse whickering behind him. He turned.

Amyus Crowe lay in the dusty road. In the reddish light of evening, the blood on his forehead seemed almost to glow with a demonic intensity.

"Is he—?" Sherlock started to ask, but he couldn't bring himself to finish the question.

"He's still breathin'," Virginia answered in a rush. Her accent had become more obvious.

She reached into a pocket and removed a scrap of linen—a handkerchief, Sherlock supposed. She was about to use it to wipe her father's head, but Sherlock took it from her.

"I'll wet it in the river," he said.

She nodded gratefully.

He dashed across to the point where the diving American gunman had cut a swathe through the rushes with his body before emerging and shooting Amyus Crowe. Getting as close to the river as he could without falling in, Sherlock moistened the handkerchief, then returned to where Amyus Crowe lay. Virginia had straightened out his arms and legs so that he was lying more normally, not twisted up in the way he had landed. As Sherlock bent to join her, he noticed that Crowe's chest was moving up and down and his eyelids were fluttering. It seemed like ages since Crowe had fallen from his horse, but Sherlock realized that it could only have been a couple of minutes at most. The fight with Gilfillan hadn't been long, but it had been intense, and that had made it *seem* long.

Virginia was running her hands up and down her father's arms and legs. "No broken bones, far as I can tell," she said. "Don't know about his ribs, although I'd be surprised if he hadn't cracked a couple. He's got a whole load of cuts and grazes, mind."

"He was lucky," Sherlock pointed out. "This close to the river, the ground is soft and muddy. If he'd come off the horse earlier, where the ground was baked hard, he might be dead by now."

Virginia took the handkerchief from him and ran it across Crowe's forehead. It came away bloody, revealing a long scratch that immediately began to bleed again.

"I think this is where the bullet hit," she said.

"Another bit of luck. A couple of inches to the left and it would have gone through his temple." Sherlock took a deep breath and tried to stop his hands from shaking. "We ought to find a doctor."

Virginia shook her head. "We need to get him back to the cottage. I can look after him there. As long as there's no broken bones, what he needs is rest." She sighed. "I've got a feeling he's been through worse than this and survived." She glanced at Sherlock, glanced away, then glanced back again, noticing his various bumps, scrapes, cuts, and bruises. "Are you okay?" she asked.

"I've had worse while playing rugby," he said.

She frowned and shook her head.

"It's a game that I don't like and that I don't play very well. The point is, I'll be all right."

"Did you get him?" she asked angrily.

"I stopped him," Sherlock replied, "but I think your father and my brother will want to talk to him, so I didn't hurt him too much. Even though I could have done."

"Maybe you should have," she said darkly.

Thinking about head injuries, Sherlock asked: "What about concussion? The ball injured your father's head, and he may have hit it as well."

Virginia gazed at him. Her expression was fixed and angry, but her eyes told a different story. They were desperate.

"We'll have to watch him," she said. "Look for signs of dizziness, sickness, nausea, or confusion."

"I've suffered from all of them in my time," Crowe said, faintly but distinctly. "Can't say I enjoyed 'em much, but they were mainly self-inflicted. This time it wasn't my fault."

"Father!"

Eyes still closed, he reached up and patted her clumsily on the shoulder. "I rolled when I hit the ground. Technique was taught to me by a rodeo rider in Albuquerque. If a body relaxes all its muscles and rolls up like a porcupine, it can probably survive a fall worse than that." He glanced at Sherlock, "I can see that you found out the same thing yourself." He paused, closing his eyes momentarily and breathing slowly. "What happened to the coach?"

"They got away," Sherlock said angrily. "With Matty."

"An' the man who stayed behind an' shot me?"

"Alive but unconscious. We can take him back and question him, I suppose."

"Yep," Crowe said darkly, "I s'pose we can."

Sherlock thought for a moment. "I can tie him up," he said. "Then we can sling him over my horse. If you're all right to ride, Virginia can ride Sandia and I'll walk."

"We need to move fast," Virginia said. For some reason she was blushing, and she wouldn't look at Sherlock. "Walking would take too long. You can ride behind me."

"Are you sure?" Sherlock asked.

"Don't look a gift horse in the mouth," Crowe said, chuckling. "The ideas are good, but what are you goin' to use to tie the man up?"

Sherlock thought for a moment. They didn't have any ropes with them. He could use the reins from his horse, he supposed, but how would they make sure that it stayed with them when they rode off? Could he make some bindings from the reeds on the riverbank? Too wet, and it would take too long. "My belt," he said finally. "I can tie his hands behind his back with my belt."

Crowe nodded. "Sounds good to me," he said. "Or you can use the twine in my pocket." He glanced up at Sherlock. "There's some things a man should always travel with—a knife, wax matches, an' a ball of twine. There ain't much you can't do with a combination of knife, matches, an' twine."

Sherlock took the twine from Crowe and tentatively walked back down the road to where Gilfillan still lay. It was nearly dark by now, and for a terrifying moment Sherlock couldn't locate the man in the shadows, but eventually he found where he was lying. He tied the man's hands, wrist crossed over wrist, then left him and walked back to where his horse was cropping grass by the side of the road as if this kind of thing happened every day. Leading the horse back, he left it beside Gilfillan and bent down, trying to work out how to get the man up and onto the horse. Eventually he managed to manoeuvre the American, still unconscious, to his knees, then slipped himself underneath the man as he slumped forward, taking the weight onto his upper back. He straightened, pushing with his knees and feeling his muscles protesting as he stood, head bowed forward, Gilfillan's body balanced precariously across his shoulders. For a moment he panicked, unsure how to proceed, but by that time Amyus Crowe was standing upright and Virginia could come across to help him. Between the two of them, they got Gilfillan slumped across the saddle of Sherlock's uncomplaining horse. To stop him sliding off, Sherlock tied Gilfillan's wrists to the stirrup on one side and his ankles to the stirrup on the other. Finished, he stepped back to admire his handiwork.

"I been meanin' to ask," Virginia said from beside him, "what did you end up callin' your own horse?"

"I haven't given it a name," Sherlock replied.

She seemed surprised. "Why not?"

"Couldn't see the point. Horses don't know they have names."

"Sandia knows his name."

"No, he knows the sound of your voice. I doubt he understands words."

"For a kid who knows so much," she said critically, "you sure don't know very much."

The four of them made a sorry-looking bunch as they cantered back to Amyus Crowe's cottage—Crowe slumped forward on his horse, Virginia on Sandia with Sherlock pressed close behind her, and his own horse bringing up the rear with Gilfillan lying across it. The journey back seemed to take forever. Tiredness weighed Sherlock down like a heavy blanket. His scratches itched, and all he wanted to do was to roll into bed and sleep for as many hours as he could possibly cram in.

It was well and truly night when they arrived back, and Mycroft was standing in the doorway.

"Sherlock!" he called, "I was—" He stopped. His voice, it seemed to Sherlock, was higher pitched than normal. He seemed to be struggling with some great emotion.

"It's all right," Sherlock said tiredly. "We're fine. I mean, Mr. Crowe has been shot, we have a prisoner, and we didn't get Matty back, but we're all still alive."

"I had no way of knowing what had happened," Mycroft said as Sherlock slipped off Sandia's back. "There were several courses of action open to me, but I was not sure which one was best."

"Shouldn't you have caught your train by now?" Sherlock asked.

Mycroft shrugged. "If necessary, I can find a comfortable hotel for the night."

"But won't your superiors be annoyed when you don't turn up to work tomorrow?"

Mycroft frowned, as if the notion of a "superior" was a curious concept. "Yes," he said, drawing the word out. "I suppose so." He brightened. "Although what is happening here may well have a direct impact on international relations, and so does fall within my ambit. If necessary, however, I can always charter a special train to take me back to London overnight."

Sherlock gazed at him, wide-eyed. "You can *do* that?"

"I have never had to, so far, but I believe my Terms of Reference do permit me the occasional indulgence, yes. Now, tell me everything."

While he and Virginia helped Amyus Crowe off his horse and the four of them went inside, leaving the American unconscious and strapped to Sherlock's horse, he told his brother the events of the night since they had left the cottage earlier. Virginia filled in some details that he had missed, and when he was talking about the fight with the American he felt Virginia's hand resting on his arm in concern. Mycroft too winced at how close Sherlock had come to death on several occasions.

"It is not clear what the best course of action is," Mycroft said eventually, when they were all settled in chairs with drinks in front of them. "Until your prisoner wakes up, we seem to have made use of every bit of information we have. Time and resources are not on our side."

"I could wake him up," Crowe said quietly. "And then have a quiet word with him. Civilized, like."

"Forceful questioning is not an option," Mycroft said warningly. "The man may be a villain in at least two countries, but he has the right to be treated in a civilized manner until he is actually convicted of a crime, and even then he is not something that can be treated roughly at the behest of anyone in authority. As one of the oldest and one of the youngest civilized countries, Britain and America have an obligation to set an example to the rest of the world. If we act barbarically then we have no right to stop anyone else from acting barbarically, and the world will slide into anarchy."

"Even if politeness leads to the injury or death of someone we should be protectin'?" Crowe asked.

"Even then," Mycroft said. "We must maintain the moral high ground, no matter what tempts us down into the valleys of iniquity."

"I have an idea," Sherlock said, surprising himself. It was true, something was rolling around in his mind like a marble in a tin tray, but he hadn't quite figured out the full implications of it yet.

"Go on," Mycroft said. "If it can prevent Mr. Crowe from pulling out our prisoner's fingernails with a pair of pliers, then I, for one, am all for it."

"That man—the American—jumped out of the carriage to stop us when it looked like we might prevent the carriage getting them to the docks and out of England."

"Correct," Crowe rumbled.

"From what he said to me, he was prepared to send a telegram to the others telling them that he'd either succeeded or failed."

"Accepted," Mycroft said.

"And if he doesn't send a telegram, if one isn't waiting for them when they get to the end of their journey, they will have to assume that we overcame him," Sherlock pointed out. "They will assume that we rendered him incapable of sending a telegram and that we are still chasing them, in which case their best option is to kill Matty because he's not useful to them as a hostage anymore."

"Oh no!" Virginia whispered.

"Where would he have sent the telegram?" Sherlock asked. "I mean, it's not as if the others were going to stay at a hotel until he arrived. They were heading straight for a ship, as far as we know."

Crowe and Mycroft looked at each other.

"The boy has a point," Crowe said after a few moments. "They would need some way of getting a message back and forth. Maybe some agreed place near the ship—a local post office, or something, where any message he sent would be picked up."

"They would have had to agree on it in the few seconds before he jumped out of the carriage," Sherlock pointed out. "What are the chances of him remembering in the stress of the moment—?"

"Unless one of the others wrote it down for him," Mycroft finished. "Sherlock, you have a fine mind on those bony shoulders of yours. We need to search that man's pockets for an address."

Crowe levered himself up from the chair. "I'll go," he said. At Mycroft's warning look, he added, "Don't worry, I won't try to wake him up if he's unconscious, and if he's already awake then I won't do any more than ask him a polite question before riffling through his pockets." He raised an eyebrow enquiringly. "I take it that theft is acceptable, even if pressured questioning is not?"

"We'll make an exception," Mycroft said calmly. "In this case."

Amyus headed outside to search Gilfillan. Sherlock noticed that Virginia watched her father leave with a troubled expression on her face. He wanted to ask her about it, but Mycroft gestured him over with a flipper-like hand.

"Sherlock . . ." he said quietly, then hesitated. "Sherlock, I suspect that I am failing in my duty to look after you properly. I am sorry."

Sherlock gazed into his face, trying to work out if he was serious or not. "What do you mean?"

"Our father entrusted you into my care. He looked to me to ensure not only that your education continued, but that you were kept happy and safe. In the time since he left for India with his regiment I have abandoned you into the care of relatives whom you had never even met and then stood by while you became engaged first in the lunatic schemes of a mad Frenchman with delusions of grandeur and now in some bizarre attempt to return to America the man who killed its former president. During the past couple of months you have spent more time looking death in the eye than most men experience during the course of a lifetime. You have been knocked out, kidnapped, whipped, drugged, chased, shot at, burned, and nearly stabbed, not to mention forced to survive unsupervised in the dangerous London metropolis, in a foreign country, and in rough Channel waves at night. If I had known everything that would happen to you, I would—"

He stopped, apparently overcome with emotion. He turned his head away. Sherlock thought he saw the gleam of tears in his brother's eyes. He reached out tentatively and put a hand on Mycroft's broad shoulder.

"Mycroft . . . you've always been the steadiest thing in my life. I've always come to you for advice, and you've always been more than generous with your time. You've never made me feel like I'm bothering you, even when you've had more important things to do."

Mycroft tried to say something, but Sherlock kept going.

"We've never been the kind of brothers who would climb trees together in the garden. You've never had the energy and I've never seen the point. That doesn't matter. You are the person I've always looked to for guidance, and you've never let me down. I doubt that will ever change. You are what I want to be when I grow up—successful, important, and self-reliant. You have never let me down, and you never will."

Mycroft looked at him and smiled. "When you grow up," he said, "I suspect you will carve a path for yourself in the world that nobody else has ever carved. I can foresee a time when I will be coming to you for help and advice, not the other way round. But despite everything you have said, I have stood by while you have been in danger."

Sherlock shook his head. "I think there's always danger, wherever you go. You can either ignore it, or you can wrap yourself in blankets so it doesn't hurt you, or you can walk towards it and dare it to do its worst. If you do the first thing, then the danger takes you by surprise. If you do the second thing, then you spend all your time swaddled up in the dark, letting the world pass you by. The only logical course of action is to go towards the danger. The more you get used to it, the better you can deal with it."

Mycroft smiled, and for a moment Sherlock could see, within the folds of fat that now encased his brother's frame, the boy that he had once been. "I collect information and amass knowledge," he said softly. "But you—you have developed wisdom. There will be a day when everybody in the world knows your name."

"And besides," Sherlock said, trying to lighten the

mood, "I've had the time of my life recently. If anyone had told me that by the end of the summer holidays I would have learned to ride a horse, fought in a boxing match, sailed across the Channel, and fought a duel, I would have laughed. I'll bet the most the other boys from school have done is flown a kite and had a picnic on the lawn. There's still a part of me that thinks I'll wake up to find out this has all been a dream."

Mycroft's gaze flickered across the room to where Virginia was still watching the door, waiting for her father to return. "And I suppose there are other compensating factors," he said.

"What do you mean?" Sherlock asked, suddenly uncomfortable.

"I mean the attractions of companionship." Mycroft's face was suddenly pensive. "I am a . . . solitary . . . man," he said. "I do not suffer fools gladly, and I prefer to spend my time alone with a book and a decanter of brandy. Do not let my example become your exemplar. If friendship—or, dare I say it, affection—comes into your life, then embrace it enthusiastically."

Sherlock's spirits suddenly fell as Mycroft's words reminded him of Matthew Arnatt, somewhere out there in the hands of kidnappers. "I don't mind embracing the danger," he said somberly, "but I don't want it to affect my friends."

"They make their choices, as you make yours," Mycroft pointed out. "The same arguments apply. They are not puppets, and you cannot keep them safe, just as I apparently cannot keep you safe. If they want to be with you, they will be. They accept the risk." He raised an eyebrow. "Certainly by now young Matthew must have worked out that being around you is neither safe nor boring."

"We will get him back, won't we, Mycroft?"

"I will not let my heart write a cheque that life will not allow me to cash," Mycroft said gently. "I cannot know the future for sure, but I can use my knowledge and experience to predict the shape of it. I believe there is a high probability that Matty will be returned to us unharmed, although what other events may transpire along the way is another question."

The door opened and Amyus Crowe entered the room. He was holding a piece of crumpled paper.

"I found this in the prisoner's pocket," he said. "Looks like some kind of code. Not sure what it means."

"Was he conscious?" Mycroft asked.

"He was either flat out or a good actor. I had a quick look at his clothes, though. The cut of the material and the labels inside are mainly American."

"Let us have a look at that paper. It might give us a clue to where he had to send his message."

Crowe spread the paper out on his desk. Mycroft and Sherlock crowded around him. Virginia stayed back, smiling now that her father had returned.

The paper had a series of letters and numbers scrawled across it in handwriting that had obviously been scrawled in a moving carriage in a hurry. Sherlock read ten groups of five characters each:

snes9 opst4 noses tsgrt htrnn
avede mfaos pftcd tieka ocaDy

"What does it mean?" Sherlock asked.

"It appears to be a simple substitution cipher," Crowe replied. "Substitution ciphers were used a lot during the War Between the States to keep messages from falling into the wrong hands. The idea is simple. Instead of 'a' you write somethin' else, say 'z' "—he pronounced it "zee"—"an' instead of 'b' you maybe write 'y.' As long as you an' the person you're sendin' the message to both know which letters substitute for which other letters—what the key is—the message can be coded and decoded safely."

"But we don't know what the key is, do we?" Sherlock said.

"That's right. If we had a longer message we might be able to work it out through frequency analysis, but we don't."

"Frequency analysis?"

"This is hardly the time for a tutorial." Mycroft sighed, but Crowe answered anyway.

"A clever man many years ago worked out that in messages written in English, certain letters occur with more frequency than others. 'E' is used more often than anythin'. 'T' comes next, then 'a', then 'o' an' then 'n.' 'Q' an' 'z' are, unsurprisin'ly, the least used. If you have a large block of text where the letters have been substituted for other letters, look for the most common. That's prob'ly 'e.' The next most common is prob'ly 't.' It's a process of elimination. With a bit of luck you can decode enough of the message to work out the whole thing." He looked at the message on the paper in front of them. "This one I'm not so sure about. We don't have enough letters to do a frequency analysis, but I'm wonderin' if they had enough time to work one out, or code up a message if they did. I reckon this is much simpler."

"Simpler how?" Sherlock asked.

"Ten groups of five letters each. That makes me think of a grid, or a table."

Crowe quickly scribbled down the letters again underneath the originals, but in a more ordered arrangement:

s n e s 9
o p s t 4
u o s e 5
t s g r t
h t r n u
a o e d e
m f a o s
p f t c d
t i e k a
o c a 0 y

"Now there's two ways a body can write a five-by-ten grid," he mused, "this way, or the reverse."

Quickly, he wrote another grid, this time longer across than it was wide:

s o u t h a m p t o
n p o s t o f f i c
e s s g r e a t e a
s t e r n d o c k 0
9 4 5 t u e s d a y

" 'Southampton Post Office,' " Sherlock read breathlessly, " 'SS Great Eastern Dock, 09.45, Tuesday.' That must be the place to send the message, the name of the ship, and the time it leaves."

"Not a particularly clever code," Crowe mused, "but prob'ly the best they could manage in a speeding carriage." He glanced at Mycroft. "I guess we both know what comes next, don't we?"

Mycroft nodded. "I'll get started."

Sherlock looked from one to the other. "*What* comes next?" he demanded.

The two men stared at each other. It was Mycroft who eventually spoke.

"They've booked themselves on a ship leaving Southampton tomorrow at a quarter to ten. While we are dealing with things here, they'll be at Southampton. By the time I can get the local police roused, the ship will have sailed."

"So they've got away," Sherlock said.

"Not necessarily," Mycroft replied. "There are ships sailing for America every day. Most of the ships take passengers, but their main function is carrying letters and parcels. That's where the money can be made. If we can book tickets on a ship leaving tomorrow, or the day after, for the same destination, then we can get there shortly behind them. Or perhaps even ahead of them. Our ship may be lighter, or more powerful. They did not choose their own ship because they thought they would be chased, but because they wanted to get out of the country as fast as possible."

"We?" Sherlock asked.

"Mr. Crowe will have to go," Mycroft replied, "because he has jurisdiction in his own country. He can call upon the assistance of the local police. He will obviously take his daughter because he would not leave her here unaccompanied. I, on the other hand, will stay, because I need to ensure that the British government is apprised of events, and to provide Mr. Crowe with any long-range diplomatic support he needs."

"Can't he just send a cable to the Pinkertons, telling them to intercept the *Great Eastern* when it arrives?"

Mycroft shook his head, his prominent jowls wobbling as he did so. "You forget," he said, "that we have no clear descriptions of the men; certainly not enough to secure their arrest. Apart from John Wilkes Booth, they cannot be identified by anyone apart from you."

"And what *about* me?" Sherlock asked, barely able to breathe.

"You are the only one of us who saw the other men," Mycroft said gently. "I cannot tell you to do this, Sherlock. I cannot even in all conscience *ask* you. I can merely point out that Mr. Crowe cannot apprehend the men if he cannot find them."

"You want *me* to go to *America*?" Sherlock whispered.

"I can tell Uncle Sherrinford and Aunt Anna that I have arranged an educational trip," Mycroft said. "Lasting perhaps a month or so. They will be against it, of course, but I think I can persuade them."

"Actually," Sherlock said, thinking about Mrs. Eglantine and the strange power she seemed to exert in his aunt and uncle's household, "I think you'll find it a lot easier than you expect to convince them to let me go away for a while."

SEVEN

The docks at Southampton were a bustling mass of men, women, and children dressed in their Sunday best. Some of them were streaming like ants up the gangplanks leading from the dockside up to the decks of ships, some of them were coming down the gangplanks from other ships and gazing around wide-eyed at the sight of a new country, while the rest were either saying goodbye to friends and relatives or greeting newcomers with open arms. And in and around them wove uniformed porters wheeling piles of luggage precariously mounded on trolleys and dockworkers in rough clothes and bandannas moving goods onto and from wooden pallets. Above it all towered the wooden cranes that were taking net-covered pallets from the dockside up to the decks of the ships or from the decks down to the dockside, as well as the cliff-like wooden or iron sides of the ships and the masts and funnels that rose like a forest all around.

And everywhere Sherlock looked he could see evidence of a hundred crimes being committed: pockets being picked, fixed card games being played, netted bales of goods being cut open so that small items could be removed, children being separated from their parents for heaven knew what reason, and newcomers paying in advance for transportation to boardinghouses and hotels that didn't exist or were nothing like the florid descriptions that were being given.

It was humanity at its best and at its worst.

The past twenty-four hours had been possibly the most hectic in Sherlock's life. Following the conference in Amyus Crowe's cottage and the unexpected decision that they would be going to America—a decision that Sherlock still couldn't quite believe had been made—he and Mycroft had returned to Holmes Manor, diverting to Farnham to send a carefully worded telegram to the post office at Southampton Docks persuading Ives and Berle that Gilfillan had succeeded in stopping them. Once at Holmes Manor, Mycroft had gone into the library to talk with Sherrinford Holmes while Sherlock had headed up to his bedroom to pack his meagre possessions into the battered trunk that had once belonged to his father. Sherlock had slept badly, disturbed partly by his memories of the fight with Gilfillan and the stinging of his wounds, but partly also by the excitement of being on the verge of leaving the country—for America! Breakfast was a strained affair, with neither Sherrinford nor Aunt Anna sure of what to say to him and with Mrs. Eglantine smiling coldly from behind them. And then Sherlock had climbed into a carriage with Mycroft, watching as his trunk was hauled up and strapped to the back, and then they had set off for the long drive to Southampton.

On the way, Sherlock had found himself thinking

about, of all things, the coded message that Amyus Crowe had found on Gilfillan's unconscious body. He'd never really thought about codes before, but there was something about the rigorous way they were put together, and the logical processes that could be used to deconstruct them, that appealed to his orderly mind. He found himself imagining all kinds of codes, from simple reorderings like the one they had encountered yesterday, through more complicated substitutions where symbols replaced letters, to even more intricate arrangements in which the substitution changed according to a different code, so that the first time "a" appeared it would be replaced with one thing, and the next time with something else, and so on, all driven by an underlying algorithm. In that case, a simple frequency analysis of the kind that Amyus Crowe had outlined would be useless. How could that kind of code be cracked? he wondered. The world of codes and ciphers would require some further research.

Eventually they arrived at Southampton. Amyus and Virginia Crowe were already waiting for them—Crowe with a discreet bandage wound around his forehead, nearly hidden by the brim of his hat. Sherlock guessed they had ridden down and then arranged for their horses to be stabled while they were gone.

"I have your tickets and travel documents," Mycroft said, handing a sheaf of paper across to Amyus Crowe. "You are booked on the SS *Scotia*. That's her over there. She belongs to the Cunard Line—a fine British ship. The tickets are first class, of course. I would not expect you to endure the rigours of steerage—not with your daughter and my brother in your charge."

Sherlock followed Mycroft's gesturing hand, and saw a huge ship that appeared to be fully as long as a rugby pitch. A massive paddle wheel was set halfway along the side of the vessel. Presumably there was a similar one on the other side. As well as the paddle wheels, it also had two masts with sails that were, at the moment, furled. Sherlock assumed that the paddle wheels were driven by steam engines inside the massive hull—two funnels emerging from the deck were probably there to carry the steam away—and that the sails would be used when there was wind to fill them while the steam-driven paddle wheels would drive the ship when the wind dropped.

His logical mind chased the thought down. If the paddle wheels were driven by steam engines then the steam engines had to be driven by burning coal, which meant that the ship must have reserves of coal stored on board, on the basis that there was no way to take on more coal in the middle of the Atlantic. That meant extra weight, which meant extra coal would be needed just to move the coal around. But how did you work out how much coal was needed for the voyage when for every extra ton of coal you added you had to add some more just to move that ton around, and knowing that as that ton was used up then the amount you needed to move it around got less and less? There was a complex mathematical calculation there, just out of reach, which reminded him strangely of the example Amyus Crowe had given him some weeks ago of the way the numbers of foxes and rabbits varied over time. Was everything in the world driven ultimately by equations?

"Grateful as I am for your help, Mr. Holmes," Amyus Crowe said, strangely diffident, "I'm not a rich man. We have not talked about the question of financial recompense."

"No need." Mycroft waved a hand, obviously embarrassed at this discussion of money. "The British government has paid for these tickets. At some stage in the next week or so I will have a conversation with your ambassador and suggest that he help defray the cost, on the basis that we are assisting your nation with your own internal politics, but for the moment rest assured that you will not be left destitute upon your arrival in New York. I presume you have access to funds there?"

Amyus Crowe nodded. "Grateful, nevertheless, Mr. Holmes."

Sherlock glanced to Amyus Crowe's side, where Virginia stood. She was looking nervous, and her face was bloodless, white.

"Are you all right?" Sherlock asked, moving over to her while his brother and her father continued to talk.

She nodded. "I don't want to talk about it," she said.

"I thought you'd be pleased about returning home?"

She glanced at him with an expression that could have

cut through glass. "Which part of 'I don't want to talk about it' did you not understand?"

Sherlock raised a placating hand and backed away, the way one would with a wild animal. Virginia, he told himself, and not for the first time, was probably the most complicated person he'd ever met.

"What news of the *Great Eastern*?" Crowe was asking Mycroft.

"As the coded message indicated, she left this morning from a pier near here, bound for New York. I have checked the passenger manifest, but can find no names that mean anything to us. One passenger failed to turn up—I can only presume that was the unfortunate Mr. Gilfillan, who even now resides in the care of the Farnham police. I will have him transferred to the Metropolitan Police later today. It will make it easier for any investigation to take place."

"Don't be too harsh on the man," Crowe said lightly. "Remember, he ain't been convicted of anything yet."

Mycroft raised an eyebrow but did not respond. Instead he turned to Sherlock. He put one hand on Sherlock's shoulder and with the other hand pointed towards the SS *Scotia*. "Launched six years ago, built and operated by the Cunard Line, here in England," he explained. "She is three hundred and seventy-nine feet long and weighs three thousand nine hundred tons. Her captain's name is Judkins, and he is Cunard's most trusted operative. She carries three hundred passengers, as well as cargo, and burns one hundred and sixty-four tons of coal a day. She can make the trip from Southampton to New York in eight days and a handful of hours. Imagine that—one week and you will be in the Americas. In the days of the pioneers, first settling that majestic country, the trip would have taken months."

"Have you ever been to America, Mycroft?" Sherlock asked.

A shudder ran through his brother's large frame. "Southampton is foreign territory as far as I am concerned," he said. "America might just as well be the Arctic."

Mycroft turned back to Crowe. "Your luggage will already be on its way to your cabins," he said. "I have, after some thought, reserved three berths in two cabins. One is for you and Sherlock to share. The other is for Virginia, but I understand she will be sharing with another female traveller. I have not been able to ascertain the name of this traveller, as the decision apparently rests with the ship's purser, but you can be assured that any woman travelling first class will be of gentle breeding."

"I'm sure Virginia can manage," Crowe said. He seemed awkward.

"One other thing," Mycroft went on. "I have taken the precaution of reserving seats for the three of you at the first dinner. I am told, by people who know these things, that the seats you get at the first dinner determine your social position for the rest of the voyage. The best seats are those nearest the captain, nearest the doors in case of seasickness, and furthest from the engines. I know the journey is only eight days, but you might as well be as comfortable as possible during that time." He shuddered again. "I cannot say I envy you. These days, the journey from my lodgings to my office and my office to my club is enough to exhaust me. I cannot conceive of any force that could move me from that routine."

Crowe smiled. "You may be surprised, Mr. Holmes, at what disturbs us from our orbits. It may be the simplest thing. I suspect you too may discover the joys of foreign travel."

"God forfend," Mycroft said.

And then it was time to go. Sherlock stuck out his hand. Mycroft did the same. They shook soberly, like gentlemen meeting in the street.

"Be safe," Mycroft said, "and do what Mr. Crowe tells you. Your presence on this trip is important—we may not know how important for some time, but I remind you that only you can identify these rogue Americans. At the very least, they are criminals and political refugees who should be taken into custody and tried for their crimes. At most, there is some plot afoot that needs to be scotched, lest the fragile political situation in America be affected for the worse. And, for heaven's sake, enjoy yourself. It's not that many children of your age who get the chance to travel abroad."

He reached into a pocket and withdrew a small book. Handing it to Sherlock, he said: "You will need something to pass the time. This is a copy of *The Republic*, by the Greek philosopher Plato. It takes the form of a dramatized set of dialogues between Plato's mentor Socrates and various other Athenians and foreigners in which they discuss the meaning of justice, and examine whether or not the just man is happier than the unjust man. Plato also uses the dialogues to propose a society ruled by philosopher-kings, as well as discussing the roles of the philosopher and the poet in society. *The Republic* is one of the most influential works of philosophy and political theory, and I commend its study to you."

"Is it translated?" Sherlock asked dubiously.

"Of course not," Mycroft said, taken aback. "I know how fast you read. If it was translated, you would finish it in an afternoon. If you have to translate as you are going along, then I have some confidence that the majority of the voyage will have passed by before you have completed it. Besides which, translations are always at the mercy of the skill of the translator. If you want to read and understand something properly that is in a foreign language, you need to learn that language." He hesitated. "Knowing your love of the grotesque and the criminal, I would point out that although Plato succumbed to old age, his mentor Socrates died when he was forced to drink poison by the Greek authorities. I do not know if that will help you in reading the book, but knowing your penchant for the melodramatic I give the knowledge to you as a gift to do with as you wish."

"I'll see you again," Sherlock said, feeling an unaccustomed choking sensation in his throat. He didn't know if he meant it as a statement of fact or a question, but Mycroft looked away for a moment, his eyes glistening.

"Sherlock," he said, "I will never have children—I am too accustomed to my own ways, and too intolerant of change to set up in a household of others—but if I ever had a son I could love him no more than I love you. Take care of yourself. Take great care."

And then, in a rush, they boarded, up a long gangplank that led from the dock to the deck. At the top their tickets were checked, and they were escorted down wooden stairs and along windowless corridors inside the ship to their rooms—going first to Virginia's room, where her companion had not yet arrived but where Virginia's luggage was waiting—and then to the room that Sherlock and Amyus Crowe were to share. The rooms were small and panelled in wood—about nine feet across, with two bunk beds on one side and a comfortable sofa across from them. Each end of the cabin had a washbasin and a mirror. Above the sofa a round window let in light and air, but Sherlock noticed with some trepidation that it could be shut and screwed tight. Was that in case of storms? And if so, how often did storms occur? And how would they get proper ventilation if the storm lasted for more than a few hours?

Amyus Crowe investigated the bunk beds. "Best if I take the bottom and you take the top," he growled. "If

I fall out in rough seas, I'd prefer to have less far to fall. An' remember—I'm a deal heavier than you."

Remembering what he'd thought about the window and possible storms, Sherlock noticed that both bunks had a wooden lip running along the side of the mattress and extending above it, presumably to stop people rolling over in their sleep and falling out onto the floor, but he could imagine that if the waves were rough enough then people could just be rattled back and forth in their bunks like marbles in a biscuit tin.

"Not sure about these mattresses," Crowe said disparagingly, testing their thinness. To Sherlock they looked thicker than his mattress back at Holmes Manor, but he discreetly said nothing.

With the knowledge that their luggage was safely aboard, they returned to the main deck to watch the preparations for departure. The gangplank was being pulled up as they arrived, and the crowds on the dockside were clustering around, waving to the people on the ship. A part of Sherlock wanted to scan the crowd for Mycroft's moonlike face, but another part of him knew that Mycroft would already have gone. Sherlock's brother was not a sentimental man, and he hated goodbyes.

Sherlock's hand crept down to the jacket pocket where he had stowed the copy of Plato's *Republic* that Mycroft had given him. It had been an unexpected gift, and Sherlock intended to read the whole book, even if it was in Greek.

The ship's engines, deep within its belly, were running

up to speed now, and Sherlock could not only hear their rumbling but feel it through the wood of the deck as well. He had a sudden, horrible realization that the noise of the steam engines would be their constant companion for the next eight days. How would he sleep? How would he be able to hear anything anyone said to him? The only consolation was that he would probably get used to it, but at the moment he couldn't see how that would be possible.

The ropes attaching the SS *Scotia* to the dockside were being released now from the bollards they were tied to, fluttering down to the side of the ship like ribbons even though they were hawsers as thick as Sherlock's fist. The enormous paddle wheels started to turn, churning the water beneath them and gradually levering the ship forward. A steam whistle sounded, and at the signal the crowd on the dock let out a huge cheer, as if nobody had ever seen such a sight before. Caps and hats and bonnets were flung into the air, and the passengers gathered on the ship's deck responded in kind.

A sudden shaft of guilt and sadness penetrated Sherlock's heart. He wanted Matty to be there with them. He wanted Matty to be *safe*. His mind kept sidling around to images of what might be happening to his friend, and he kept having to force them away. Ives and Berle had no reason to hurt Matty. He was their insurance policy.

The question was, did Ives and Berle think as logically as Sherlock?

Looking around to distract himself, Sherlock noticed a man nearby. He was standing by himself, holding what appeared to be a violin case, but instead of gazing at the crowd he was looking in the other direction, out to sea. He was thin, with black hair longer than was usual in a man, and his jacket and trousers appeared to be of corduroy. Sherlock guessed him to be in his thirties. He raised a hand to shield his eyes from the sun, and Sherlock noticed that his fingers were long and thin. He suddenly looked sideways at Sherlock, and he smiled, touching his forehead in a casual salute. His eyes, Sherlock noticed, were green, and the wideness of his smile revealed a gold tooth set far back in his mouth.

"The start of an adventure," he called. His voice held a slight Irish brogue.

"Eight days at sea with nothing to do but walk around and read books," Sherlock called, emboldened by the excitement of their departure into talking to a complete stranger. "Not much of an adventure."

"Ah, but think of the miles and miles of water that will lie beneath us as we travel. Think of the wrecks of other ships that litter the bottom of the sea, and the strange creatures that swim there, in and out of the portholes and around the bones of drowned sailors. Adventure is all around, if you know where to look." He raised the case that he carried. "And if all else fails, I can take some time to practise my music on deck, beneath the stars, and serenade the mermaids."

"Mermaids?" Sherlock asked sceptically. "More likely to be dolphins, or some other kind of marine life."

"A man can dream," the stranger said. He nodded genially at Sherlock, tipped his cap, and moved away through the crowd. Sherlock kept track of his long black hair for a while, but eventually lost him in the press of people.

"If you want to wander off and explore," Amyus Crowe said from behind him, "you go ahead. We're gonna be on this ship for a week or more, an' I have no intention of shepherding you all that time. As long as you don't fall overboard, there ain't nowhere you can go. I'm gonna go back to Ginny's cabin an' introduce myself to her companion, make sure the woman's not a drunk or a lunatic or both. We'll meet up in our cabin, by an' by, an' then we'll see what's happening for dinner."

Sherlock wandered up towards the front of the ship—the bows, as sailors called them. He passed the bridge on the way—the raised area where the captain stood, immaculate in his uniform and peaked cap, along with the helmsman who steered the vessel via a huge wheel, the same size and construction as the wheel of a cart, as far as Sherlock could tell. Behind them was a small cabin, shielded from the wind and the rain, but the majority of the bridge was actually open deck. Set to one side was a strange metal object on a pole, something like an alarm clock with extra-long hands that could be moved around the face, but instead of being marked with hours and minutes the face of the device had words—"Ahead," "Full Steam," "Stop," and "Slow." It took only a few seconds before Sherlock worked out that it must be a communications device, allowing the Captain to give his orders to the engine room, far below the deck. The hands, as they were moved to cover particular words, probably rang different bells down in the engine room which the stokers would then respond to.

Further ahead, just before the bows, was a roofed-over enclosure, like a long barn. It even smelled like a barn. Sherlock took a look inside, through one of the openings that lined its walls, and was surprised to see animals, all penned together in a small space. It had been built up in three stories, with cows, pigs, and sheep clustered on the bottom, ducks and geese in the middle, and chickens on top. Each animal was protesting against the vibration and the cold sea wind that whipped across the ship. Presumably they would provide eggs and milk, and even meat, as their numbers were gradually whittled down. By the end of the voyage, the barn, like the coal-storage area, would probably be almost empty. Sherlock hadn't expected there to be live animals on board, but he supposed it made sense. Fresh food could not be expected to keep for the period of the voyage, especially if storms or mechanical breakdown delayed them. Presumably, somewhere else on the ship, vegetables and fruit were either being stored or, perhaps, even grown, and somewhere else would be barrels filled with fresh water. And presumably several hundred bottles of wine, champagne, port, brandy, and whisky for the first-class passengers.

Something flickered at the edges of his vision. He turned his head quickly. A dark figure faded back into the shadow of a lifeboat. Sherlock took a couple of steps forward, but the figure had vanished. He shook his head. It was probably just one of the passengers.

Moving further forward, Sherlock watched for a while as the coast slipped away on their right-hand side. The ship would undoubtedly hug the coast as it headed west, around Cornwall, and then strike out to the coast of Ireland. Once past there, it would head out into open waters, across the three thousand or so miles of ocean that lay between that coast and the harbour at New York for which they were bound.

He was surprised how stable the ship felt. There was barely any swaying from side to side. Perhaps things would be different out in the Atlantic, but the ship's size and weight seemed to protect it against the relatively small waves here along the English coast. Sherlock couldn't help remembering the small boat in which he and Matty had sailed from Baron Maupertuis's offshore Napoleonic fort to the coast near Portsmouth. That journey had been grim, and he had no intention of experiencing anything like that again.

He suddenly felt very lonely. England, and everything that meant to him—his home, his family, even his school—was slowly falling away, and all that was ahead of him were surprises—a new world, a new set of people and customs. And danger. He didn't know what the men who were keeping John Wilkes Booth captive wanted, but they obviously had a plan, and it was one that they were willing to kill to keep secret. And here he was, just a boy, getting involved with intrigues beyond the limits of his world.

And Matty. What about Matty? Sherlock doubted that he was as comfortable as the three of them looked likely to be, here on the SS *Scotia*. Matty was probably tied up, or at least confined to a cabin somewhere. Maybe his captors had come to a deal with him—since they were all aboard a ship and he couldn't escape, if he promised not to cause trouble they would let him roam free—but Matty could be stubborn, and he might have refused.

That was assuming he was still alive. Amyus Crowe and Mycroft had both deduced that he was, but Sherlock was acutely aware that deductions were just projections into a sea of fantasy based on a few known facts. If the facts were wrong, or if the projection wasn't done in the right direction, then the final destination would be wildly inaccurate. And Matty might be dead. The Americans might have decided they didn't want the burden of a live captive throughout the journey, and just slit Matty's throat and dumped him by the side of the road back in England. The message might just have been a hoax, a wild attempt to stop Amyus Crowe from interfering, but with nothing to back it up.

Morosely Sherlock wandered back along the rails that lined the deck. He had to ask directions of a steward at one point: a thin man with an immaculate uniform and short blond hair beneath his cap. Having found out where he was going, he walked past groups of excited travellers, past the two funnels and the two huge, trunk-like masts, past the long, low shape of the communal first-class saloon with its windows looking out onto the deck, and back to the stern of the boat. The white wake of their passage trailed behind them like the tail of a comet. Sea birds followed them, diving into the wake for disturbed and disoriented fish.

At the back of the boat, a narrow stairway led down into the depths of the ship. Roughly dressed men hung around the top of the stairs smoking and casting glances forward at the better-dressed passengers. Sherlock guessed these were the steerage passengers, crammed into unsanitary and cramped conditions belowdecks, sleeping in rough hammocks or on benches, but paying much less for their tickets. People looking to start a new life in America, rather than travellers on business or pleasure as the first- and second-class passengers mainly appeared to be.

He sensed a presence beside him. Before he turned, he knew that it was Virginia.

"How's your cabin?" he asked.

"Better than I had on the way to England," she replied. "Father will tell you that the food and the accommodations were better, but don't let him fool you. We weren't travelling steerage, but we weren't first class either, and just because it was an American ship instead of a British ship don't automatically make it better."

"What about your companion?"

"She's an elderly widow heading out to join her son, who moved to New York five years ago. She's got a maid in the servants' area, an' she's planning to start readin' the Bible now an' finishin' when we get to New York. Good luck to her, I say."

"Do you want to take a walk around the deck?" he asked nervously.

"Why not? Might as well make ourselves acquainted with the place. After all, we're goin' to be spending the next eight days here."

They wandered forward along the other side of the ship to the one Sherlock had come back along. When they got to the first-class saloon, Sherlock gestured to Virginia to stop.

"I just want to take a look inside," he said.

The door opened outward and was on a stiff spring, presumably to stop it being pulled open by the wind on a regular basis. Sherlock tugged it open and glanced inside. The room was empty apart from two white-clad stewards laying silver cutlery on the single long table that dominated the room. Fifty or so chairs were set around the table—matching, presumably, the number of first-class passengers. The stewards glanced up at him, nodded, and continued on with their work.

The saloon was panelled in dark wood, with mirrors set around it to increase the illusion of depth. Where there weren't mirrors there were artistic murals set into the wooden panels. Oil lamps hung from the panels on sturdy supports.

"So we all eat in here?" he said.

Virginia nodded. "All in together," she replied. "It was the same on the boat we came out on."

"Lords and ladies mixing with industrialists and theatrical impresarios," he went on. "Very democratic. Nowhere for the *hoi oligoi* to escape from the *hoi polloi*."

"No cabin service," Virginia agreed. "People eat here or they don't eat at all."

One of the stewards began to set out place cards around the table. Sherlock wondered where Mycroft's bribe had placed them. Now they were at sea, all bets were off. Despite the payment, they could be seated at the far end of the table, away from the captain and the doors, and over the engines, and they wouldn't be able to do anything about it apart from complain. Sherlock presumed they were at the mercy of the purser, a man who had already demonstrated that he could be bribed.

Sherlock stepped back and let the door swing shut. Something moved in the corner of his eye. He glanced sideways, towards where the first-class saloon ended at an alley running between it and the nearest funnel. A figure was just ducking back into the alley. He didn't recognize it—sailor or passenger, he couldn't be sure. The only thing he caught was the sun hitting a flash of iridescent blue around the figure's wrist as it withdrew into the shadows. A blue shirt cuff, maybe? He wasn't sure.

He ran quickly down to the end of the saloon and glanced around the corner, but the alley was clear. A hatch halfway along led down into the depths of the ship. Whoever had been watching them was gone, but Sherlock knew that it wouldn't be left at that. This was the second time he'd spotted someone watching him from the shadows. Someone on this ship was interested in them, and that could mean only one thing.

The Americans who had kidnapped Matty had someone on the ship.

EIGHT

The daily routine of the voyage to New York was established within the first eighteen hours, as far as Sherlock could tell. Despite the huge size of the ship, the areas where the passengers could go were pretty restricted. Once a person had walked the deck, taken a meal, checked out the smoking room and the library, and had a couple of conversations with other passengers about the unusually calm weather, all the options had been exhausted. Between meals most people seemed to spend their time either alone on deck, reading a book in a comfortable chair, or gathered in small groups at tables in the smoking room or the bar, playing bridge or whist. When the sun went down the stewards went around the ship turning the oil lamps on, but setting them as low as possible, and everyone headed for their cabins to sleep.

Sherlock had spent the first few hours watching his home country recede from him until it was just a dark line on the horizon. He missed the moment when it actually vanished. He must have blinked, or turned to watch something else, but one moment England was there and the next the ship was alone on an endless ocean, heading towards the sunset, with the white wake that stretched away behind them the only thing to indicate they were moving.

He and Amyus Crowe and Virginia had joined the rest of the passengers for dinner, but while Amyus Crowe talked easily with everyone around him, Sherlock found that he had nothing to say. He ate his food and watched everyone else, wondering who they were, where they had come from, and where they were going. Amyus Crowe had already taught him some of the ways one could tell a person's occupation—the stains on their sleeves, the patterns of wear on their jackets, the calluses on their hands—and he was pretty sure that he'd already pegged one man as an accountant and two others as horse trainers.

Captain Charles Henry Evans Judkins was a tall man with an impressive set of white whiskers adorning his cheeks. His uniform was black, spotless, and perfectly pressed; decorated with bright gold braid; and he carried himself with an upright, military bearing. He was a hit with the ladies, who had all dressed in their finest clothes for the occasion, and he told many strange stories of his time working for the Cunard Line. The ones that impressed his audience the most concerned creatures such as whales and giant squid that were sometimes seen in the distance, and great storms that sometimes appeared on the horizon like black walls and which tossed ships about on the waves so much that at times the deck appeared to be as vertical as a cliff face. Judkins told these stories with a showman's flair, pulling his attentive audience in with his words and giving the impression that sea travel was a dangerous activity which they would be lucky to survive, but Sherlock could tell that he was acting a part and providing a form of entertainment that would tinge the way the passengers saw the rest of the voyage. After all, if he told them it was as boring as a walk in the park, then what stories would *they* have to tell to their friends when they disembarked?

One story in particular that he told caught Sherlock's attention. Judkins had been talking about the various attempts to lay a cable across the Atlantic, from Ireland to Newfoundland, in order to allow the sending of telegraphic communications. If that could be done, then rather than a message taking well over a week to make it across from one country to the other in mail bags in the hold of a ship, information could be passed almost instantaneously via electrical pulses. The idea of telegraphic communication fascinated Sherlock. He could already see, after what had happened back in Amyus Crowe's cottage, that the letters of the message would have to be replaced by easily transmitted codes—long and short pulses, maybe, or just a simple "on" and "off" arrangement—but the idea of laying a cable some three thousand miles long, from one coast to another, across the bottom of the sea without it breaking under the strain, made Sherlock's mind boggle. Was there nothing that the mind of man could not accomplish, once it set itself to the task? The original method, according to Judkins, had two ships starting out in the middle of the Atlantic and laying their cables in different directions until they both hit land, but that had immediately run into problems when the crews tried to splice the cables together in the middle of a storm. The next attempts had taken place with ships setting out from Ireland and heading for Newfoundland, laying out the cables as they went, but the cables often broke and had to be dredged back up so that the crews could repair the breaks and keep going.

"I recall one occasion," Judkins said in a low, deep voice, "when a broken cable was dredged up from the abyssal depths of the ocean, *and there was a creature holding onto it*!" He glanced around the table, his eyes bright beneath bushy brows, while the various passengers who were hanging on his every word gasped. "A godless creature like a marine earwig, if you would credit it; white in colour, but fully two feet long and with a set of fourteen clawed legs that gripped hard onto the cable and would not let go. It was still alive when they dragged the cable onto the deck, but it soon died, being removed from its natural habitat amongst the murk of the ocean floor."

One woman let out an inadvertent shriek.

"I understand from the men who were there," Judkins continued, "that the creature tasted something like lobster, when cooked."

His audience dissolved into relieved laughter. Sherlock caught Amyus Crowe's eye. Crowe was smiling too.

"I've heard similar stories," Crowe murmured, just loud enough for Sherlock to hear. "The things are called 'isopods.' They're something like prawns, but the conditions at the bottom of the ocean allow them to grow to prodigious size."

The steward who was serving Sherlock's part of the table—up near the captain, as Mycroft had promised—was the thin man with short blond hair who had helped Sherlock with directions earlier. He nodded at Sherlock as he reached out to place a dish of soup in front of the man sitting opposite.

There was no lobster, which was probably a blessing.

After dinner Sherlock had headed for bed, leaving Amyus Crowe in the bar, and if Crowe had come to bed at all then Sherlock had been asleep in his bunk when he had done so. When Sherlock woke up and got ready for breakfast, Crowe had already left the cabin. He seemed to be able to survive on small amounts of sleep.

Despite the fact that it was being cooked at sea in a cramped galley, the food was excellent. Each meal had something different in it, and waiting to see what would arrive on the plate at breakfast, lunch, or dinner was one of the highlights of the day. Everything was prepared fresh, of course—it would be difficult to store anything for very long—but even though the numbers of animals on the foredeck would diminish during the voyage there was no obvious sign of their being slaughtered—no washes of blood across the deck, no piteous bleats as the animals were taken away to their final end. The crew clearly had their own routine, which they had been following for years.

The skies on that first day were clear and blue, and the waves were small enough in comparison to the size of the ship that they just slapped across its sides without making it pitch and toss at all. Sherlock had read about storms at sea, and he overheard a couple of the passengers who were scaring the rest by telling stories of horrendous previous passages across the Atlantic where vast waves had hung above the ship before crashing down and sweeping animals overboard. But so far the ocean had been calm enough that some people were actually playing bowls in a clear area on deck.

The steerage passengers had their own fenced-off area of deck for walking and for washing their clothes. It was at the top of the stairs that led down to the dark areas of the ship where their hammocks were slung. The smell that sometimes wafted up was an eye-watering mix of bodily odours. Presumably, down there where there was no breeze and nobody could see the sky and the horizon, seasickness was a constant companion. When they came on deck they either watched the first-class passengers with subdued malice in their eyes or stared at the deck in weary depression. Every time Sherlock passed them by he thanked God that Mycroft had paid for them to travel first class. He wasn't sure he could have survived steerage. He didn't know how anyone could.

The massive paddle wheels on each side of the ship were in constant motion, driven by the steam engines whose rumbling could be felt whenever one touched a wooden surface. The paddles that were spaced around their circumference pushed against the sea as they rotated, propelling the ship forward. The captain had ordered the sails to be unfurled shortly after Southampton dropped out of sight beneath the horizon, but the way they hung limply suggested to Sherlock that there wasn't enough breeze to keep the ship moving very fast.

Surprisingly, for much of that first day after breakfast he hadn't seen much of Amyus and Virginia Crowe. She had seemed subdued and had taken to her cabin, and her father seemed to be spending his time alternately checking that she was all right and brooding in the cabin that he shared with Sherlock. Something was bothering her. Casting his mind back, Sherlock tried to remember whether Virginia had mentioned anything about the trip from America to England that she and her father had taken apart from the fact that they hadn't travelled first class but weren't in steerage either. He had a feeling that she had said something important when they first met, but he couldn't remember what.

Somewhere towards the back of the ship Sherlock could hear music playing. He turned from his position staring out at the waves, trying to trace its source. The music floated overhead, as light as the seagulls that followed in the wake of the ship and hung in the air, barely moving their wings. It sounded like a violin playing a melody that swept up before pausing at the topmost note and then crashing down again.

Leaving his place at the rail, Sherlock walked back towards the stern, looking for the source of the music. There was precious little entertainment on the ship as it was: anything that broke up the monotony of the day should be investigated and treasured.

Past the long single storey of the saloon, in a clear area of deck, a man stood playing the violin. It was the man he had seen the day before when they had been leaving Southampton—the man with long black hair and green eyes. He was still wearing the same corduroy jacket and trousers, although he appeared to have changed his shirt. The violin was pressed into his neck and his head was tilted, chin holding the body of the instrument steady while his left hand fingered the neck and his right hand sawed the horsehair bow across the strings. His eyes were closed and his face bore an expression of intense concentration. Sherlock had never heard a piece of music like that before: it was wild, romantic, and turbulent, not ordered and mathematical, like the pieces by Bach and Mozart that he was used to hearing in the occasional recitals at Deepdene School for Boys.

Several other passengers were gathered around the man, listening to him with quizzical smiles on their faces. Sherlock watched and listened, as he swept to a climax, held the note, and then stopped. For a moment he kept the violin up to his chin, eyes still closed and a smile on his face, then he let it fall and opened his eyes. The crowd applauded. He bowed. His violin case was on the deck in front of him, Sherlock noticed, and some of the passengers threw some coins in before they wandered away.

After a few moments, only the violinist and Sherlock were left. The violinist bent to scoop the coins from the case, then glanced up at Sherlock.

"Did you enjoy that, my friend?"

"I did. If I had some money I'd give it to you."

"No need." He straightened, having left the violin and bow in the case. "The money offsets my expenses and allows me a little extra for the occasional drink, but I'm not trying to make a living by playing. Not here on the ship, anyway. I do, however, have to practise, and my roommate does not appear appreciative of anything apart from German polkas."

"What was that piece?" Sherlock asked.

"It's a newly written violin concerto in G minor by a German composer by the name of Max Bruch. I met him in Coblenz, last year. He gave me a copy of the score. I've been trying to get it right ever since. I think one day it will be a part of the repertoire of every classical violinist."

"It sounded incredible."

"He uses some ideas from Felix Mendelssohn's works, but he gilds them with a particular glint of his own."

"Are you a professional musician?"

He smiled; an easy, unforced grin that revealed strong white teeth. "Sometimes I am," he said. "I can turn my hand to many trades, but I seem to keep coming back to the violin. I've played in orchestras in concert halls and string quartets in high-class tearooms, I've busked on the streets and accompanied singers in music halls while beer glasses fly overhead and shatter against the stage. My name, by the way, is Stone. Rufus Stone."

"I'm Sherlock Holmes." Sherlock walked over and extended his hand. Rufus Stone took it, and they shook for a few moments. Stone's hand was firm and strong. "Is that why you're going to America?" Sherlock continued. "To play the violin?"

"Opportunities are drying up in England," Stone replied. "I was hoping that the New World might have some use for me, especially after the cream of their manhood was cut down in the War Between the States." His gaze flickered up and down Sherlock's frame. "You have the build of a good violin player. Your posture is upright, and your fingers are long. Do you play?"

Sherlock shook his head. "I don't play any instrument," he admitted.

"You should. All the girls love a musician." He tilted his head to one side, almost as if the violin were still there. "Can you read music?"

Sherlock nodded. "I learned at school. We had a choir, and we had to sing every morning."

"Would you like to learn the violin?"

"Me? Learn the violin? Are you serious?"

Stone nodded. "We've got a week before we dock, and that time will pass awfully slowly if we don't find some way to amuse ourselves. When I get to New York I'm going to be looking for employment as a violin teacher. It would help if I could actually say that I've taught somebody. At the moment I have some good ideas about how to do it, but I've never turned them into practice. So—what do you say? Are you willing to help me out?"

Sherlock thought about it for a moment. He didn't play whist or bridge, and the only alternative was laboriously translating the copy of Plato's *Republic* that Mycroft had given him. This sounded far more interesting. "I can't pay," he said. "I haven't got any money."

"There will be no financial encumbrance on you. You'll be doing me a favour."

"What can you teach me in a week?"

Stone considered for a moment. "We can start with posture," he said. "The way you stand and the way you hold the violin. Once I'm happy you've got that right, we can move on to getting the various right-hand techniques correct—*détaché*, *legato*, *collé*, *martelé*, *staccato*, *spiccato*, and *sautillé*. Once I'm happy with that, we can move on to the left-hand techniques—finger dropping and lifting, shifting, and *vibrato*. And then, I'm afraid, it's practice, practice, practice—scales and arpeggios until the tips of your fingers are sore."

"I said I can read music, but I can't hold a note," Sherlock admitted. "Our choirmaster said I had a cloth ear."

"No such thing," Stone said dismissively. "You may not

be able to sing, but I guarantee I can get a tune out of you by the end of the week that people will throw coins for, even if it is just a German polka. What do you say?"

Sherlock grinned. Suddenly the voyage seemed like it might be a lot more interesting than he'd expected. "It sounds good," he said. "When do we start?"

"We start now," Stone said decisively, "and we run on until lunchtime. Now, pick up the violin. Let's see how good your stance is."

For the next three hours, running from the end of the breakfast session to halfway through lunch, Sherlock learned how to stand properly, how to hold a violin, and how to hold a bow. He even played a few notes, which sounded like a cat being strangled, but Rufus ("Call me Rufus," he had said when Sherlock called him Mr. Stone. "When you say 'Mr. Stone' it makes you sound too much like a bank manager for my liking") told him that it didn't matter. The purpose of the morning's session, he pointed out, was not to learn how playing the violin *sounded* but to learn how it *felt*. "I want you to be relaxed, but ready. I want your arms and fingers and shoulders to know all the shapes that a violin can make against them. I want that violin to feel like an extension of your own body by the time we've finished."

By the end of the time, Sherlock's body was aching in places he didn't even think he had muscles, his neck was cramping, and the tips of his fingers were tingling from where he'd been pressing the catgut strings down. "I've just been standing in one spot!" he protested. "How come I feel like I've been running a race?"

"Exercise isn't necessarily about moving," Rufus said. "It's about muscles tensing and relaxing. You don't often see fat musicians. That's because although they're sitting down or standing in one place, their muscles are continually at work." He paused, face creasing in thought. "Except for percussionists," he said eventually. "They get fat."

"What next?"

"Next," Rufus said, "we have luncheon."

While Rufus returned his violin case to his cabin, Sherlock went looking for Amyus Crowe. The big American had emerged from wherever it was he had been sequestered, but there was no sign of Virginia. As they all sat at the communal table, Sherlock introduced Crowe to Rufus Stone.

"Pleased to make your acquaintance, sir," Crowe said, shaking Rufus's hand. "You're a musician, I perceive. A violinist."

"You heard me?" Rufus said, smiling.

"No, but you've got fresh dust on your shoulder. In my experience dust on a man's jacket means one of three things: he's a teacher, he plays billiards, or he plays the violin. There ain't any billiards table aboard this ship, to my knowledge, an' I'm not aware there are enough children on this ship to make it worthwhile settin' up a classroom."

Sherlock checked the shoulder of his own jacket. Indeed, there was a fine patina of dust across it. He rubbed some between his thumb and forefinger. It was an amber-brown colour and felt sticky.

"This isn't chalk," he said. "What is it?"

"Colophone," Rufus explained.

"A form of resin," Crowe interrupted. "Called 'rosin' by musicians. It's collected from pine trees an' then boiled an' filtered before bein' formed into a cake, like soap. Violinists coat their bows with it. The adhesion the resin causes between the strings and the bow is what makes the strings vibrate. Of course, the resin dries out and becomes a dust, which is deposited on the shoulder as that's the bit of the body closest to the instrument." He glanced at Sherlock's jacket and frowned. "You've been playin' the violin as well. No, you've been *learnin'* the violin."

"Rufus—Mr. Stone—has been teaching me."

"You don't mind, Mr. Crowe?" Rufus asked. "I only offered to help us both pass the time."

"I never put much store in music," Crowe rumbled. "The only tune I know is your national anthem, an' that's only because folks stand up when it's played." He glanced at Sherlock from beneath shaggy eyebrows. "I was intendin' to continue our studies while we were on the ship, but Virginia ain't taking too well to the voyage." He shook his head. "I can't rightly recall if I mentioned it but her mother—my wife—died on the last transatlantic voyage we made. That was from New York to Liverpool. The memory weighs heavily upon her mind. An' on mine." He sighed. "Memory's a funny thing. A person can slide memories of just about anythin' to one side an' ignore them, but sometimes the slightest thing can set them off again. Usually it's smells an' sounds that recall memories the best. Ginny's not talked about her mother for a while now, but the smell of the ocean an' the smells of the ship have brought it all floodin' back."

"I'm sorry," Sherlock said. It seemed inadequate, but he couldn't think what else to say.

"Bad things happen to people," Crowe said. "It's the one acknowledged truth of the human condition." He sighed. "I'm goin' to trust you to spend time on that translation your brother gave you," he said. "An' I'll try to spend an hour or two a day with you, talkin' over what your eyes an' ears can tell you while you're on this here ship, but the opportunities for proper consideration are scant. The rest of the time is your own. Use it as you will."

The rest of the meal was conducted in uncomfortable silence. As soon as it was finished, Sherlock excused himself. He had a feeling that he'd somehow disappointed Amyus Crowe, and he didn't want to add to that disappointment by going straight back to his violin lessons. Judging by the slight nod that Rufus Stone gave him as he left, the violinist understood.

He spent an hour in a chair on the deck, reading through the difficult Greek of Plato's *Republic*. The process of translating from Greek to English in his head was so laborious that he hardly understood the sense of what he was reading—he could get the words right, but by the end of the sentence he'd lost track of where it had started and what it was trying to say.

He looked up at one point, wrestling with a particularly difficult transitive verb, to see a white-uniformed steward standing beside him holding a tray. It was the same man who had helped him with directions and who had served at dinner the night before.

"Is there anything I can get for you, sir?" the steward asked.

"A Greek dictionary?"

The steward's lined, tanned face didn't change. "I'm afraid," he said, "that I cannot help you there, sir. We do have a library on board, but I do not believe there is a Greek dictionary upon its shelves—especially a dictionary of *ancient* Greek, which is what I suspect you need."

"Do you know *every* book that's in the library?" Sherlock asked.

"I have been with this ship ever since she launched," the steward replied. "Not only do I know every book in the library, I know every cocktail on the menu, every plank on the deck, and every rivet in the hull, yes?" He nodded his head. "Grivens is the name, sir. If you need anything, just ask."

Sherlock's gaze was drawn towards the hand that held the tray. It was tattooed from the wrist upward, the design disappearing into the man's sleeve. It looked to Sherlock like a pattern of tiny scales, coloured a delicate, gold-flecked blue that shone in the sunshine.

The same colour that Sherlock had seen on the wrist of the figure that had been observing him from the shadows the day before. Coincidence, or not?

Grivens noticed the direction of Sherlock's gaze. "Is something wrong, sir?"

"Sorry." Sherlock thought quickly. It was obvious that he'd spotted something odd, but he had to cover for his gaffe. "I was just noticing your . . . your tattoo. My . . . brother . . . has one just like it." In his mind he formed a quick apology to Mycroft, who was the last person in the world Sherlock would expect to have a tattoo. Except perhaps for Aunt Anna.

"Had it done in Hong Kong," Grivens explained. "Before I joined the *Scotia*, that was."

"It's beautiful."

"The man who did it was a wrinkled little Chinaman in the back alleys of a marketplace in Kowloon," the steward continued. "But he's famous among sailors all over the world. I swear there's nobody to touch him, not anywhere else. There's colours he uses that nobody else can even mix. Anytime I see a tattoo done by him on another sailor, or if another sailor sees my tattoo, we just nod at each other, 'cause we know we've both been to that same little Chinaman. It's like being in a club, yes?"

"Why do so many sailors have tattoos?" Sherlock asked. "As far as I can tell, every member of this crew has a tattoo of some kind, and they're all different."

Grivens glanced away, out to sea. "It's not something we tend to talk about, sir," he said. "Especially to passengers. The thing of it is, and forgive me for being indelicate, but if there's a shipwreck then it might take some time for the bodies of the sailors to wash ashore—that's assuming they ever do. There have been instances where bodies couldn't be identified, even by their closest relatives. The action of saltwater, harsh weather, and the fishes of the deep, if you take my meaning. But tattoos last a lot longer. A tattoo can be recognized long after a face is gone. So that's how it started—a means of identification. Gives us some measure of comfort, knowing that after we're gone at least our families have a fighting chance of being able to bury us properly."

"Oh." Sherlock nodded. "That makes sense, I suppose. Thanks."

Grivens nodded. "At your service, sir. Are you going to be here for a while?"

"Where else would I go?"

"I'll check back with you later, then. See if you need anything else."

He moved away, looking for other passengers to serve, but leaving Sherlock thinking. If this was the man who had been watching him from the shadows—if he *was* being watched from the shadows, which was itself an assumption based on a scuffle and a movement—then why was he so concerned as to whether Sherlock would be staying there on deck? Did he want to search Sherlock's cabin for some clue as to what Sherlock knew? Or did he intend going after Amyus Crowe and Virginia? Whatever the answer, Sherlock couldn't stay there. He quickly got up and headed off along the deck and down the stairway to the corridor where his cabin was located.

The door to his cabin was open a crack. Was it the steward, searching it, or was it Amyus Crowe inside?

Sherlock moved closer, trying to look through the crack to see what was happening. If it was Grivens, then he would go and fetch Amyus Crowe, tell him what was going on.

Something shoved him hard in the small of his back. He fell forward, stumbling into the cabin. Another push and he was on the floor, just managing to miss the edge of the bunk bed by twisting his head and curling up. The carpet burned against his face as he hit it. He curled round, looking up at the doorway.

Grivens shut the door behind him. His faded blue eyes were suddenly as cold and as hard as marbles.

"You think yourself clever, yes?" he snapped. Sherlock caught his breath at the abrupt change of attitude from servitude to anger. "I've broken better men than you in half. You think I didn't realize you were going to follow me here to see if I was searching your cabin? I noticed you examining my tattoo, and I could tell by your eyes that you recognized it from yesterday, when I was watching the two of you. So I made you think I was going to search your cabin, and I lured you back here."

"To do what?" Sherlock asked. He was finding it difficult to catch his breath lying on the floor, twisted around like that.

"To get you off this ship. You, then the other two."

"Off this ship?" Sherlock's mind took a second or two to catch up. "You mean—*throw* us off? Into the *Atlantic*? But we'll be missed!"

"The captain might even turn around, steam back and look for you, but it won't do any good. You won't last half an hour in that water."

Sherlock's mind was racing, trying to work out how this had happened. "You're not part of this. You *can't* be. The men we're following wouldn't have known which ship we were going to take—if we were going to take one at all."

"All I know is they paid me to keep an eye out for three travellers—a big man in a white hat and two kids. Maybe with another man—a fat man—maybe not. A third of the money now and two-thirds if they see a report in the papers of three or four passengers vanishing overboard."

"But how did they know we'd take this ship?" Sherlock asked. Then he realized. "They paid off someone on *every* ship?"

Grivens nodded. "Every ship leaving for the next few days, anyway. That's my guess. They found most of us in the same place—a bar where the ships' stewards gather between voyages."

"But how much would that cost them?"

Grivens shrugged. "Not my problem, as long as they have enough left to pay me when I get to New York. They didn't seem short of cash. They said they'd pay extra if I could get you to tell me how much you know about their plans. You can do it the easy way, without pain, and I'll do you the favour of making sure you're unconscious when I throw you over the side, yes? Or you can do it the difficult way, in which case I'll have to snip your fingers off with a cigar cutter, one by one, until you tell me, and then throw you overboard still conscious."

"I'll shout out!" Sherlock blustered. "People will hear."

"Didn't I mention?" Grivens said. "I started off as a ship's chandler, making sails, before I became a steward. Your fingers never forget the feel of an iron needle going through canvas. I'll sew your lips shut with thick twine, boy, just for the pleasure of looking into your frightened eyes when I throw you overboard." He paused. "Now, answer the question. How much do you know about the plans of these Yanks?"

He leaned forward, grabbing for Sherlock's hair. The iridescent blue tattoo on his wrist seemed to glow in the darkness of the cabin.

Sherlock lashed out with his booted foot, catching Grivens in the groin. The steward folded nearly double, grunting in pain.

Sherlock scrambled to his feet. Grabbing Grivens's shoulder, he pulled him forward. The man fell, and Sherlock scrabbled to get past him and through the doorway.

The steward's hand grabbed for Sherlock's ankle. He pulled hard, dragging Sherlock back into the room. Sherlock twisted, lashing out with his free foot and catching Grivens above the eye. He released Sherlock with a spat curse and fell backwards.

Sherlock knew that he had to escape, and then he had to get to Amyus Crowe. He launched himself towards the door and pulled it open. The light from the oil lamps hanging on the corridor wall outside streamed into the cabin. He scrambled out, pushing the door closed, and ran off down the corridor. Behind him he heard the crash of the cabin door hitting the inside wall as Grivens pulled it open, and the thudding of feet as the steward chased after him. The corridor ended in a junction; Sherlock went left, heading for the stairs up to the deck and to safety, but he must have gone wrong somewhere because there was no sign of the stairway. Instead the corridors took him deeper and deeper into the bowels of the ship.

Faced with the choice of a stairway that led down and going back again, he chose to go down. This wasn't passenger territory anymore: the walls were cruder wood, without the ornate panelling of first class, and the oil lamps were guttering and yellow. There was only bare floor beneath his feet, not soft carpets.

From somewhere behind him, Sherlock heard footsteps. Grivens was still on his trail. He kept moving.

The sound of the ship's engines was closer now, like the hammering of some huge mechanical heart, and the atmosphere was noticeably warmer. Sherlock was sweating, partly because of the chase and partly because of the steam in the atmosphere.

He went round a corner to find a large door ahead of him. It was shut. He glanced briefly over his shoulder, but there was no point going back. He could only go onward.

He opened the door and went through.

Into Hell.

NINE

Heat hit him in the face, nearly knocking him down. It was like walking past the open door of a baker's oven. He felt the short hairs on his neck curling up and the sweat springing out on his face and neck. The air itself was so thick and so hot that it was hard to catch his breath.

The doorway opened on a wrought-iron balcony that looked down on a cavernous inferno filled with machinery: pistons, wheels, axles, all moving in different directions at different speeds—side to side, up and down, round and round. It was the *Scotia*'s engine room, powering the huge paddle wheels on the sides of the ship. Somewhere nearby, Sherlock knew, there would be a separate boiler room, where sailors would be shovelling coal into a massive furnace where it would burn and produce heat, which would turn water in a boiler above into steam and force it through a network of pipes into this room, where pistons and joints and wheels would convert the pressure of the steam into rotary motion that would be fed to the paddle wheels via massive axles. If it was hellishly hot in here, then the boiler room would be worse than working inside a volcano. How could men stand it?

The noise was deafening: a combination of clanging, hissing, and thumping that made Sherlock's head hurt. He could feel the vibration through the door frame where his hand was holding on and through the air itself. It was like being punched repeatedly in the chest. It would be next to impossible to hold any kind of conversation in conditions like this. The men who worked here would have to communicate by sign language. Deafness would be an occupational hazard.

Illumination was provided by dirty oil lamps that hung from the walls at various points, and also by gratings in the ceiling that let in a meagre trickle of light from the world above, but the light petered out quickly in the smoky, dusty, steamy atmosphere: and there were great pools of black shadow everywhere Sherlock looked. Air also entered through the gratings, providing a welcome cool breeze for anyone standing underneath. Coal dust and water vapour eddied in the atmosphere, restless spirits uncertain which way to go.

Sherlock quickly looked around, trying to work out where *he* could go. The engine room seemed to take up several levels inside the centre of the ship. Walkways were bolted to the walls and crossed from side to side at various levels. Wrought-iron ladders led up to the walkways. Massive iron beams crossed the room, giving it some stability and providing anchors for the various pipes and wheels. It all seemed to be designed so that any pipe, any piston, any wheel, any axle could be reached by a man with a spanner in case something broke.

Some of the smaller pipes terminated in pressure gauges—large instruments about the size of Sherlock's clenched hands with dials showing the steam pressure in the pipes. Presumably the engineers could check the gauges and tell if the ship's engine needed more coal or whether the pressure was building up too fast and needed to be vented. Other pipes had large metal wheels attached that probably opened or closed valves, allowing the steam into different pipes at differing rates.

Looking up, Sherlock could see two large pressure vessels in the ceiling space. A lot of the pipes led towards them. They seemed to open out to the deck level. It took him a moment to work out that they probably led to the *Scotia*'s two funnels, providing a means of venting the steam that had done its work.

Everything was made of thick, black metal that was hot to the touch, and everything was fastened together with rivets the size of Sherlock's thumb. The machinery wavered in the heat-haze caused by the burning coal, the air itself rippling and making it hard to judge distances.

The smell of the engine room made Sherlock's nose prickle uncomfortably. Mainly it was a sulphuric smell, like rotten eggs, but there was a tarry odour beneath that, and something else that reminded Sherlock of the taste of blood in his mouth but which was probably hot iron.

A figure moved out of the shadows. Sherlock flinched, expecting it to be Grivens, but it was another member of the crew, an engineer. He was naked to the waist and massively muscled, and where his skin wasn't blackened with coal dust it was streaked by sweat, so that his face and body were covered with a series of black-and-white stripes, like the engravings of zebras that Sherlock had seen in books about Africa in his father's library. His moleskin trousers were sodden with sweat, and he carried a shovel over his shoulder. His entire demeanour—the way he carried himself, his expression, everything—spoke of bone-aching weariness. As Sherlock watched he walked along past the pounding engine and vanished through another doorway without looking up, probably heading for a swinging hammock in the dark depths of the ship.

Aware that Grivens was only moments behind him, Sherlock hurried along the balcony until he got to a ladder that led both upward and downward. Which way to go? Upward would lead him towards the deck, but there might not be a way out up there. He'd certainly never seen any of the engineers or stokers on deck. They were probably forbidden from emerging into the open, condemned to spend the entire voyage in the darkness below. Down, then, and he just had to hope there were other ways out of the engine room.

He clambered down the iron ladder as fast as he could, his fingers burning on the hot rungs. The vibration of the engines was transmitted through his hands to the point where he could feel his teeth shaking. The heat and the lack of breathable air were making him feel weak; twice his sweat-slicked hands slipped off the rungs and he nearly fell. Eventually he got to the bottom, and rested his forehead gratefully against the ladder before he pushed himself away and moved off.

Up on the balcony, the door smashed open again. Sherlock could hear it striking the wall. Silence for a moment, and then a pair of booted feet clanked on the metal grille flooring.

Sherlock slipped into an alley running between two large parts of the engine: irregular masses of black iron festooned with pipework. His shoulder brushed against one of them and he flinched back. It was boiling hot.

The alley ended in a rivet-covered curved metal surface, part of a pressure vessel of some kind. It was a dead end. No way out.

The shadows between the parts of the engine shielded him. He tried to make himself as small and as quiet as possible.

Footsteps on the ladder, and then silence as the newcomer reached the floor.

"Kid," shouted Grivens's voice, "let's talk about it. Got off to a bad start, we did. I overreacted. Come out into the light, there's a good boy, and we can chat it through like old friends. We'll laugh about this all, one day, I promise we will, yes?"

Sherlock didn't trust the man's words and he didn't trust the man's tone of voice. If he came out, he knew he'd be killed.

"All right," Grivens went on. "All right, then." It was difficult to hear him above the clanging and thudding of the machinery. "You're scared. I understand that. You think I'm going to do you harm. Well, let's talk about money, then. I've been paid to off you, that much you already know, but I'm a practical man. A businessman, if you'd credit it. I'm sure the big Yank can more than match the money I'm being paid by the blokes who hired me. Let's you and me go up to see him together and set the situation out, like men of the world. He can write me a cheque, and I'll forget all about the three of you. How's that sound?"

It sounded like a trick, but Sherlock wasn't stupid enough to say so. Instead he just kept silent.

Somewhere nearby, a valve snapped open and released a plume of steam with a deafening *hisssss*.

"Kid? You still there?" The voice sounded closer this time, as if Grivens had moved. He was looking for Sherlock, not content with just hoping that his reassuring words would persuade him to emerge from hiding. "I know we got off on the wrong foot, but I want to make it up to you. Come out and talk."

Sherlock realized that his back was pressing against a pipe, or a section of engine, that had steam in it. The heat was spreading through his jacket and his shirt, blistering his back. He tried to edge forward, but that meant moving part of his body into a patch of light. He moved slowly, but the heat was too much and he had to jerk away before he was badly burned. His foot hit a section of pipe. The noise rang out round the engine room like a bell.

"So, you *are* here." Grivens sounded as if he was just a few feet away. "Well, that's a start, anyway."

A shadow fell across the mouth of the alley in which Sherlock was hiding. In the ash-grey light that shone through the gratings above, Sherlock could make out the silhouette of Grivens's head and shoulders. He was holding something in his hand, which was raised above his head, ready to strike. It looked like a spanner; a very large, very heavy spanner.

It occurred to Sherlock that down here, in the bowels of the ship, Grivens didn't even have to worry about getting Sherlock's body up to the deck and throwing it overboard. He could just chuck it in the fire and let it burn. All he would have to do was to bribe the stokers with a couple of shillings to look the other way, and Sherlock would be reduced to grit and dust.

"Come out, come out, wherever you are," Grivens sang. His body now blocked out all the light entering the alley. He seemed to sense where Sherlock was. Rather than moving on, he turned into the alley.

Sherlock ducked down, trying to stay in the shadows. Another few seconds and Grivens would see him, and then it would all be over.

His hand touched the warm floor, and it took him a couple of seconds to realize that it had slipped past where the pipe he was pressed against should have met the deck. He moved his hand around, exploring. It seemed as if the pipe didn't go all the way down to the floor, but curved around underneath. It was sitting on struts that were bolted to the floor, but there was enough room for Sherlock to slide underneath. Hopefully there would be a way out on the other side. If not, he would still be as trapped as he was now but considerably more uncomfortable.

He dropped to his hands and knees, then to his stomach. The floor was uncomfortably hot against his skin. His shirt was wet with sweat, and it stuck to the floor as he tried to slide under the machine. He reached out and grabbed one of the struts supporting it, hoping he could pull himself along, but the strut burned his hand and he cried out in pain.

"Aha!" Grivens rushed into the alley, his spanner clanking against the pipes. "Where are you, you little cur?"

Sherlock braced himself and reached out for the strut again. The metal seared his palm but he endured it, pulling hard, scrabbling with knees and feet, dragging himself under the engine part and away from Grivens. He suddenly sensed space above him, and climbed shakily to his feet. His hand throbbed, but he was in a different part of the engine room. Another alley led away from him, the walls formed by an interlocking series of pipes. He ran down it, looking for a ladder or a door.

Something went *clang* behind him. He turned, to find Grivens standing at the end of the metal-walled alley. He'd just hit his spanner against a metal stanchion.

"All right, kid. End of the line. You've had a good run, but it's time to call it a day. Let old Grivens just put you out of your misery, yes?"

"Is it too late for that deal you mentioned?" Sherlock temporized.

Grivens smiled. "Far too late," he said. "Sad to say, I'm a man of my word. I shook hands on a deal, and I have to see it through. Couldn't really break my contract now, could I? What kind of man would that make me?"

"So it was just words."

He nodded. "Just words. There was always a chance you'd believe them and come out of your own accord, but I didn't have much faith."

He began to walk forward, swinging the spanner.

Sherlock looked around frantically for something he could use to fight with. It looked like fighting was his only option now.

Clang! The spanner hit an iron pipe, sending shock waves reverberating around the engine room.

"Just look at me," Grivens said in a calm, low voice. "Just look at me, kid. Look me in the eye. Don't look for a means of escape. Accept the inevitable, yes?"

Sherlock felt the calmness of the voice, the reasonableness of the words, and the heat of the engine room lulling him into a trance. He shook his head abruptly. He couldn't let himself be hypnotized by the steward.

He glanced desperately from side to side. Something caught his eye—something leaning against a ladder. A shovel! One of the stokers must have left it there at the end of his shift. Its handle was black with coal dust and its blade was partly melted, as if it had been pushed by accident too far into the flames. Sherlock reached out and grabbed it, holding it across his body with the blade up by his face.

"So the cur's got some spirit in him, yes?" Grivens's face was set into a grim mask. "Just means I have to work a bit harder for my cash."

He lunged forward and lashed out with the spanner, trying to catch the side of Sherlock's head. Sherlock ducked back, and the spanner hit the side of an iron tube. Sparks flew across the room. Sherlock felt them burn his face. He brushed at his hair in case any of them had caught in it.

Grivens snarled and pulled the spanner back. Raising it over his head, he brought it crashing down towards Sherlock's scalp.

Sherlock blocked the blow clumsily with his shovel. The spanner hit the wooden shaft at its halfway point and dented it, nearly knocking Sherlock to his knees.

The vibration transferring from the shovel felt like it might tear his arms from their sockets. He managed to bring the shovel around and caught Grivens's kneecap with the blade. Grivens screamed and staggered back, mouth open in an "O" of disbelief.

"You little beggar!" he cursed. Swinging the spanner like a club, he lunged at Sherlock again.

Sherlock brought the blade of the shovel up to meet the spanner. The two connected with a sound like the crack of doom. Grivens bounced backwards, the spanner whirling away from him and disappearing into the darkness of the engine room. Sherlock's suddenly nerveless fingers dropped the shovel on the floor.

Grivens was standing in a half crouch, cradling his right elbow in his left hand. His face was twisted into an animalistic snarl.

Sherlock turned and ran.

The alley ended in another junction, with more alleys heading left and right. Sherlock took the right-hand one and tore along it, stopping only when he came to a ladder leading upward. He glanced back over his shoulder. No sign of Grivens. Feeling the weakness in his shoulders from where the steward had brought the spanner down on his shovel, he clumsily climbed up the ladder to a walkway.

The walkway ran parallel to the main axle that crossed the room, exiting through a gap in the engine-room wall and driving one of the paddle wheels. Sherlock had lost track of which way was forward and which was back. He wasn't sure which paddle wheel the axle was turning. Maybe both of them. Not that it really mattered. The axle turned slowly alongside him, as thick as his body, glistening with grease. Further back towards the centre of the engine room was the complicated arrangement of toothed gear wheels, pistons, and offset cams that drove it.

Leaning over the barrier that ran alongside the walkway, he tried to see where Grivens was. No luck. The steward had vanished.

The fight seemed to have attracted no attention. Was the engine room always this deserted, or had Grivens bribed the crew to stay out while he dealt with Sherlock?

Something grabbed at his ankle and pulled. Sherlock fell to the walkway, feeling his leg being tugged over the edge. He grabbed hold of the barrier to stop himself being pulled over. Grivens's face was pressed up against the metal grille of the walkway. It was his hand that had grabbed Sherlock's ankle.

"You're really going to make me earn this money, aren't you?" he hissed. "Just for that, I'm going to make the Yank and his daughter suffer. Just think about that as you're bleeding to death here."

Sherlock's only response was to kick out with his other foot, scraping the sole of his boot down his leg until it hit Grivens's fingers. Grivens grunted in pain and released his grip. Sherlock rolled away and pulled himself to his feet.

Grivens's face appeared at the top of the ladder, followed by the rest of him. His teeth were exposed by the grimace of hatred on his face.

"This isn't about money anymore," he hissed. "This is personal."

Sherlock backed away slowly. The steward reached the top of the ladder and moved on to the walkway. His shoulders were hunched, his fingers curled into claws. His previously immaculate white uniform was now grey and streaked.

Sherlock felt something hard pressing into the small of his back. He glanced down quickly. He'd reached the end of the walkway. He was pressed into one of the wheels that controlled the flow of steam through the pipes. Alongside him, the massive cylindrical axle rotated endlessly around on its bearings. He'd reached the area where the offset cams transferred the linear motion of the pistons into rotary motion, driving the axle. There were several of them, and they looked like grease-smeared metal horses' heads bobbing up and down in a complicated rhythm. For a second Sherlock found himself appreciating the sheer brilliance of the engineering at work in the ship. How could people just assume these things worked without wanting to know how?

Not that he would be getting the chance to ever learn anything again. Grivens was still stalking towards him, closing the gap. He reached out for Sherlock's throat with both hands.

"I should get a bonus for this," the steward whispered. His fingers closed around Sherlock's throat and he squeezed tight. Sherlock felt his eyes bulge with the pressure. His chest wanted to suck air in, but no air was getting through. Frantically he clutched at Grivens's wrists, trying to pull them away, but the steward's muscles were locked tight, hard as iron. Sherlock shifted his grip to the man's fingers. Maybe he could pry them away from his throat. His vision had turned red and blurred, and black dots were beginning to swim around in front of him, obscuring Grivens's face. His chest burned in agony.

Desperately he twisted his body with his last ounce of strength. Caught off balance, Grivens half fell onto the barrier running along the side of the walkway, but his grip on Sherlock's throat did not slacken. The cams were pumping up and down beside them now: chunks of metal pounding the air just inches from their faces. Grivens's expression was feral, his eyes pinpricks of black hatred.

Sherlock let his body drop, as if he'd run out of energy. Grivens, taken off guard, let him drop. Instead of falling to his knees, Sherlock shifted his hands from the steward's fingers to his leather belt. Grabbing the belt, he straightened up again, pushing as hard with his legs and pulling as hard with his arms as he could. Grivens's feet left the walkway as Sherlock lifted him up by his belt. Already twisted around as he was, the weight of Grivens's body carried him sideways to the edge of the barrier. Sherlock expected him to let go then, scrabbling for purchase on the barrier, but he kept his grip on Sherlock's throat, pulling him over as well.

Until his sleeve caught in one of the pounding cams. It caught the material and pulled. Grivens screamed—a short, despairing cry of fear and rage—as his body was jerked off the walkway and into the machinery. Sherlock let go of the man's belt and brought his arms up, knocking the steward's hands away from his throat and allowing him a lifesaving breath as the steward's body was pulled away, wrapping around the rotating axle and catching in the cams as they hammered up and down.

The engine didn't even falter, but Sherlock had to turn away before he had seen more than a fraction of what happened to Grivens's body as it was pulled into the rotating metal.

Sherlock bent over, hands on his knees, trying to pull as much of the hot air into his lungs as possible. For a few moments he thought he was going to suffocate as his body demanded more oxygen than he could give it, but gradually his gasping subsided. When his vision wasn't red and blurred anymore, and when he could breathe without his chest hurting, he straightened up and looked around.

There was no sign of Grivens. The black grease on the axle and the cams looked redder and shinier than it had before, but that was all.

Eventually Sherlock climbed down the ladder and crossed the engine room, looking for a way out. He wasn't sure if the door he found was the one he'd entered through or another one, but it didn't matter. Outside, it was cool and the air was fresh. It was like leaving Hell and entering Heaven.

People stared at him when he emerged on deck, but he didn't care. He just wanted to get back to his cabin, wash the grime and the grease off his body, and change his clothes. He would put the ones he was wearing in the laundry. Maybe the laundresses on board could clean them, maybe they couldn't. In the end, he just didn't care anymore.

Amyus Crowe was in their cabin when Sherlock pushed the door open. "I think someone's been in here, searchin'," he said, then turned and saw the state of Sherlock's face and clothes. "My God, what happened?"

"The people we're following to New York—they spread some money around the port," Sherlock replied wearily. "There's probably one man on every ship leaving this week who's been promised money if he kills the three of us."

"At least one," Crowe said. "But we can worry 'bout that later. Who was it?"

"One of the stewards."

"An' where is he now?"

"Let's just say they're going to be down one member of staff at dinner," Sherlock said.

He told Crowe the story while he washed off and changed clothes. The big man listened silently the whole time. When Sherlock started repeating himself, Crowe raised his hand.

"I think I understand the full story," he said. "How do you feel?"

"Tired, dehydrated, and sore."

"That's understandable, but how do you *feel*?"

Sherlock glanced at him in puzzlement. "What do you mean?"

"I mean a man's died, an' you were the cause. I've seen men spiral into a morass of guilt an' sadness after an event like that."

Sherlock thought for a minute. Yes, a man had died, and Sherlock was responsible, but it wasn't the first. Baron Maupertuis's thug Clem had almost certainly drowned when he fell off Matthew Arnatt's boat, but that had happened because Matty had hit him on the back of the head with a metal boathook. Maupertuis's right-hand man, Mr. Surd, had been stung to death by bees, but that could arguably have been classed as an accident—he'd fallen backwards into the hive. And there were the people who'd been on the Napoleonic fort when it had exploded in flames—they may have burned to death or drowned when they jumped into the sea, but their fates seemed several steps away from anything Sherlock had directly done. Was Crowe right? Was this the first death he'd directly and unequivocally caused?

"I'm not what you'd call religious," he said eventually. "I don't believe there's a God-given instruction that 'Thou shalt not kill,' but I suppose I believe that society functions better when there *are* laws and when people can't just go around killing other people. That's part of what Plato argues in *The Republic*, which my brother gave me to read. But the steward *was* trying to kill me, and if I hadn't done the same to him then he wouldn't have stopped. I didn't *choose* to kill him. He picked the fight, not me."

Crowe nodded. "Fair enough," he said.

"Was that the right answer?"

"There is no right answer, son; least, not as far as I can make out. It's a dilemma—society works because people follow rules an' don't go round murdering each other, but if people choose to live outside those rules, what do you do? Let them get away with their behaviour, or fight them with the same weapons they use to fight you? If you follow the former course, they get to take over society, 'cause they're always prepared to fight harder and dirtier than you are. If you follow the latter course, then how do you stop yourself becomin' as bad as them?" He shook his head. "In the end, the only advice I can offer is—if you get to the stage where a man's life don't matter to you, then you've gone too far. As long as death bothers you, as long as you understand it's your last resort, not your first, then you're probably on the right side of the line."

"Do you think Mycroft knew something like this would happen?" Sherlock asked. "Do you think that's why he gave me the book?"

"No," Crowe replied, "but your brother is a wise man. I think he knew that at some stage you'd be askin' yourself these questions, an' he wanted to make sure you had the tools to answer them with."

TEN

He slept for a while, even though it was only mid-afternoon: a disturbed sleep, full of images of Matty, tied up and helpless in the dark, crying to himself, wondering where his friends were. When Sherlock awoke he found his cheeks were wet with sympathetic tears, and it took him a few moments to remember where he was and what had happened.

His muscles ached and his lungs burned, and he could feel the bruises on his throat from where Grivens had clutched at it. He tried to find some trace of horror inside him over what he'd done, but there wasn't anything that strong. Regret, yes. He regretted the fact that a man was dead, but that was about as far as it went.

Lying awake and thinking about Grivens, to distract himself from worrying about Matty, Sherlock found himself thinking about the iridescent blue tattoo on the man's wrist, the one that had first made Sherlock realize that the man had been watching him. If he'd thought of tattoos at all, then he'd thought of them as something decorative, but there was obviously more to them than that. They were a means of recognition, of identification. In this case, they'd led him to identify a man who might be watching him on behalf of the fleeing Americans.

And, based on what the steward had said, you could recognize a tattooist by his style, just like you could recognize a painting by Vermeer or Rubens. Or, Sherlock thought, remembering the paintings in the hall at Holmes Manor, by Vernet. His mind was filled with the idea of an encyclopedia of tattoos, cross-referenced back to the places they were done and the artists who did them. Would such a thing even be possible?

After a while he decided that lying in bed wasn't going to accomplish anything. He got up and went outside.

The sun was shining strongly on the deck of the SS *Scotia*. All around them the horizon was a flat line. It was as if they were at the centre of an upturned blue china bowl. There was no sign that they were moving at all; even the sea birds hung motionless in the air.

After a few minutes, he realized that he had been hearing a violin playing for some time without noticing. Rufus Stone? Probably. The chances of there being two violinists on board were fairly slim, and he thought he was beginning to be able to detect some elements of Stone's style—the flourishes he threw in at the end of certain phrases, and the way the fingers of his left hand sometimes struggled with complicated arpeggios.

He went looking for the man and found him in his usual spot near the bows of the ship. This time there was no crowd around him. Perhaps they'd all got bored.

"I was beginning to wonder if you'd decided to abandon

our lessons like a man throws away a threadbare handkerchief," Stone called, still playing.

"I had . . . a busy afternoon," Sherlock responded. "But I'm here now."

"Then let's start." Rufus stopped playing and lowered the violin. "Any questions before we see how much of your stance you remember from this morning?"

Sherlock thought for a moment. "What's your favourite piece of music?" he asked. "Is it the Bruch you were playing this morning?"

Rufus considered. "No," he said eventually. "I have a sneaking fondness for the work of Henryk Wieniawski. He has written several violin concertos, of which I prefer the second, in D minor. And then there's Giuseppe Tartini's famously difficult violin Sonata in G minor. That is a true test of a violinist's skill."

"Difficult?" Sherlock asked.

"It's known as the Devil's Trill Sonata. Tartini claimed that he'd had a dream of the Devil playing the violin. When he woke up he tried to write down the piece of music the Devil was playing, and this was the closest he could get. It's so fiendishly difficult that some critics have suggested that Tartini had to have sold his own soul to the Devil in exchange for the skill to play it."

"That's rubbish."

"Of course it is. But it makes for a good story, and it helps to swell an audience if they think there's something spooky or bizarre about the music you're going to play." He held the violin out to Sherlock. "Now let's see how much has stuck."

For the rest of the afternoon, Sherlock held the violin under Rufus Stone's critical eye and tried, one after the other, different ways of using the bow to elicit notes from the instrument without actually worrying about which note it was. At the moment it was the technique that Rufus wanted him to master. He started with simply bowing the string in long, smooth, flowing gestures—*détaché*, as Rufus described it—while just supporting the neck of the instrument with his left hand rather than actually holding down any strings. That in itself took hours until Rufus was satisfied, first on one string and then on the others, as Sherlock tried hard to attain an even tone to the note no matter how long it lasted.

And that was how the rest of the voyage went. After breakfast, Sherlock would join Rufus Stone on deck for two hours, then they would move to the saloon for lunch. Another two hours of practice and then Sherlock would head back to his cabin for a break to read some more of Plato's *Republic.* Two more hours with Rufus Stone, and then dinner. Following that, Sherlock usually spent some time with Amyus Crowe in the library before heading to bed, but Crowe's day was mostly taken up with seeing to Virginia, and he had little time to continue with Sherlock's education. Little time, and little in the way of props or examples. Sherlock had already noted that Amyus

Crowe's preferred method of teaching was to take something that he saw or had found and use it as the basis for a lesson. In the middle of the ocean, with no land in sight, there was precious little opportunity for him to do either.

Virginia stayed in her cabin, unwilling to come out on deck or talk to anyone. Sherlock saw her only once or twice during the entire journey. Her skin was so pale and translucent compared with the red of her hair that he worried she might not survive the voyage, but Amyus Crowe told him that she was going to be all right. She was just reliving the original journey over from New York to Liverpool, during which her mother had died. "A mental disturbance," Crowe said one night in the library, "aggravated by the monotony of the journey and the fact that she misses Sandia terribly. Ginny's an outdoor girl, as you have probably realized by now. She hates to be cooped up anywhere. Once we disembark she'll be back to normal."

The weather was surprisingly stable during the whole journey. Apart from one day of dark skies and squalling showers, during which Rufus Stone and Sherlock had to retreat to Sherlock's cabin to practise, the skies were blue and the sea was calm. Or, at least, the waves were small enough compared to the size of the hull that the *Scotia* could just carve its way through them.

Once, on the fourth day, there was some excitement when the captain announced that they had sighted another ship. Passengers took turns with a telescope to look at the distant speck on the horizon. Amyus Crowe did use this as the basis for a lesson, asking Sherlock to calculate the likelihood of two ships being within line of sight of each other, given the vastness of the ocean and the relatively small number of ships, but Sherlock had already realized that although the Atlantic Ocean was large and the distance between Southampton and New York was long, most ships tended to follow the same narrow corridor across, and there were tens, perhaps hundreds, of ships afloat at any one time. Given that, the chance was actually quite high.

Both Sherlock and Amyus noticed an exchange of flashing lights between the ships as night fell. Sherlock watched the crew on the *Scotia* sending their message using a lantern with a shutter across the front that could be opened or closed. Part of him worried about secret messages being sent to and from conspirators on both ships concerning him and Amyus and Virginia Crowe, but that would mean most of the crew would have to be part of the conspiracy, and that wasn't likely. And besides, there had been no other attempts to search the cabin or to do anything to the three of them, either before the other ship was sighted or afterwards. It seemed as though Grivens was the only person on the *Scotia* who had been recruited by the conspiracy.

The disappearance of the steward caused a small amount of consternation among the crew, and less among the passengers. The captain didn't try to turn the ship around and search in case he had fallen overboard. Sherlock could only assume that shreds of Grivens's clothes had been found among the machinery in the engine room, and that the captain had deduced that he'd fallen into the engine while drunk.

As time went on, Sherlock learned the main styles of bowing—*legato, collé, martelé, staccato, spiccato,* and *sautillé*—and he'd just started to use the fingers of his left hand to hold down the four strings in various ways to form notes and chords. He still hadn't played anything more musical than long, sustained tones. Rufus Stone was fanatical about building up technique and ability before letting a student loose on actual music, but Sherlock could appreciate Rufus's approach. It was logical. It made sense.

"What happens when we land?" Sherlock asked one day, late in the voyage, in a pause during a lesson.

"What happens is that I wander off into a new and glittering world of opportunity, looking to establish myself as a music teacher first, and then, if I'm lucky, find some suitable orchestra that will pay me to play. You, on the other hand, will join the estimable Mr. Crowe and his mysteriously absent daughter and do whatever it is that you've come to do in New York."

During the fifth day of the voyage, during a break from his almost incessant violin practice, Sherlock spent some time at the bows of the ship, leaning on the rail and staring ahead at the distant blue line of the horizon.

He was not alone. Several other passengers were also in the bows of the boat, watching the wind and the waves and the clouds. Perhaps even watching for land, although it was far too early for that. Maybe the captain's stories about great storms and monstrous sea creatures had fired their imaginations and they were watching for the first sight of something out of the ordinary. As far as Sherlock was concerned they were more likely to see a drifting iceberg.

One man, wrapped in an overcoat against the cold wind, attracted Sherlock's attention. He had a trim black beard that curled out at the edges and a moustache that had been waxed so that it curled up at the ends. Instead of staring out across the ocean ahead, he had his back to it and was scribbling lines in a notebook with a pencil.

In fact, as he watched, Sherlock realized that the man was not scribbling lines but sketching something. Sherlock shifted his position, trying to see what the man was drawing, but all he could see on the paper of the man's notebook was a cylindrical object with pointed ends, something like a fat cigar. It seemed to be separated into sections by some internal walls, or barriers.

"You are interested in my drawing, yes?" the man said, glancing up. His voice had a strong accent: German, Sherlock thought.

"Sorry," Sherlock said, blushing. "I just wondered why you weren't looking ahead, like everyone else."

"I *am* looking ahead," the man said. "A long way ahead, to a time when journeys such as ours are conducted not by boats, which are subject to storms and waves, but by balloon."

"*Balloon?*" Sherlock echoed. He nodded towards the sketch in the notebook. "Is that what that is?"

The man stared at Sherlock critically. "I think you are unlikely to be an industrial or a military spy," he said. "Too young. And your face tells me that you have an open mind and a keen intellect, which is not my experience of spies." He laughed, although it was more of a snort than a laugh. "I have been . . . criticized . . . in my own country for my ideas. I am hoping that in America things will be different."

"I'm Sherlock Holmes." Sherlock extended his right hand. "Pleased to meet you."

"And I am Ferdinand Adolf Heinrich August Graf von Zeppelin," the man said, bowing stiffly, then extending his hand to shake Sherlock's hand. "In your country, I would be referred to as Count Zeppelin. You may just refer to me as Count." He turned his notebook around so that Sherlock could see it. "Now, tell me—can you conceive of a gigantic balloon made of varnished silk braced with hoops of some kind, a rigid airship, if you will, filled with a gas that is lighter than air and flying across the ocean at a height such that below the balloon you see clouds, not waves?"

"What gas would you use?" Sherlock asked.

The Count nodded. "An excellent question. The French have been using hot air for smaller balloons, although I cannot see that working for larger ones, and the American army have had good results with coke gas, which is derived from burning coal. I would favour hydrogen, if it could be purified enough."

"And how would you move the balloon?" Sherlock was fascinated by this strange man's ideas. "Surely balloons would just float off?"

"This ship on which we find ourselves does not just float. It moves. It has engines. It has paddles. If paddles can move a ship through the water then they could move a balloon through the air."

Sherlock looked at him dubiously. "Are you sure that would work?"

Von Zeppelin smiled coldly. "I have conducted an extensive study of lighter-than-air flight. Four years ago I was in America, acting as an observer for the Northern Potomac army in their war against the Confederate States. While I was there I made my first ascent in a tethered reconnaissance balloon. I also met Professor Thaddeus Lowe, who is probably the world's greatest expert on lighter-than-air flight." Von Zeppelin's rather rigid face seemed to light up when he talked about balloons. It was obvious to Sherlock that the subject enthused him. "Professor Lowe had previously built a balloon intended for transatlantic flight, just like this ship, which he named the *Great Western*. It was 103 feet in diameter and could lift twelve tons. Before the war, he used it to make a successful flight from Philadelphia to New Jersey, but his first attempt to cross the Atlantic was halted when its skin was ripped open by a wind." He shrugged. "The start of the war meant that Professor Lowe's plans were halted. He formed the Union Army Balloon Corps at the express request of President Lincoln. Wars are strange things. On the one hand they drag men of intellect away from their pursuit of progress, but on the other hand they also accelerate the need for progress. Without the War Between the States, would the president have been interested in the possibilities of balloons?"

"Sherlock!"

The voice was female, and young. It was Virginia. Sherlock turned to see her standing a little way off, in the lee of a lifeboat. She was still looking pale, but she was smiling.

"Excuse me," he said to the Count. "I need to go."

The Count bowed stiffly again. "Of course. The fair sex takes precedence over everything."

"Are you married?" Sherlock asked.

"I am engaged to be married," Zeppelin said. His stern face lit up as he smiled. "Her name is Isabella Freiin von Wolff, from the house of Alt-Schwanenburg, and she is the most beautiful woman in the world." He glanced towards Virginia, then back to Sherlock. "Although you would not think so, I think."

Sherlock smiled at him. He quite liked the German count.

"I'll see you later," he said.

"It is a small ship," the Count replied, "and there are only so many of us on board. We are bound to bump into each other again."

Leaving the Count behind, Sherlock walked towards Virginia.

"I was afraid you were going to spend the entire voyage in your cabin," he said awkwardly.

"So was I," she replied. "I hate bein' cooped up in a small room, but I don't see as I had much choice." She blushed, the colour suddenly flooding into her pale cheeks, and she looked away. "I guess . . . I guess my pa told you that this voyage reminded me too much of the last voyage we took together, when my ma died."

"He did," Sherlock confirmed.

"And, to make it worse, I get seasick. You wouldn't believe that someone who rides a horse could get seasick, but I've been as sick as a dog."

He couldn't help smiling. That complete honesty was one of the things he liked most about Virginia. No English girl would have dreamed of discussing matters of the stomach like that.

"How are you feeling now?" he asked.

"The lady I'm sharing a cabin with made me some herbal tea. This is the first day I've managed to keep any down, but I think it's helping."

"I'm sorry about your mother," he said awkwardly. "And I'm sorry this trip reminds you of her. I think being in England keeps on reminding you of her."

"It does." She paused. "I don't know if she was ill when she boarded, or whether she caught somethin' on board, but she was mightily sick for a whole week. She got thinner an' thinner, and whiter an' whiter, an' then she just slipped away." A tear slid from her eye and began a slow trickle down her cheek. "They buried her at sea. The captain said he couldn't keep her body on board, not for the rest of the voyage, so they wrapped her in a canvas sheet an' said some pretty words an' then just tipped her over the side. That's the worst thing. I haven't even got a grave I can visit." She gestured with her open palm at the expanse of ocean. "Just this."

Sherlock was silent for a moment, then he said: "My mother's ill." He didn't know he was going to say that; the words just spilled out of him.

"What's the matter?" Virginia asked.

"Nobody will talk about it." He paused. "I think it's consumption."

"Consumption?"

"Tuberculosis. She's pale and thin, and she's tired all the time. And I sometimes see blood in her handkerchief when she coughs, but I know my brother and my father try to stop me from seeing it." He couldn't seem to stop himself from talking, now that he had started. "So I went into my father's library and I looked in as many books as

I could until I found those symptoms. She's got tuberculosis, and she's going to die. There's no cure. It just makes people waste away, bit by bit."

Virginia moved close and rested her head against his shoulder for a moment before moving away. "At least my ma was taken away quickly," she said, gazing up at him. "I'd never thought about it before, but I guess that was a blessing. Seeing her slippin' away over weeks, months, years . . . that must be terrible."

Sherlock turned away so she couldn't see the gleam of the tears that he felt pricking in his eyes.

"Are we really goin' to find him?" she whispered.

"Find who?"

"Matty."

Sherlock felt his breath catch in his chest. He'd been asking himself the same question, and he was still no closer to an answer.

"We'll find him," he said. "And he'll be all right. The men who kidnapped him have every reason in the world to keep him alive."

"That's not a real answer," she said softly, "and you know it."

"Have you seen the ship?" he asked, deliberately changing the subject.

"Not that much of it. I've been asleep most of the time."

"Then let me show you."

He escorted her around the deck, showing her everything from the bows to the stern, including the pen where the animals were kept—now somewhat depleted in number after five days of the voyage. In the bows of the boat, she put her hand on his arm.

"Pa said you'd got into a fight," she said. "Are you okay?"

"I'm always getting into fights," he replied.

"You should learn to fight better."

"Hey, I've managed so far. I've survived."

"What happened? Tell me!"

So he told her everything that had happened with Grivens, the steward, and unlike the time when he'd told the story to Amyus Crowe he found himself getting emotional and having to stop a couple of times in order to get his feelings in check. Somehow, telling Virginia the story made it more real. It wasn't just a collection of facts anymore.

When he'd finished, she squeezed his arm. "Are you all right?"

"I will be, I suppose."

"It's a shock, isn't it?"

He glanced at her, puzzled. "What?"

"Being responsible for the death of a human being. And knowing that it might have been you."

He shrugged awkwardly. "I guess it is. I just . . . don't know how to react to it. I don't know what's appropriate."

"I remember," she said, "when we were livin' in Albuquerque, an' when Pa used to come back from his trips, he'd just slump into a chair an' want to drink whisky.

We'd try to talk to him, but he wouldn't respond. I didn't know then what he did, or where he'd been. I only found out later that he'd been trackin' some killer, or a traitor, an' that sometimes it didn't end well." She paused for a moment. "I guess what I'm tryin' to say is that when it starts to not matter, when you find you don't have a reaction, that's when you need to worry, 'cause that's the point where you ain't quite human anymore."

She leaned up and kissed him briefly on the cheek: a touch of warmth in the cold air. "I'm goin' to go an' lie down for a while. I'll prob'ly see you at dinner."

She walked off. He could still feel the warm trace left by her lips on his cheek.

The last three days of the voyage were filled with anticipation, and with a strange betting fever that swept over the passengers as they wagered on everything from the exact day, hour, and minute that they would see land to the first name of the pilot who would come aboard to guide them into New York harbour. Sherlock kept himself away from it, throwing himself with equal feverishness into his violin lessons with Rufus Stone. He practised the shapes of notes and chords with his left hand until the pads of his fingers were blistered. Only on the last day did Stone actually allow him to combine what he had learned about his stance, about his use of the bow, and about how his left hand should grasp the neck of the violin, and actually play for real.

It was one of his proudest accomplishments.

"You need to get yourself a violin," Rufus told him. "A good one, not something made out of boxwood and held together with horse glue." He scowled at Sherlock. "You have a certain natural talent, my friend, and your fingers are as long, as thin, and as flexible as pipe cleaners. You could go far. I'm not saying you could be a great concert violinist—I'd have needed to start teaching you at the age of five for that to happen—but I reckon if you keep practising you could earn your living in a theatre orchestra, for sure."

They were interrupted by a commotion among the passengers at the front of the ship. Land had been sighted!

Sherlock rushed to look. The trip had been long enough that he'd almost forgotten what it was like to walk on a surface that didn't move under his feet.

America was a dark shape on the horizon that, over the course of several hours, resolved itself into a craggy line of hills and cliffs topped with trees. Strangely, it didn't look much different from the landscape of southern England, but there was something in the air, some indefinable scent, that suggested they were indeed somewhere else.

The ship turned so that it was heading down towards New York with the coastline on its starboard side. Despite the fact that there were still several hours to go before reaching port, some of the passengers rushed off to pack their bags.

The last meal before they arrived was a party, with special courses and a celebration cake along with crates of champagne. Sherlock ate sparingly and left as soon as he could in order to get some sleep before arrival. He had a feeling he was going to need it.

And then they were arriving in New York harbour. Despite his intentions, Sherlock stood out on deck with everyone else, watching the various small islands slide past them. The ship moved carefully, cautiously, under the control of the pilot—the local expert seaman who had joined the ship from a small boat that had come up alongside it.

"Complex area," Amyus Crowe said from beside Sherlock. "One of the most intricate harbours in the world. There's three separate bodies of water that meet here—the Atlantic Ocean, the Hudson River, and the Long Island Sound. Add that to the fifty-odd islands in the vicinity, along with the thirty-odd rivers, creeks, an' streams apart from the Hudson that empty out here, an' you get a very complicated system of tides an' currents."

"What do we do now?" Sherlock asked.

"First thing I got to do is make contact with the authorities. We're goin' to need help in this business, an' I owe it to them to tell them I'm back. There's men around this city that owe me some favours, an' I intend callin' in those favours, see if anyone remembers seeing young Matty and his captors, for a start. Your brother should have already telegraphed them to let them know we're comin', so I'm expectin' to be met at the dockside. And then we find out when the SS *Great Eastern* docked, assumin' it already has. If not, we wait for it. If it's already here then we track down where three men, one of them a mental invalid, along with a child, went. We can find them, I'm sure of it." There was something hard in his voice, and when Sherlock glanced up it was as if Crowe's face were carved out of some heavy stone. "An' when we do find them, they will wish they had never been born."

Eleven

Disembarkation at New York was a chaotic affair. Everyone was trying to get down the gangplank at the same time with their luggage, and the number of passengers seemed to have doubled, with everyone from steerage suddenly appearing on deck and blinking at the bright sunlight. Eventually, however, all the passengers ended up in a large warehouse-type building, where lines formed and people were called forward to a row of desks where immigration officials in uniforms and with serious, humourless faces checked everyone's documents. Sherlock could make out hundreds of voices talking in as many different accents, and mentions of final destinations like Chicago, Pennsylvania, Boston, Virginia, and Baltimore.

Sherlock caught sight of Rufus Stone in a different queue. The violinist had his case slung over his shoulder. Apart from that he seemed to have precious little in the way of luggage. He turned and caught sight of Sherlock and winked. Sherlock smiled back.

The German—Count Ferdinand von Zeppelin—was also in another queue. His stiff back and his frown suggested that he wasn't used to waiting, or to mixing with people of such a different social class. He didn't look around at all. Instead he just stared straight ahead, apparently wishing he was anywhere else but there.

The ship had docked alongside many other ships belonging to different shipping lines, all set along the extensive harbour area. Most of them were iron- or wood-hulled with two huge paddle wheels on the sides, but Sherlock noticed a smattering of smaller wooden ships that still used sails, and some more modern iron ones that appeared to have a set of metal blades on an axle at the back.

The weather was hot and stifling. It reminded Sherlock of the engine room of the SS *Scotia*, but with an additional smell of sewage added on top. He tried to breathe as little as possible, standing with Virginia behind Amyus Crowe as the big American dealt with a particularly dour immigration official, then following Crowe outside into the open air of America.

America! He was in a different country! Excitedly, Sherlock looked around, trying to catalogue the differences between England and America. The sky was the same blue, of course, and the people looked identical to the ones he'd left behind, but there was something indefinably different. Maybe it was the cut of the clothes, or the architectural style of the buildings, or something he couldn't even put his finger on, but America was *different* from England.

Crowe managed to secure a cab—one of hundreds

that were queuing up for the disembarking passengers—and they set off through the amazingly wide streets of New York. Most of the buildings were made either of wood or of a brown stone that must have been quarried locally. The wooden buildings were typically only one or two storeys tall, but the brownstone ones could be four or five storeys, and many of them had a basement level accessible via steps. A large number of the buildings nearest the harbour were either hotels, boardinghouses, restaurants, or bars, but as the cab headed into the city Sherlock spotted more and more shops and offices, as well as large tenement buildings where hundreds of people lived together but in their own separate sets of rooms. Now *that* was something you didn't see very often in England, except possibly in the dangerous Rookery areas of London.

And there were boys on every street corner selling newspapers, four or six sheets of small-print text that they waved over their heads while they called out the juicier headlines—bodies found without their hands, robberies carried out at gunpoint, politicians found to have taken bribes. All human life appeared to be there—well, the seamier side of human life, at least—and each boy seemed to be selling a different newspaper, the *Sun*, the *Chronicle*, the *Eagle*, the *Star* . . . an endless parade of names.

The cab stopped outside a hotel that appeared to be significantly more salubrious than the ones closer to the harbour. Presumably, Sherlock thought, there was some kind of filtering effect going on—the steerage passengers would end up in dingy, dirty, cheap boardinghouses close to the water, while the passengers with more money could get further and further away, into the better, cleaner, but more expensive areas.

"This is the Jellabee Hotel," Crowe said as he got out and helped Virginia to the street. "I've stayed here before. It's a decent place—at least, it was. The Pinkerton Agency uses it a fair amount. They're just around the corner. We'll head in and see if there are any rooms available, then go off for dinner at Niblo's Garden. Best place in the city."

While Crowe went up to the front desk to book rooms, Sherlock looked around. Inside, the hotel was, if anything, even hotter than outside. It was, however, neatly kept, with decent carpets underfoot, and the people in the lobby were well dressed. Most people spoke with an accent similar to that of Amyus and Virginia Crowe, and to the men they had followed to this country, but Sherlock noticed a smattering of other languages—French, German, Russian, and several others that he couldn't place.

Crowe ambled back, smiling. "I've secured a suite of rooms for us," he said. "A sittin' room plus three bedrooms. When we get Matty back, he'll have to double up with you, Sherlock."

"Of course." Sherlock took heart at the way Crowe said "when" rather than "if."

They took the stairs to the third floor, where their rooms were located. Oddly, Sherlock noticed, it was on the second floor.

"Ah," Crowe rumbled. "Good point. That's one of the differences between England and America. In England you have a ground floor, a first floor, a second floor, and so on. Here in America the ground floor is called the first floor, so we just have a first floor, a second floor, and so on. No ground floor."

"What else do I need to know?" Sherlock asked.

"What you call a pavement, we call a sidewalk. Apart from that, it's pretty much the same. The money is different, though. We have dollars, dimes, and cents, not pounds, shillings, and pence. I'll give you both some money later on. Don't flash it around."

The rooms were good—the sitting room had two sofas and several comfortable chairs, along with a writing desk, and a window with a view over the street outside. Sherlock's bedroom was smaller, but the bed was far softer than the one he had left behind at Holmes Manor. The hotel wasn't exclusive by any means, but it obviously catered to guests with money and expectations.

"Can I go out for a walk?" he asked Amyus Crowe.

Crowe thought for a moment. "You're a smart kid. You think you can find your way back?"

"I'm sure I can."

"The city's laid out on a grid system: pretty logical to follow." He crossed to the writing desk and picked up a sheet of letterhead. "If you get lost, ask for the Jellabee Hotel. The address is on here. Don't get involved with any street corner card games, don't flash any money around, an' don't give anyone any cheek. If you find yourself in a location called 'Five Points,' then get out as quickly as you can. You'll know you're in Five Points because of the smell—the place is full of turpentine distilleries, glue factories, and slaughterhouses. Follow those rules and you'll be okay." He delved in his pocket and handed over a fistful of notes and coins. "That should buy you somethin' to eat, if you get hungry, or a cab to get you back."

"What are you going to do?"

"I'm goin' to find out when the SS *Great Eastern* docked. An' if it hasn't docked I'm goin' to find out when it's due in."

Sherlock turned to see whether Virginia wanted to come with him, but she had already retreated into her room.

Crowe shook his head. "Leave her," he said. "There's too many memories here for her. Let her come to terms with it herself."

Outside, in the sunshine, the smell of sewage and rotting vegetables was much stronger. Sherlock wandered along the pavement—the *sidewalk*, he reminded himself—taking in the sights and the sounds of this new city in a new land.

He passed shops with signs outside offering "notions," which seemed to be household items of various kinds, and bars serving everything from "gumption"—which he guessed from the smell was a kind of cider—to something called "port wine negus." Alleys led off the main street, narrow canyons between the buildings in which he was surprised to see not only cats and dogs but also wild pigs rooting through the piles of discarded rubbish for something they could eat. There were also restaurants on every corner, offering food from various nations. Sherlock was particularly struck by the sheer number and variety of oyster bars, usually serving beer and wine and the mysterious "gumption" as well as oysters that had been fried, boiled, broiled, grilled, or just served on ice. Oysters seemed to be the most common food around New York.

As well as the bars, restaurants, and shops, there were churches made of white stone, with white steps up to their front doors and with sharply pointed steeples, and warehouses where all kinds of goods coming off the ships, or heading for them, were stored. Within the space of a few blocks Sherlock saw more variety than he'd seen in several villages and towns in England all put together.

And someone was following him.

He became aware of it after about half an hour of wandering. The same brown bowler hat kept turning up in the crowd behind him. He recognized it because it had a distinctive green band around the crown. He made a point of checking the crowds for other hats like that, but there was only one and it was always behind him.

He tried going into a shop looking around at the various "notions"—washing boards, soap, pegs, and suchlike—that were on display, but when he came out the man in the brown bowler hat was loitering on a corner, reading a newspaper that he'd obviously bought from one of the street boys. Sherlock then tried ducking down a rubbish-strewn alley to a parallel street, but somehow the man in the brown bowler hat guessed what he'd done and ran down another alley, so that when Sherlock looked behind him again the man was still there. Sherlock couldn't see the man's face, but he was bulky and he walked with a roll of his shoulders, as if he'd just come off a ship that had been gently moving under his feet and he wasn't used to the feel of solid ground.

Sherlock's mind raced. He didn't know whether the man had picked him up at the hotel or just seen him in the street and started following. If he'd just seen Sherlock in the street, then the last thing Sherlock wanted to do was to lead him back to the hotel where Amyus and Virginia Crowe were staying. He had to get rid of the follower somehow. No, he thought suddenly, he needed to reverse the situation; follow the follower to see where he was based. Because Matty might be held there as well.

This wasn't going to be easy.

He ducked into another of the general purpose stores. This one seemed to have a fair selection of clothes—jackets, caps, and trousers. Estimating that his follower was going to stay outside for a while, Sherlock quickly picked out a flat cap and a jacket and noticed with relief that the shop had another exit onto a side street. He took his items to the counter, where the man looked him up and down and said: "You know, a kid like you ought to think 'bout buyin' a sling. We just got a new batch in. Are you interested?"

"A sling?" The word stumped Sherlock for a moment. Was a sling some local term that he ought to know about? Then he remembered, thinking back to Bible study at Deepdene School. Hadn't David used a sling to kill Goliath in the First Book of Samuel? It was some kind of weapon that you could use to throw stones accurately and with force.

"All the boys around here are carryin' them," the man added.

"How much?" Sherlock asked.

The price didn't add much to the cost of the clothes, so Sherlock agreed. If possessing a sling helped him blend in, then all the better. After he'd slipped the jacket and cap on he examined it as the man wrapped his own jacket—the one the follower would recognize and be looking for—in brown paper for him to take away. The sling was a simple pouch of leather that would hold a stone, with leather thongs on either side. One thong was designed to be tied around the wrist; the other looked like you held it, whirled the sling around and then released it, letting the stone fly off.

"You'll need some ammunition," the man said, handing Sherlock the parcel containing his old jacket. "I'll give you a bag of ball bearin's for free."

Sherlock paid with the money that Amyus Crowe had given him. He slipped the sling and the ball bearings into a pocket, taking the brown paper parcel tied up with string. He pulled the cap low on his head and left the shop at a fast walk through the side exit, trying to put some distance between himself and the man in the brown bowler hat. When he could see a corner coming up ahead, he accelerated his pace even more.

Heading around the corner, he called to the nearest paperboy.

"How much for all the papers?"

The kid looked like he couldn't believe his luck. "Ten cents a copy," he said, "an' I got fifty left, ain't I? That makes . . ." He paused, calculating. "Six dollars straight."

Sherlock estimated that he had just over forty newspapers left, and even if it was fifty the total price would only be five dollars. "I'll give you five dollars for the lot," he said.

"Done!" the kid cried. He handed over the pile of newspapers, and Sherlock gave him five dollar bills. As the kid ran off, waving the money in the faces of his friends and laughing, Sherlock started to sell newspapers.

"Read all about it!" he cried in the best approximation of a New York accent he could manage. He knew it was probably mangled by having been listening to Amyus Crowe and Virginia for so long, but as long as it wasn't an English accent it probably didn't matter that much. "Terrible murder at"—his mind raced—"Five Points! Police baffled! More murders expected!"

The other paperboys checked their headlines, wondering where he'd got that from, but he'd already got three customers taking newspapers off him when the man in the brown bowler hat came around the corner.

It was Ives—the man from the house in Godalming. The burly, pale-haired man with the gun.

Sherlock tried to scrunch himself down, letting his shoulders drop and hunching himself, as though he was tired and hadn't eaten properly for a while. It worked. Ives's gaze passed over Sherlock, ignoring him in the same way a man might ignore a gas lamp or a horse trough. He stopped, scanning the street ahead, presumably looking to see where Sherlock had gone. When he couldn't locate him, Ives cursed under his breath. He stood there uncertainly for a moment, barely six feet away from the boy he was searching for, then abruptly turned around and walked away.

Sherlock threw the papers at the feet of the nearest paperboy. "Here, sell these," he said.

"That's the *Sun*," the kid said. "I only sell the *Chronicle*."

"Expand your inventory," Sherlock replied, and sped off after Ives.

Ives headed off at a fast walk, head down and hands in his pockets. He looked dejected. Perhaps whoever his employer was would be angry at the fact that he'd lost

Sherlock. The fact that he didn't head back to the Jellabee Hotel meant that he probably didn't know where Sherlock and the other two were staying.

The sun was slipping down in the sky now, barely clearing the tops of the buildings and casting an orange light over everything. It shone directly into Sherlock's eyes, making him squint so that it was hard to track where Ives went. They must have covered five blocks or more before Ives turned off the street and headed into a boardinghouse.

Sherlock looked around uncertainly. He didn't know if this was Five Points or not, but it certainly didn't look as appealing as the area where the Jellabee Hotel was located, despite the presence of a dilapidated clapboard church with a wonky steeple at the end of the street. It stank, but he wasn't sure if it was the smell of turpentine distilleries and slaughterhouses or just the general smell of decay and sewage that seemed to hang over New York like an invisible fog. This place looked dangerous. The people hanging around on street corners weren't paperboys anymore, they were men in ripped shirts and dirty trousers who watched everyone going past with hard eyes. Somewhere, a man was playing a mournful trumpet. The instrument was out of tune, but so much else around there was out of tune as well that it seemed to fit.

Sherlock needed to blend in even more than he had earlier. He ducked into an alley and rubbed his cap in the dirt, then ripped one of the sleeves of his jacket so that the lining was exposed.

That should do the trick. He looked like he belonged now.

Heading back to the street, limping slightly to make his gait appear different, he walked down to the boarding-house. The door was open, and he glanced inside.

There was no lobby, as there was back in the Jellabee. If he walked into the hall he would just have a choice of doors or the bare stairs. It wasn't like he could go around knocking on doors looking for Matty. He had to think of something else.

Glancing around, he saw that the building opposite had a metal staircase bolted to the brickwork outside—some kind of fire escape, perhaps. Ladders led down from one floor to the next, attached to narrow metal balconies. If he climbed up, he might be able to see inside some of the windows of the boardinghouse. If the curtains were open. And if the glass was clean enough.

Stop procrastinating! he told himself. Crossing the road, he waited for a moment when nobody was passing by and quickly scrambled up the fire escape to the first floor. Or was that the second floor? He wasn't sure.

He scrunched himself down against the metal grille of the balcony and stared across the road. Four windows, none of them with any curtains, which was a blessing. One room with a man inside whom Sherlock didn't recognize, pacing back and forth. Another window with a woman staring out. She appeared to be wearing a nightgown. She caught Sherlock's eye and smiled sadly at him. Two rooms that were currently unoccupied.

He scrambled up the next ladder. The metal creaked and swayed beneath him. Sherlock wondered when it had last been checked for safety, and then he wondered if it had *ever* been checked for safety.

The next balcony looked across onto another four rooms.

The first two were deserted.

The third window gave onto a room with four men standing with glasses in their hands, drinking and talking. One of the men was Ives and one was Berle, the doctor. The other two men were unknown to Sherlock.

The important thing, however, was that Matthew Arnatt was standing with his elbows on the window ledge, looking out at the street. His gaze roved curiously from person to person, thing to thing. He looked unharmed; no bruising, no grazes. He also looked like he'd been fed; or at least he didn't look thin and hungry. He just looked bored and sad.

Until he saw Sherlock. Then his eyes lit up and his face creased into a huge, beaming smile.

Sherlock's heart surged to see that Matty was alive, and apparently in good health. The fear he'd been repressing throughout the entire journey suddenly released, threatening to overwhelm him. He blinked back tears of relief.

Sherlock raised a finger to his lips, shushing Matty. The boy nodded, but he was still beaming. Sherlock knew if the men in the room saw that smile they'd know something was up. Sherlock placed his fingers at the corners of his mouth and dragged them down into an exaggerated sad face. Matty frowned at him. Sherlock tried again, letting his eyebrows droop sadly as well, and Matty's own eyebrows shot upward into his hairline as he suddenly understood. The smile faded away from his face and his mouth moved back into the same downward curve that Sherlock had first seen on it a few moments ago, but his eyes were still gleaming.

"Are you all right?" Sherlock mouthed.

Matty nodded slightly.

"Are they treating you well?" Sherlock mouthed again.

Matty frowned.

"Are . . . they . . . treating . . . you . . . well?" Sherlock mouthed again, separating the words to make it easier for Matty to understand.

Matty nodded again, very slightly.

"We're going to get you back!" Sherlock told him.

Matty opened his mouth and formed the words "I know!"

The men behind Matty seemed to conclude their discussion. Sherlock had a feeling that there wasn't much time. "Where are they taking you?" he mouthed.

Matty's lips moved, but Sherlock couldn't understand what he was trying to say. He frowned, trying to indicate that he didn't know what Matty was saying. Matty tried again, but whatever words he was forming were unfamiliar to Sherlock.

Matty's hand moved on the window frame, as though he was writing something. Was he leaving a message for Sherlock, etched in the dirt and dust? Then he pointed to the sill outside the window, then across the street at the old, dilapidated church Sherlock had noticed earlier. He raised his eyebrows, asking if Sherlock understood. Sherlock shook his head. Matty tried again—miming writing a note on the window frame, pointing to the windowsill, and then pointing at the church. In fact, he pointed at the top of the church. Then he added more gestures—holding two fingers up, then pointing at Sherlock, pointing at himself, and then holding up three fingers and shrugging, as if confused.

This was madness. Whatever message Matty was trying to convey, it wasn't getting through.

Sherlock was just about to indicate again that he didn't understand when one of the men crossed the room and grabbed hold of Matty's shoulder, dragging him away from the window. He didn't look outside, so Sherlock assumed he had grabbed the boy because he wanted Matty to go with them, not because he'd seen him communicating with someone. Sherlock looked away and tried to be inconspicuous. When he looked back, the room was empty. The men had gone, taking Matty with them.

Sherlock rushed down the ladder to the ground and raced across the road towards the boardinghouse. He wasn't sure what he was going to do, but he had to do something.

He was too late. While he and Matty had been trying to communicate, one of the men must have come down to get a cab, while another had taken their luggage downstairs. By the time Sherlock had crossed the road they were already climbing into the cab. Sherlock got one last look at Matty's frightened face before the horses were whipped up and the cab drove off.

He looked around for another cab, but the street was empty of anything apart from people.

He felt a blanket of dark despair falling over him.

No. No time for that. He raced back towards the hotel as fast as he could, retracing the route he'd taken and unconsciously memorized, knowing that he had the hotel's letterheaded paper in his pocket if he got lost. His mind was working as fast as his legs, trying to sort out what Matty's last message had been. A clue, obviously. An answer to the question Sherlock had asked. But what?

Charades, perhaps? Was Matty trying to spell out the name of the place he was going in the form of syllables? As the stores, hotels, and street corners flashed past, and as the air whistled in Sherlock's throat and burned in his lungs, he tried to decipher the clues.

Writing. Pencil? Pen? Words? Letters?

The windowsill. Did he mean the sill itself, or the stone it was made from?

And the church. As his feet pounded on the sidewalk and as he pushed past slower pedestrians, Sherlock tried to remember what was on top of the church. A spire, obviously. And on top of the spire was—

A weathervane, moving to show the direction of the wind.

And suddenly it all fell into place. Pen-sill-vane. There was a place in America, somewhere nearby, called Pennsylvania. Pennsylvania. Was *that* what Matty had been trying to convey?

But what about the other message—the two fingers, pointing at himself and Sherlock, then looking confused while holding up three fingers? What did that mean?

Two—that might mean "to." "Pennsylvania to—" where?

The Jellabee Hotel was in sight now. Sherlock's muscles were screaming in pain, but somehow he kept on running.

Matty and Sherlock and a third thing, something missing. Virginia! It had to be Virginia. That was a place as well as a girl's name!

"Pennsylvania to Virginia." It still didn't make much sense to Sherlock, but Amyus Crowe might be able to explain it.

He burst in through the hotel front door and pelted up the stairs, virtually collapsing against the door to the suite.

He hit his fists against it. The door opened and he fell inside. Virginia was standing over him, looking startled.

"Where's your father?" he gasped.

"He's not back yet. He must still be with the Pinkerton Agency."

"I've seen Matty. They're taking him now." He was having to force the words out past his gasps for breath. "Matty got a message to me—'Pennsylvania to Virginia.' I think he was trying to tell me where they were taking him, but I don't understand. Are they going to Pennsylvania or Virginia? Or both? They're both places, right?"

Virginia shook her head. "It's simpler than that. The Pennsylvania Railroad runs trains out of its own station in New Jersey, across the Hudson River. They have a line heading to Virginia. That's where they're taking Matty. Must be."

"We need to find your father and tell him."

"There's no time," she said. "If they're heading for the station, then we need to take a ferry and get there now and intercept them, try to get Matty back. We can't wait for Pa. I'll leave a note."

She moved quickly towards a table, opened a drawer, and took out a roll of bank notes. "Pa left this here so it wouldn't get taken from his pocket on the streets. Not that anyone would have tried, but he's always careful. Anyway, we might need it."

She scribbled a note to her father on one of the letter-headed sheets from the writing desk, then together they ran downstairs and exited the hotel. A cab was just depositing a passenger; Virginia jumped in and pulled Sherlock after her. Virginia called up to the driver; Sherlock couldn't hear what she said, but the cab set off at a fast trot.

"I promised him double the fare if he gets us to the ferry in ten minutes," she said, grinning.

Sherlock and Virginia held on tight as the cab clattered through the streets of New York. Twice, potholes in the road caught the wheels, throwing them together, but they quickly drew apart.

By the time the cab pulled up outside the ferry terminal on Manhattan's west side, Sherlock was sore from the bouncing journey. After Virginia paid the driver, they just managed to catch a ferry as lines were being cast off. On the short trip across the traffic-filled water, there was no sign of their quarry aboard the boat. No doubt they had caught a vessel from a different terminal.

After the boat docked, Sherlock and Virginia were first down the gangplank, racing into the massive train station. It was a scene of controlled chaos, with people heading in all directions across a massive marble hall. At the opposite side of the hall a series of arches led to what Sherlock assumed were the platforms. Boards hung on hooks announced the destinations of the trains, and the stops along the way. Even as he watched, some boards were being taken down and others put up.

Sherlock ran along the line of arches, checking all the

signs. After a few moments he became aware that Virginia was running beside him.

Chicago, Delaware, Baltimore . . . It occurred to Sherlock with a sickening lurch that Virginia was a state, but the destinations on the boards were *towns.* Back in England he would have known that Southampton, for instance, was in Hampshire county, but here, in America, he had no idea which state contained which towns.

"There!" Virginia called. "Richmond—it's the state capital of Virginia. Track 29."

She led the way through an arch, and Sherlock followed. A guard in an impressive blue uniform and peaked cap scowled at Sherlock's ripped jacket and dirty cap and tried to stop them, but Virginia ran past him. He tried to grab Sherlock's arm, but Sherlock pushed him out of the way.

They were running along the platform now, beside the carriages of a seemingly endless train. The engine at the front was invisible around a curve. Unlike in British stations, where the platforms were raised to the same level as the doors at either end of the carriages, in here the platforms were lower and steps led up to each door.

Sherlock was scanning the windows as they ran, looking for Matty's face, but it was the burned, scarred face of John Wilkes Booth that he saw first. He pulled Virginia to a halt, then drew her back along the carriage to the end.

"We don't have much time," he gasped.

Virginia looked in both directions along the train. Apart from a small group of people boarding further up, there was nobody who might help. Even the ticket collector who had tried to grab them just now had vanished—possibly to fetch the police.

"We need to find a guard on the train," she said, and started climbing up the steps. "He can stop the train from going."

Sherlock could only follow her up the steps. He wasn't sure she'd thought this through, but then again he wasn't sure that he had any better ideas.

They found themselves inside a carriage. An aisle ran down the centre, between wooden seats covered with upholstered cloth.

Halfway down, in facing seats, were Ives, Berle, John Wilkes Booth, and a kid who was, judging by the shape of the back of his head, Matty. The men were talking intensely and Sherlock ducked down between two seats before they saw him.

Virginia looked around for the guard. Sherlock's heart flipped in his chest when he heard a whistle blow outside, a sharp, shrill burst of sound.

The next thing that happened was that the train began to move.

TWELVE

Sherlock's initial instinct was to run back to the door and jump off the train. He grabbed Virginia's arm and pulled her towards him, but she resisted.

"We need to get off!" he hissed. "We haven't got tickets, and we're leaving your father behind!"

"We can get tickets from the conductor on the train," she replied, "or tell him that our pa has the tickets and he's in another compartment. And we can telegraph back to Pa when we stop and tell him where we are. The important thing is that we don't lose the men who have Matty. If we do, we've lost them forever. We need to track them until they settle in another hotel, or a house, or something."

"But—" he started.

"Trust me! This is my country, I understand how it works. I've made train journeys by myself before. We'll be okay."

Sherlock subsided. They'd ended up where they were by accident, but they ought to make the best of it, now they were there. Getting off the train and going back to the hotel would waste all the effort they'd gone to in getting to America so far.

"Very well," he said. "We'll stay."

"We don't have a choice now," Virginia pointed out. She indicated the window. Outside, the platform had vanished and the train was speeding up as the line cut across wide dirt streets. He could feel, as well as hear, the *clack-clack clack-clack* as the wheels of the carriage passed over the joins in the track every hundred yards or so.

Sherlock glanced back down the aisle, towards the men who were holding Matty. "They're all settled down," he said. "We should find a seat and work out what we do next. Are we just following them, or are we going to try to get Matty away from them?"

"Depends on what happens," Virginia replied. "Why do you think they ran for the train so fast?"

"That's my fault," Sherlock admitted. "One of them saw me on the street but I managed to hide so he headed back to their hotel. They must have decided to clear out. That's when Matty managed to tell me where they said they were taking him." He paused, looking around. "There's two spare seats over there. Let's sit down at least."

The seats were facing backward, away from the group of men who were holding Matty captive. An elderly conductor came by and collected their fares. As they sat, Sherlock glanced out of the window. The train was heading around a curve up ahead, and he could see the engine that was pulling them. Naïvely, he'd expected it to look like the ones back in England that ran from Farnham through Guildford to London, but this one was different. The basic cylindrical boiler shape was the same, but the small funnel that British trains had was replaced with a massive thing with sloping sides, sticking up from the front of the boiler. And there was some bizarre object attached to the front of the train: a metal grille with a pointed front that seemed to be designed to sweep things off the tracks.

"Buffalo," Virginia said succinctly, following his gaze.

"What?"

"Buffalo. And cows. They wander across the tracks and sometimes just stay there. The train has to slow down and that thing pushes them out of the way."

"Oh." He thought for a moment. "What about telling the ticket collector?"

"Telling him what?"

"That Matty's being held hostage."

"What's he going to do?" Virginia shook her head, copper-coloured hair swirling around her. "The ticket collector's an old man coming up to retirement. He won't be able to do anything."

The train pushed on. As Sherlock watched, the buildings and roads outside the window gave way to open ground and patches of trees. The bright sunshine made the green vegetation seem to glow of its own accord.

"How long does the journey take?" he asked.

"To Richmond?" She thought for a moment. "The better part of a day, maybe. Depends if we stop anywhere. And we might have to change trains somewhere."

"A *day*?" This country was *big*. "What about food?"

"There might be a restaurant car at the back. If not, there'll be people selling food in the stations we stop at. The train stops for long enough that we can get off and grab a bite to eat. And we might even be able to send a telegraph message to Pa at the hotel, or via the Pinkertons, especially if we write it out first and just hand it in. Most stations have a telegraph office attached."

"We'll have to be careful we're not seen," Sherlock pointed out.

"We'll manage," she said reassuringly.

Sherlock glanced over his shoulder to check that the men hadn't moved. One of them was coming towards him, down the aisle. Sherlock quickly turned back, hoping the man hadn't seen him. It was Berle, the balding doctor. He passed by, and Sherlock watched his back as he moved off down the carriage. He'd have to watch out for the man coming back in the other direction. He'd be facing them then, and he would certainly recognize Sherlock if he saw him again.

It occurred to Sherlock that the most obvious way to disguise his face would be to turn around and kiss Virginia when Berle came back. That way, all Berle would see would be the back of his head. He turned to Virginia and opened his mouth, ready to propose the course of action. She glanced at him, her eyes bright and violet in the sunshine.

"What?" she asked.

"I was just thinking . . ." he said hesitantly.

"Thinking what?"

It was a simple thing to say—"I might need to kiss you so we don't get recognized, so don't be surprised if I do"—but for some reason he couldn't get the words out. Her face was just a few inches away from his, close enough that he could count the freckles. Close enough that he could just lean forward and touch his lips against hers.

"Nothing. Don't worry."

She frowned. "No, what?"

"Really, it's nothing." He turned away, keeping an eye out for Berle's return. If he saw the man he would just look out of the window or something. He realized he was still wearing the flat cap he'd bought in the notions shop. He could just slide it down over his eyes and pretend to be asleep. That would work. Probably.

He glanced out of the window again. Telegraph poles were flickering past, one after the other, paralleling the track. Idly, he counted seconds between the poles—one, two, three, four—and then again—one, two, three, four. The poles were spaced equally apart, as far as he could tell. If he knew how far apart they were, then he could use the information about the time between them to work out how fast the train was travelling. Not that the information would be any more than just interesting, but it would pass the time.

A small town flashed past, gone as soon as it appeared. All Sherlock had was a sense of low wooden buildings and four-wheeled carts, and lots of horses.

The movement of the train was making him sleepy. He'd used up a lot of energy in running back to the hotel earlier, and the constant tension was beginning to get to him. His body craved rest.

He might have dropped off to sleep for a while, because the next thing he knew he was looking out of the window onto a long drop down to the glittering water of a river. The train was on a bridge, crossing a ravine. From what he could see, the bridge was made of wood, and barely wider than the train.

Virginia sensed his sudden tension. "Don't worry," she said, "it's perfectly safe. These bridges have been around for years."

Shortly after that, the train began to slow down.

"Coming into a station," Virginia said.

"Or there's a buffalo on the line," Sherlock responded. His mind started sorting through possibilities. Arriving at a station gave them a whole series of options, from just getting a bite to eat, through sending a telegraph message to Amyus Crowe, and all the way to making an attempt to rescue Matty. If they could get him off the train somehow, then they could either wait in the town until Amyus Crowe got to them or they could just get a train back again—assuming they ran more than one a day, or one a week. It occurred to him that he had no idea of the timetables in this country.

"We need to get out on the platform," he said. "If we get a chance, we need to separate Matty from those men."

The train slowed down even more. They were passing a huge field of tall plants with bulbous tops. The only fence Sherlock could see stretched from the train line to the horizon. The sound of the train's steam whistle suddenly cut through the air: a mournful hoot like the call of some mythical creature. They passed by a smattering of barns and houses, then more houses, and then a whole town materialized as the train gradually heaved itself to a halt alongside a boardwalk that was barely raised above the ground.

"Let's get off," Sherlock said as the voice of the distant ticket collector bellowed: "This is Perseverance, New Jersey. Ten-minute stop, ladies and gentlemen; ten-minute stop. This is Perseverance."

Sherlock pulled Virginia out of her seat and towards the door. Someone outside opened it, and the two of them jumped to the boardwalk.

"You get food," he said. "You've got the money. I'll check that they haven't got off here."

The boardwalk was crowded with people in dusty clothes made of denim, cord, or some kind of patterned cotton that looked a bit like a summer tartan. Sherlock pushed his way through them and moved into the shade of a wall. Some people were leaving the train for good, some were just leaving for a few moments, and some were getting on.

Ives exited the train with Matty. Berle, the doctor, was probably looking after the half-mad John Wilkes Booth.

Matty was looking pale, but Ives seemed to be treating him reasonably well. He wasn't pushing him around or hitting him at least, but his hand was resting on Matty's shoulder. He pushed the boy towards a row of small wooden buildings, little bigger than a garden shed, that sat off to one side of the track. Toilets, Sherlock assumed. Probably just holes in the ground, shielded for privacy.

Ives pushed Matty into one of the outhouses and closed the door. He stood there for a moment, then walked away, grimacing and holding his hand across his face. The smell was obviously driving him away.

Sherlock ran around to the back of the outhouses and counted along to the one he thought Matty had gone into. The wood at the back was almost rotted away at the bottom. Ives had been right. The smell was nauseating.

"Matty!" he hissed through the cracks in the wood.

"Sherlock!" Matty's voice shouted. "I saw you and Virginia on the train!"

"Did *they* see us?"

"No. They would have said."

"Right." Sherlock tested the wood at the base of the outhouse. "Help me make a hole."

Together, with Sherlock pulling and Matty pushing, they snapped enough bits of wood off to make a hole big enough for Matty to scramble through. Sherlock grabbed his hand and pulled. Within moments the two boys were standing together.

"Are you all right?" Sherlock asked breathlessly.

"Better now." Matty frowned. "I was scared on the ship, but they treated me pretty well, and they fed me. And I knew you'd come for me."

"Let's get out of here."

Together they snuck along the back of the outhouses. Sherlock peered around the side. Ives was still standing off to one side, waiting.

"Where's Virginia?" Matty asked.

"She's getting food."

"What about Mr. Crowe?"

"He's back in New York," Sherlock admitted.

"How did that happen?"

Sherlock shook his head. "A whole set of circumstances, all coming together at the same time. It wasn't part of the plan."

Ives wandered away, holding his nose. While his back was turned, Sherlock grabbed hold of Matty's arm. "Come on!"

Together, the two of them ran across the open ground to the simple clapboard building that housed the ticket office and waiting room. Sherlock led Matty around the side, out of sight if Ives turned around. Virginia was there waiting for them. She handed Sherlock two twists of paper with something hot inside, then grabbed Matty and gave him a huge hug.

"I'm so glad to see you again!" she said.

Matty squeezed her back. "Me too," he said, heartfelt.

Sherlock peered around the edge of the building. The

crowd was thinning out now—people who were getting on the train there had already boarded, and people who were getting off there had already dispersed. Only a few passengers who had got off to stretch their legs and grab some food were left. The conductor was standing beside the train, looking up and down its length and checking his pocket watch. Up at the front, the driver was refilling the engine with water from a tank by the side of the track, raised up on stilts.

"All we have to do," Sherlock said, "is wait here until the train goes, then we get the next train back to New York."

"It's not going to be as easy as that," Virginia warned.

"Why not?"

She pointed back towards the outhouses. "Look!"

Berle and Ives were standing together. Ives was obviously explaining something, and Berle was looking furious.

"They've realized Matty has gone," Sherlock said. "They'll start searching."

He was right. Berle and Ives split up, heading off in different directions. Berle went back down the length of the train, looking underneath to see if anyone was standing on the other side, while Ives stalked towards them. No, in fact he was stalking towards the station. He went inside, checking the waiting room.

"Quick!" Sherlock said. "This way!"

He led the other two back towards the train.

"We can't get back on there!" Virginia protested.

"We have to," he said. "Ives and Berle will check all around the station and the outhouses. If we can get on the train and then off the other side, we can make a run for it, then come back when the train has gone."

He scrambled up the steps leading onto the train. Virginia and Matty followed. He could sense their reluctance.

Sherlock quickly moved across to the other side of the carriage and tried the handle of the door.

It was locked.

He twisted harder. No result.

Virginia was at the other door. "They're coming back!" she called.

Sherlock glanced down the carriage. "We can get to the next door," he said urgently. "Come on."

Fortunately they had boarded a different carriage from the one they had left. As they pushed through the central aisle, past people who were standing up, checking their luggage, or just wandering up and down, they didn't see any of the men they were trying to avoid.

At the far end, Sherlock checked the door leading off the train and away from the station. This one was unlocked, but as the door swung open and he prepared to jump off, he caught sight of the burly, blond Ives standing on that side of the train. He was looking away from Sherlock, out into the countryside. Sherlock pulled the door closed quickly.

Virginia was checking the station side. "The bald man is still there," she called. "He's checking both sides of the train."

Outside, the conductor blew his whistle. "All aboard!" he called.

Sherlock's brain was whirling. There was no way off.

"We'll just have to try again at the next station," he said decisively. "At least we've got Matty off them."

The conductor's whistle blew again, and seconds later the train jerked and began to move, slowly at first but accelerating gradually. Virginia glanced out of the window. "The bald man has got back on," she said.

Sherlock checked out of his side. "So has Ives."

"So everyone's back on," Matty pointed out. "Great. And I didn't even get a chance to go to the toilet like I needed to."

"At least we've got food," Virginia said.

"Let's find some seats," Sherlock said. "Preferably as far away as possible from those men. The other end of the train, if we can." He turned to head away, towards the rear of the train, but something in the silence behind him made him turn back.

Berle and another man whom Sherlock didn't recognize were standing behind Virginia and Matty. They must have come along from the other carriage without their noticing.

Sherlock glanced back over his shoulder.

Ives was striding down the aisle of the carriage Sherlock had been planning to head into. He wasn't looking happy.

"Don't be a fool, kid," Berle said. "Ives is angry enough already. Don't make him worse. He kinda gets . . . out of control sometimes. Bad things happen then."

Sherlock glanced back and forth between Ives and Berle. Between the devil and the deep blue sea.

His heart felt leaden in his chest. No way out. Two choices, each of which led to captivity.

No, he told himself. What would Mycroft say? What would Amyus Crowe say? When you've only got two choices, and you don't like either of them, make a third choice.

He opened the door of the carriage and stepped out into the open air.

The green, lush landscape of the New Jersey countryside flashed past in a blur. He heard Virginia gasp behind him, and Ives curse. He kept his left hand gripping the door frame and his left foot wedged against the point where the frame met the floor, and as the wind whistled past him it pushed him backwards, and he swung out and around, into the area between the carriages. He'd spotted a ladder there earlier, leading up to the roof of the carriage, and he grasped for it with his right hand. His fingers closed on a rung, and he stretched with his right leg, trying to get purchase on the ladder. After what seemed like minutes but was probably only a second or two, his foot hit a rung. Releasing his grip on the doorframe, he pulled himself up the ladder.

A hand closed on his left foot before he could pull it up. He kicked downward, feeling his heel hit someone's face. The grip released abruptly, leaving an ache behind where the fingers had clamped down hard.

Within a moment he was on top of the train.

He had to crouch and keep one hand gripping the guide rail that ran along the roof from front to back.

Ahead of him he saw the train curving away. Smoke from the funnel was streaming backwards. It made his eyes water and breathing difficult.

He hesitated for a moment. Rather than be captured he had taken the only other option—escape—but his escape was limited. He was still on the train—literally *on* the train—and he didn't have a plan. No matter where he went, Ives and the other men would find him. Find him and probably kill him. And he couldn't just escape, just jump off the train into a convenient river or something. He had to rescue Virginia and Matty.

He felt despair looming over him like a black wave, but he pushed it backwards with a massive effort of will. Time for that later. Now he had to think.

If he could scramble along the roofs of the carriages to the front of the train, then maybe he could alert the driver. Maybe he could find a way to get a message to the authorities, or get the points switched around to take them back to New York, or something. Anything!

Still crouching, he scrambled along the roof of the carriage. The wind was against him, pushing on him like a giant hand in the centre of his chest, but he pushed back. He had to. His eyes were streaming with tears where the steam was stinging them, and his breath was catching in his chest, but he couldn't stop. Matty and Virginia depended on him.

The train shuddered over some rails, and Sherlock nearly lost his grip. He swayed back and forth for a moment or two, trying to get as low as he could, before he thought he was safe.

Well, saf*er*, he thought, glancing around at the landscape that flashed past in green and brown blurs.

A river was coming up. He could see it ahead of the train, which was curving around towards a bridge that looked like it was made out of matchsticks. He felt his heart pounding.

And then it threatened to explode completely as Ives's head and shoulders appeared at the junction between the carriage Sherlock was climbing along and the one ahead of it. The man must have doubled back along the carriage and climbed up the next ladder.

He pulled himself up to the roof and stood upright. The steam from the engine, pushed backwards by the wind, billowed around him like a white cloak.

"You're not thinking straight, kid," he yelled. "Where are you goin'? You're safer down there with the others."

Sherlock shook his head. "You only need one of us to

threaten Amyus Crowe with," he yelled. "And I don't think you want to be saddled with three hostages."

"Amyus Crowe," Ives said. "Is that the big guy, the one in the white suit? Never knew his name till now, but he's persistent. An' so are you."

"You have no idea," Sherlock yelled, but he was scared. He glanced over his shoulder. No sign of Berle or the other man, but the chances of his being able to get away in that direction were slim. They were probably waiting for him at the next couple of carriage junctions, one of them holding Virginia, the other holding Matty.

When he turned back, Ives was holding a gun.

"You've got moxie, I'll give you that," Ives said, raising the gun to take aim.

Part of Sherlock was wondering what "moxie" was, while another part was noticing that the train was just shifting from land onto the bridge that he'd seen a few moments before. The ground below suddenly plunged away into a chasm of rock with a glittering blue ribbon at the bottom. And a third part of his brain was trying to tell him something.

Ives fired. Sherlock flinched, but the wind and the vibration had knocked Ives's aim off, as he knew that they would, and the bullet passed harmlessly to one side.

Ives moved closer, trying to maintain his balance, and Sherlock tried to latch onto the thought that hovered just out of reach. Something he'd done recently. Something he'd *bought*.

The sling! Desperately he scrabbled through his pockets looking for the leather pouch with the two bits of leather thong attached that he'd bought at the notions store. Right-hand trouser pocket—no. Left-hand trouser pocket—no. Ives was getting ready to fire again. Left-hand inside jacket pocket—no, but his fingers brushed against the collection of cold ball bearings the store-keeper had given him. Ives was pointing his gun again, bracing it with his other hand. Left-hand outside jacket pocket—yes! Sherlock pulled out the sling and quickly slipped his right hand through the loop, then closed the other loop in his palm, leaving the leather pouch to hang loose.

Ives fired. The bullet whistled past Sherlock's ear.

He delved into his pocket with his left hand, pulling out a ball bearing, and quickly slipped it into the pouch. Before Ives could react, Sherlock whirled the weighted sling around his head twice, then released the thong he was holding. The ball bearing flew towards Ives, making a gleaming line in the sky. It caught his left ear, tearing a chunk of flesh away. Ives cried out in surprise and shock as blood splattered. His eyes went wide with disbelief.

Sherlock grabbed the loose thong again and slipped another ball bearing into the pouch.

The train was in the middle of the bridge now, and Sherlock thought he could detect a sideways motion as the bridge rocked under the weight.

Ives lurched forward and shuffled towards Sherlock,

hands outstretched to grab him. He appeared to have forgotten the fact that he still had a gun.

Sherlock whipped the sling around his head again, twice, and let go of the loose thong. The ball bearing shot across the narrowing gap between them, hitting Ives in the centre of his forehead and staying there, in the dent it had created. Ives fell backwards, eyes so wide that Sherlock could see white all around his pupils. His back hit the train roof and he rolled sideways, then vanished over the edge. Sherlock heard a despairing cry as he fell, and then there was nothing but the whistling of the wind and the mournful call of the train's whistle.

Sherlock let his breathing settle and his heart calm down before he stood again and moved backwards to the junction where he had climbed up.

One down; several more to go; but he had a weapon now.

The track clattered beneath the train's wheels as it reached the other side of the ravine. The whistle sounded again. Sherlock glanced forward, towards the engine, and saw that the line ahead split into two. One led onward, straight, while the other curved away, along the edge of the ravine.

And the train was taking the curving branch, slowing down as it passed through a gap in a fence and headed towards a station that Sherlock could see up ahead.

Not a station, he realized.

A house. A large white house. And beyond it, what

looked like a series of fenced enclosures, walled areas and cages, like a private zoological exhibition.

He scrambled down the ladder as fast as he could and swung himself back into the carriage. The conductor was moving down the central aisle, pushing past the uneasy passengers, calling, "Unscheduled stop. Please do not alight. This is an unscheduled stop."

The train drew to a halt in a long *chuff* of escaping steam. It stopped alongside a long veranda that was attached to the back of the house.

A group of eight or nine men were standing on the veranda.

Any hope in Sherlock's mind that they were police, or army, vanished when Berle and the other man stepped off the train, holding Virginia and Matty firmly by the arm, and joined them.

THIRTEEN

The train was in chaos. Every single passenger appeared to be shouting at the conductor, trying to find out why they had changed train lines, why they had stopped, and where they were. The conductor didn't seem to be sure—he was reassuring people, but there was an expression on his face suggesting that he was out of his depth.

"Unscheduled stop!" he kept shouting. "Please do *not* disembark here."

On the platform, the two men were still standing with Virginia and Matty. They were waiting for something. Waiting for him, he suspected. Off to one side he could see John Wilkes Booth. He was standing upright, but he was slowly rocking from side to side and his eyes weren't tracking anything in particular. Probably drugged to keep him quiet.

One of the men—one he'd never seen before—moved his right hand out from behind his back momentarily. He was holding a gun.

Sherlock didn't see that he had much choice, so he stepped from the train, down the short stairway to the veranda of the house.

Towards the back of the train he saw that the men who had been waiting on the platform were hauling boxes out of the last carriage. They looked like the boxes he'd seen in the garden of the house at Godalming—the ones where he thought he'd seen something moving inside. As the boxes were removed the men carried them away to a waiting cart. They seemed to be cautious about getting their fingers too close to the gaps between the slats. Two of them cursed as their box suddenly lurched and nearly fell to the ground, although Sherlock couldn't see what had made its weight shift. Maybe something inside had moved.

Although he didn't see any signal being given, the train began to heave itself away from the house with a deafening clanking as the metal connections between the carriages were pulled tight. It moved slowly at first, but increased in speed as it got further away.

"Where's Ives?" Berle asked Sherlock, raising his voice above the noise of the train. Berle was holding Virginia's arm with his right hand. With his left he was holding a carrying handle attached to a small box.

"He dropped off," Sherlock replied. He could feel his heart thudding within his chest but he tried to keep calm and project an appearance of control.

Virginia and Matty were both staring at him in concern. He looked at each of them in turn, seeking to reassure them that everything was going to be all right, but he didn't believe that and he was sure they didn't either.

"You mean he *fell* off," Berle said. "You *killed* him!"

"I can smell smoke," Booth said from behind them, with his eyes still closed. His voice was distant, dreamy.

"Quiet!" growled the third man, the one holding Matty, "or I'll take a brandin' iron to the other side of your face!" He'd probably been subjected to Booth's mania all the way from New York—perhaps all the way from Southampton—and was obviously getting towards his breaking point. Sherlock studied him for a moment. He'd not had a chance to see this man on the train. He was built like a boxer and wore trousers of denim and a denim waistcoat over a collarless shirt. He had a bright red bandanna knotted round his neck.

"Don't bait him, Rubinek," Berle cautioned. "Duke still needs him."

The man named Rubinek switched his glare to Sherlock. "What about *him*?" he growled. "Duke don't need *him* for nothin', an' he admitted he killed Ives." He brought his right hand from behind his back, the hand that wasn't holding Matty, and let the revolver he was holding point towards Sherlock.

"And what about Gilfillan?" Berle asked.

"He's in police custody," Sherlock answered.

Berle closed his eyes for a moment. "This is going from bad to worse," he said quietly. "Duke isn't going to be pleased, and I've heard about what happens when Duke isn't pleased."

"We ain't got much choice," Rubinek said practically. "The train's gone, an' we're here. So let's get rid of the kids an' go see Duke."

"We're not getting rid of the kids," Berle replied quietly, but with authority. With Ives gone he was obviously in charge. "Duke'll want to question them—see how much they know. *Then* he'll probably give them to his pets."

"I still want to kill them myself," Rubinek muttered, like a spoiled kid who had been denied a biscuit.

"At least we've got Booth and this thing," Berle said, raising the box he held to eye level and staring at it balefully. "Let's hope that's enough." He sighed. "Okay, let's get this over with."

Berle led the way down the veranda to where Sherlock noticed a round table had been set up in front of a pair of French windows. A white tablecloth had been placed over it, and there was a decanter of what looked like orange juice, a plate of bread rolls, and seven glasses sitting in the centre. Seven wrought-iron chairs, painted white, were arranged around the table. A white parasol had been stuck through a hole in its centre, providing shade from the burning sun.

Parasol. The word stuck in Sherlock's mind as they walked down the veranda towards the table. It reminded him of something, but he couldn't remember what. That was the trouble with memory, he thought—it could only hold so much information. If only there were some way of deleting all the memories a person didn't need and replacing them with the important ones. Perhaps he ought to just write down everything that might be important to him in a notebook, or a set of notebooks, listed alphabetically so he could find things quickly when he needed to.

He was just trying to distance himself from what was going on by thinking about something else, but his attempt was broken when Rubinek pushed him towards one of the chairs with the barrel of his revolver. "Sit," the man growled. Sherlock obeyed. Matty and Virginia were placed on either side of him, then Berle and John Wilkes Booth sat to Virginia's left and Rubinek sat to Matty's right.

That left one chair, Sherlock noticed. Presumably that was reserved for the mysterious Duke.

"My father will track us down if you don't release us," Virginia said.

"Your father's the big guy in the white suit?" Berle looked from Virginia to Matty and then to Sherlock. "He's not father to all of you, is he? I'd not seen you all together before." He looked more closely at Matty. "We took you because we thought it would stop him from coming after us. Shows how much we knew. We should have taken the girl."

"He still would have come after you," Virginia said. "That's what he does. He doesn't take orders well."

Berle was about to say something, but the French doors leading into the house from the veranda suddenly opened. Two servants in immaculate black tailcoated jackets held them open while another figure emerged into the sunlight.

The man was tall—over six feet, Sherlock estimated, and probably closer to seven—and painfully thin. Everything he was wearing was white—tailored suit, waistcoat, shirt, boots, broad-brimmed hat, and gloves—with the exception of the band that encircled the crown of his hat and the bootlace tie that hung down from the collar of his shirt and disappeared behind his waistcoat. They were both made of black leather. For a moment, Sherlock thought that his face was either incredibly pale or covered with white makeup, but then he realized that the man was wearing a mask of porcelain that was so exquisitely made that it looked like a fine-featured, sensitive face. The hair that emerged from beneath the hat and fell around the edges of the mask was so blond that it was itself almost white.

The eyes that stared through the holes in the mask were not white, however. The irises were so dark that they were almost black, but the area around the irises was bloodshot. The effect, set against the pristine whiteness of the mask, was to make the eyes seem as if they were glowing red.

The man's wrists, emerging from the cuffs of his shirt, were almost impossibly thin. Sherlock wondered if it would be possible to break his bones just by shaking his hand. Not that the man was extending his hand to be shaken. Both of his arms were pulled away from his body as he moved, with black leather leashes leading away from his wrists into the darkness of the house. And something was pulling those leashes tight.

He stopped just outside the doors. Sherlock thought he could see something moving behind him, at the ends of the leashes, but he wasn't sure what. Some kind of dogs, presumably, but big.

"Dr. Berle," the man said from behind the mask. His voice was light, high, and almost whispery. "Captain Rubinek. Mr. Booth. And our distinguished guests, of course. I am afraid I do not know your names. Please, in the interests of polite conversation, would you be so kind as to introduce yourselves."

"I'm Virginia Crowe," Virginia said.

Matty scowled. "Matthew Arnatt."

"Ah," the man said. "A friend from across the sea." He glanced at Sherlock with his red gaze. "And you, sir? Who are you?"

"Sherlock Scott Holmes," Sherlock replied.

"Another British visitor. How . . . entertaining."

Sherlock's attention was drawn to the hands that held the leashes. There was something wrong with them, and it took him a moment to work out what it was. There were fingers missing from both hands—the little finger on the left hand and the fourth finger on the right hand, but the gloves had actually been tailored without those fingers, so there was no empty finger hanging loose or any material pinned back.

There was something else strange about the hands as well. They were as thin as the rest of the man, but there were lumps pushing at the material of the gloves. What did those hands look like, beneath the gloves?

"You have us at a disadvantage," Sherlock said, switching his attention back to the man's porcelain mask and trying to keep his voice calm. "May I ask what your name is?"

"I am Duke Balthassar," the man said, his voice as dry and papery as autumn leaves. "That's 'Duke' as in a first name, not 'Duke' as in an honorific like 'Count' or 'Prince.' Now please, help yourselves to orange juice and bread rolls. I assure you, the juice is perfectly fresh and the rolls are still warm from the oven."

Virginia reached for the decanter. "Let me pour," she said.

Duke Balthassar moved out further into the sunshine. The leashes in his hand pulled tight, and then reluctantly two animals were pulled out onto the veranda.

For a moment, Sherlock didn't know what they were. They looked like sleek brown cats, but their heads were at a level with Duke Balthassar's waist. Their eyes were black, and their tails flicked restlessly as their gaze moved from person to person.

Virginia spilled the orange juice on the white tablecloth. *"Cougars?"* she breathed.

"Indeed," Balthassar said. He sounded pleased. "I would say 'Don't let them scare you,' but that would be bad advice. *Do* let them scare you."

"I didn't know," Virginia said, and Sherlock could hear the tremor in her voice, "that cougars could be tamed."

"Tamed?" Balthassar said. "No, they cannot. But like all creatures, humans included, they respond to fear. And they fear me." He said something in a foreign language, and the cougars scrunched themselves down on the veranda, settling with their heads on their paws.

Sherlock could see the teeth in those not-quite-closed mouths. Those teeth could bite a man's hand off his arm, and the claws that he could see, barely sheathed, could rip the arm itself out of the socket. "How do you make a cougar fear you?" he asked, not sure he wanted to hear the answer.

"The same way you make a man fear you," Balthassar said. One of his black-clad servants pulled the remaining chair out, and he sat daintily, crossing his grasshopper-thin legs. "A mixture of pain and examples of what will happen to them if they do not obey you. They have a memory. They remember the examples, and they act accordingly. Or you dispose of them and start again with another animal, and the act of disposal, if it is done properly and if it lasts for long enough, itself acts as an example of what will happen if the new animal does not obey you. You can leave the body lying around for quite some time."

There was silence around the table for a moment as everyone watched the cougars.

"I like your train," Matty said eventually.

The porcelain mask did not move, but Sherlock sensed that the man was smiling underneath. "You are very kind. It proves useful if I need to attend meetings in New York or elsewhere. I do so hate having to take a carriage to the nearest station. The roads are bumpy, and there is so much dust. It's far more preferable if the train comes to me."

"How did you arrange that?" Sherlock asked.

"I provide the train company with a great deal of business," Balthassar explained. "I am an entrepreneur. I have a number of travelling exhibitions and circuses, taking exotic animals around this fine country, and those exhibitions and circuses travel on our own trains. When I told them I wanted a spur line put in, and signals that would allow me to divert any train to my house, they agreed." He paused. "Eventually. After I provided some examples of what would happen if they did *not* agree with me."

Sherlock tried to imagine what kind of examples Balthassar was talking about, and then he tried not to. The pictures were too vivid.

"So you diverted this train because your men were on board?" Virginia asked.

"Indeed. They had cabled ahead to tell me they were on board, and with several precious cargoes." He glanced across at John Wilkes Booth, who was staring at a glass of orange juice as if it contained the secrets of the universe. "Mr. Booth here is one of them. I have been waiting for some time for him to return to this once-glorious country. I have plans for him. Another cargo was unloaded earlier and is even now being introduced to its new surroundings." He switched his gaze to the box that Berle was holding on his lap. "And I believe that this box contains the final one. Am I right, Dr. Berle?"

Berle nodded, and licked his dry lips. "You are, Duke. Do you—?"

"Not yet, Doctor. I have been waiting a long time for this particular package to arrive. I want to savour the moment." He paused and looked around the table. "I do, however, note the absence of the estimable Messrs Ives and Gilfillan," he said mildly. "Where are they?"

Sherlock knew that he had two choices: he could either let Berle tell Balthassar that Gilfillan was in custody and Ives was dead, or he could admit it first and take the initiative. He decided to take the initiative. "Mr. Gilfillan is in prison back in England," he said. "Mr. Ives I killed just now by knocking him off the train." He stared at the twin eyeholes in Duke Balthassar's mask. "Oh, and I also disposed of a steward on the SS *Scotia* who tried to kill me as well. He was being paid by Mr. Ives."

A silence settled over the table, broken only by the rumbling breath of the two cougars. They watched Sherlock intently. Somehow they knew that there was a battle for dominance going on between him and Duke Balthassar.

"How very enterprising of you," Balthassar said eventually. "Why exactly did you kill them?"

"Maybe I wanted to set an example to your other servants," Sherlock said levelly. "To make them fear me."

Balthassar laughed: a clear, high-pitched sound that made the cougars cringe backwards. "How *very* enterprising," he said. "I think I like you, Master Sherlock Scott Holmes. Not enough to keep you alive, but I do like you."

"Ain't you goin' to do anythin' to him?" the big man, Rubinek, demanded.

"For that?" Balthassar asked. "No. If they were stupid enough to let a child get the better of them then good riddance. They have saved me the trouble of dealing with them myself. No, young Master Sherlock here will not see the sunset, but not because he thinned the ranks of my servants. No, he and his friends will die because I have no use for them here."

Silence fell across the veranda.

"So," Balthassar said quietly after a few moments, "now that we have all become acquainted, and now that you're comfortable and you have refreshments, please be so good as to tell me how much the authorities know about my plans."

"We don't know anything," Sherlock replied.

"You are wrong on two counts," Balthassar said. "On the first count, you obviously know *something*, as you have managed to interfere with my schedules and to kill two of my staff. Children don't usually stumble into something this big, or if they do they back away very quickly. You, as I understand it, were first seen in the house in England where Mr. Booth was being . . . kept safe. That, at least, is where Mr. Ives and Dr. Berle first saw you. The question is, why were you at the house in the first place? Were you there by accident, or were you looking for Mr. Booth?"

Sherlock opened his mouth to say something, but Balthassar gestured to him to keep quiet.

"On the second count," he continued in the same level, pleasant tone of voice, "it doesn't matter *what* you know. The matter is of no interest to me. I have you all here, and none of you will escape. Within the next few hours, you will all die, and your knowledge will die with you. That I promise. No, the only important question is, what is known by the girl's father, and what is known by the authorities in England and here, in America?" He paused and turned the porcelain mask towards Sherlock. "Tell me, and tell me now, before I lose my patience."

Despite the hot sun shining out of a cloudless blue sky, Sherlock felt a cold breeze blow across the veranda.

"If you're going to kill us anyway," Sherlock said

carefully, "then why should we tell you anything? It's not like telling you is going to save our lives. You've already said it's not."

"A good point, well made," Balthassar conceded. "This country is built on the principles of trade and negotiation. Very well; let me make you an offer."

He turned the porcelain mask towards Virginia. "Please, extend your hand," he said.

Virginia glanced at Sherlock, panic in her eyes. He didn't know what she should do: obey Balthassar or ignore him? Sherlock didn't know what the outcome of either action would be. Despite his pleasant exterior, Balthassar seemed to be walking on a knife-edge between civility and madness.

"How tedious," Balthassar said. "Mr. Rubinek?"

Rubinek leaned across from his chair and grabbed hold of Virginia's wrist, stretching her arm out straight and letting her hand point towards Balthassar.

"Excellent," Balthassar said. He spoke a few guttural words in a language that Sherlock couldn't identify.

One of the cougars stood up and padded across to Virginia, skin sliding smoothly over slabs of muscle as it moved. She froze, breath suspended.

The cougar opened its mouth and stretched its neck out until Virginia's hand was inside its mouth. Rubinek let go and moved back into his chair. The big cat closed its mouth until its teeth were pressing into the flesh of Virginia's wrist.

"One of two things will happen now," Balthassar said conversationally. "Either you will tell me what I want to know or my cougar will bite the girl's hand off." The porcelain mask remained impassive, but Sherlock could sense a smile behind its smooth surface. "His name is Sherman, by the way. The other one is called Grant. My little joke."

Virginia's eyes were fixed on Sherlock.

"I'll tell you," Matty said urgently.

"No," Balthassar said gently. "I want Master Sherlock to tell me. He, I perceive, is the leader of this little group. He is the one who needs to learn to fear me. He is the one who needs to be *trained*." He paused for a moment. "You see, there are various ways to die. A bullet to the head is quick and painless, I believe. Bleeding to death is slow, and painful. You do not have the choice as to whether you will die: I have taken that choice away from you. You do, however, have a choice as to *how* you die: quickly or slowly, in agony or in peace."

"Very well," Sherlock said, heart pounding in his chest. "Call the cougar off and I'll answer your question."

"No," Balthassar said. "Answer the question and I will call off the cougar."

The tension in the air was almost visible. Sherlock knew that he and Balthassar were testing their willpower against one another. The trouble was, Balthassar had all the advantages.

"The authorities know about John Wilkes Booth," he said. "They know he's not dead, that he was brought to England from Japan, and that he's here in America now. The British government knows that, and so does the Pinkerton Agency. I presume they will tell the American government. They don't know what you intend doing with him."

"Good," Balthassar said. "More."

"There *is* no more!" Sherlock shouted.

"There is always more. Do the authorities know about *me*, for instance?"

"No."

"So you ended up on that train by accident? I don't think so."

"We were following them!" Sherlock said, gesturing towards Berle and Rubinek. "We were trying to get Matty back."

"And were you with anybody else on the train?" Balthassar's voice was calm but remorseless.

"No. We were by ourselves."

"How remarkably resourceful of you." Balthassar paused, and Sherlock got the impression that he was debating whether to tell Sherman to rip Virginia's hand off anyway.

Sherlock didn't bother praying. No outside entity was going to help them now. They were on their own, their fates depending on the whims of a madman.

The thought gave him an idea. Maybe he could turn that against the man in the porcelain mask.

Balthassar gave a curt order, and the cougar reluctantly pulled its head back so that its teeth were no longer pressing into Virginia's flesh. Her whole body seemed to wilt. The cougar gazed at her for a moment, then padded back to Balthassar's side.

"I have a question," Sherlock said.

Balthassar regarded him, eyes red and black behind the holes in the mask. "Did you not understand the rules? I ask questions and you answer them, and that guarantees you a quick and painless death. That was our bargain."

"But we only have your word for that," Sherlock pointed out. "*I* think you're going to get all the answers you can out of us and then torture us anyway, just because you would enjoy it. On that basis, we don't gain anything by cooperating apart from a short delay before the torture starts."

Balthassar mused for a while. "A logical analysis," he conceded. "You do only have my word, and you don't know how good my word is. What is your counterproposal?"

"We *will* take you at your word," Sherlock said, "*if* you answer our questions as well."

"Interesting," Balthassar mused. "I don't stand to lose anything on the deal, and I gain more information. On the other hand you don't lose anything, as I still get to choose the manner of your deaths either way, but you do gain information, and that apparently matters to you. So yes, I agree. Ask your questions."

"What do you need John Wilkes Booth for?" Sherlock asked. "Why is the fact that he's alive and here in America important enough that people need to die to keep it a secret?"

"Oh," Balthassar said calmly, "people need to die for all kinds of reasons, few of them important. But I like you, Sherlock Scott Holmes. You have spirit. So I'm going to tell you." He glanced at Berle and Rubinek. "After all, *they* won't understand. They just want their money."

"Hey—!" Berle started, then subsided when Balthassar stared at him.

"I realize you are British, but even you must have heard about the War Between the States," Balthassar started.

Sherlock nodded. "My brother said it was about slavery." He glanced at Virginia. "Her father said it was more complicated than that."

"Her father is correct. In the end it was about self-determination. Eight years ago we had an election in which the Republican Party, led by Abraham Lincoln, used as the basis of their campaign a pledge to stop slavery from expanding beyond the states in which it already existed. Lincoln won the election, and that resulted in seven Southern states declaring their secession from the Union, even before he took office—South Carolina, Mississippi, Florida, Alabama, Georgia, Louisiana, and Texas.

They formed a new country, the Confederate States of America, with Jefferson Davis as president. Within two months, Virginia, Arkansas, North Carolina, and Tennessee had joined them."

"What's 'secession'?" Matty asked.

"Secession," Balthassar explained, "is when a state withdraws from the Union of States and declares that it will set itself up as a separate entity. Secession is a right we believe to be guaranteed in the Declaration of Independence, but both the outgoing administration of James Buchanan, and the incoming administration of Abraham Lincoln disagreed. They considered it rebellion and declared it illegal." He sighed. "Ultimately, it doesn't matter whether you believe that a man can keep slaves or not. What we were fighting for was our right to set up our own nation, separate from the one Lincoln was leading, and doing things our own way. If slavery hadn't been the cause, then it would have been something else."

"But you lost," Sherlock pointed out. "Ulysses S. Grant and William Sherman beat Robert E. Lee in battle. He surrendered."

"He had no right to surrender," Balthassar snapped. "He did not have the authority. The war goes on, even if it's not acknowledged as such. The Government in Exile of the Confederacy still seeks to establish freedom from the oppressive regime of the Union for those states who wish it."

Sherlock's attention was distracted by a movement of

Balthassar's hand. No, not *of* his hand, Sherlock realized, but *on* his hand. The material of the white glove on his left hand was flexing slightly, just where one of the bumps that Sherlock had noticed earlier was located. As he watched, the bump seemed to *move*, edging up the hand towards the wrist. What in heaven's name was it?

"Ah," Balthassar said, noticing Sherlock's horrified gaze, "I see you have noticed one of my little companions. Allow me to make a more formal introduction."

He reached towards his left hand with his right and took a grip of the top of the glove. With a firm, careful movement, he pulled it off.

Virginia gasped, while Matty made a sound of revulsion.

Balthassar's hand—minus its little finger—and his wrist were covered with what looked for a moment like boils, but which Sherlock realized were living things, like slugs. Their skin was a reddish grey and moist, and they seemed to pulse slightly as Sherlock watched.

"What *are* they?" he whispered.

Balthassar pulled off the other glove. His right hand—this one missing his fourth finger—was similarly covered with the sluglike creatures.

"Meet my doctors," he said. "An entire medical team, dedicated to my well-being."

Reaching up with his right hand, he undid a hook behind his left ear and pulled the porcelain mask off with one quick gesture.

The cougars hissed and tried to back away across the veranda.

Balthassar's face was gaunt, the cheekbones and nose prominent, but his features were difficult to distinguish beneath the tiny boneless creatures that clung to his white skin like black drops of tar.

FOURTEEN

Virginia made a choking noise, as if she was trying to stop herself being sick. Matty said a single word that expressed his shock. Sherlock assumed it was a word he'd picked up along the waterways in his travels.

Sherlock himself was fascinated. Repelled, yes, but mainly fascinated. As he looked closer, he noticed that Balthassar's face was covered in small triangular scars. Whatever the things were that were clinging to his face, he'd been using them for some time.

"Hardly the face of a new country," Sherlock said, trying to disguise his feelings. "I can see why you have to wear the mask."

"All medical procedures have side effects," Balthassar said quietly. "Mercury, used to treat syphilis, drives men mad. I consider myself fortunate that my own side effects are limited to the purely cosmetic."

"But what *are* they?" Matty whispered.

It was Virginia who replied. "They're leeches," she said. "Bloodsucking leeches. They live in streams and ponds in hot climates."

"Bloodsucking leeches," Matty repeated. "And you're *letting* them suck your blood? You're insane!"

"At least I'm alive," Balthassar replied, unperturbed.

"My family has an inherited disease. My father died of it, as did his father. The blood flows sluggishly in our veins. Without treatment our bodies simply start shutting down, bit by bit." He raised a hand and looked at the obviously missing finger. "There wasn't a lot left of my father when he died."

"And the leeches help?" Sherlock asked.

"They have a substance in their saliva that stops the blood from clotting. They have to, otherwise they would not be able to feed. With enough leeches attached to my skin, all of them feeding, all of them secreting that substance, my circulation is quicker. The blood rushes through my veins."

"But—don't they suck your blood out?" Matty asked.

Balthassar shrugged. "A thimbleful each, perhaps. A small price to pay for good health, and one I do not begrudge them. Which reminds me . . ." He turned to Dr. Berle. "I believe you have something for me?"

Berle had a disturbed look on his face. He took the box from his lap and put it on the table, then flicked a catch on top and opened a lid. From inside he took a glass jar with a lid made of waxed paper that was fastened on with string.

Inside the jar was something horrifying.

The leeches on Duke Balthassar's face and hands—and presumably on the rest of his body as well—were small, barely larger than Sherlock's little finger. The one in the jar was the size of his clenched fist, and it was a bright, glistening red. It lay curled around the bottom of the jar, its tiny head waving blindly in the air, seeking sustenance.

Virginia clutched her hand to her mouth and turned away. The cougars, lying on the veranda nearby, tried to edge back even further. Their teeth were exposed and their eyes looked wild and scared, but their fear of Balthassar seemed to exceed their fear of the leech, and they didn't try to run.

"An impressive specimen," Balthassar said, taking the jar from the table. "When did it last feed?"

"A month or so ago," Berle replied. "Or so I'm told." He paused and swallowed before continuing. "Duke, as a doctor—as *your* doctor—I have to tell you that this—*treatment*—isn't something I recommend. In fact, I'm not even convinced it works. The things you're doing to your body . . . they're *monstrous*!"

"I'm still alive, Doctor, and I still have all of my extremities, minus two fingers and some toes," Balthassar replied. "That is all the proof I need." He pulled at a loose strand of string, and the knot holding the waxed paper on undid itself. "And with this beautiful creature I will be able to think even more clearly and my stamina will be unbounded."

He reached into the jar and carefully picked the leech out. It hung bonelessly from his fingers. He smoothed a strand of his fine white hair back from his face, then placed the leech behind his right ear.

The cougars made a mewing sound. They were terrified.

As Sherlock watched, the creature's head moved around, searching for a vein he presumed, then fastened itself onto Balthassar's skin. Its rear end manoeuvred for a moment, wriggling around, and then it too fastened itself down firmly.

Balthassar closed his eyes and smiled blissfully. "That's it," he whispered. "That's right, my beauty. Feed. Feed away."

"How . . . how long do they stay attached?" Sherlock asked.

"Days," Balthassar replied dreamily, eyes still closed. "Weeks in some cases. When they have taken their fill they detach and hibernate for a month or two while they digest the still-fluid blood. I have a large supply of leeches—most from here in America, from Florida and from Alabama—but nothing like this one. Oh no, *nothing* like this one." He smiled. "I knew it was there, in the jungles of the Far East. I could feel its presence. It called out to me, asking me to come and get it."

There was something in his tone of voice that reminded Sherlock of John Wilkes Booth when he talked about smelling smoke—sleepy, not quite focusing on reality. Could the leech be secreting something else into his bloodstream apart from the anticoagulant, some kind of narcotic that stopped its victims from caring that there was a parasite attached to them and filled them with pleasant, hallucinatory thoughts? He filed the idea away for later—if there was a later. He still had no idea how the three of them were going to get away.

Sherlock's attention was drawn by a movement down by Balthassar's feet. The cougars were edging away from him. Their attention was fixed on the giant red leech, and they didn't like it. They seemed afraid of it.

"Sherman, Grant," Balthassar hissed, then he said something Sherlock couldn't understand. The big cats stopped moving away, but their muscles were still tense.

The red leech appeared to be pulsing as Sherlock watched. Pulsing with Balthassar's blood, ingested from a vein behind his ear.

"You are wasting time," Balthassar said. "Do you have any more questions?"

Sherlock tried to pull his attention away from the leech. "You said that 'the Government in Exile of the Confederacy still seeks to establish freedom from the oppressive regime of the Union for those states who wish it,' " he quoted.

"Indeed."

"But how?" Sherlock asked.

"Try to work it out. I will tell you if you are right." As Sherlock opened his mouth to protest, Balthassar added: "Look on it as a way for me to get more information. If you can work it out, given that you know about Mr. Booth, then the authorities can undoubtedly work it out as well.

I promise, if you can't work it out, then I will give you the answer."

Sherlock thought for a moment. The longer he could keep Balthassar talking, the more he could put off the moment of their deaths. Maybe he could think of some way to escape in the meantime. Maybe Amyus Crowe would find them.

"So," he said. "John Wilkes Booth's mind has gone. He's alternately hallucinatory and violent, and he needs to be drugged most of the time just so you can move him around. He's obviously no use as an assassin, or as anything else apart from a figurehead. So you need him as a rallying point, someone you can wheel out onstage to inspire the troops."

Balthassar nodded, but the word "troops" had sparked an idea in Sherlock's brain, despite the fact that he'd only chosen it as a metaphor.

"You *are* rallying troops," he said. "That's why you need Booth—to motivate your army. To show them that there's a direct connection between the War Between the States and what you're doing now!"

Again, Balthassar nodded. "Go on."

"But I can't see you raising an army large enough to take on the Union's army. Not again. Not since you lost last time. So you need an army to do something else." His mind was racing. "But what? If the army isn't going to fight on American soil then it must be aimed at invading somewhere else." He tried to think back to some maps he'd looked at on the SS *Scotia*. "Mexico?" he asked.

Balthassar shook his head. "A good guess, but wrong. It was tried a few years back, but the plan fell apart due to lack of support. And besides, Mexico is hot and arid and has a standing army of its own that would resist us."

"What then?" Sherlock asked, but even as he did so the answer sprang into his head. "If you have an army, then you need a land border for them to cross," he said. "The United States only has two land borders: one with Mexico and one with . . . *Canada*?"

Balthassar nodded. "Well done. Yes, we have raised an army, several thousand strong, which is encamped not too far away from here. They have been finding their way here for several months, in dribs and drabs so as not to attract attention. With John Wilkes Booth as our figurehead—our *mascot*, if you like—we will march up and take the port of Halifax in order to prevent British resupply, then cut communication links between eastern and western Canada by capturing Winnipeg. We can then move through the country and capture Quebec and the Great Lakes region. Once that is done we can carve out a new nation where like-minded Confederates can join us and keep slaves, as God intended."

"But why Canada?" Sherlock asked.

"Good land for growing crops, a temperate climate—at least near the border with America—excellent harbours for trade purposes, no army to speak of to resist our advance, and of course it is a British territory, recently confederated. And Britain refused to aid us in our battle against the Union."

"The British government will never let Canada go," Sherlock said, thinking of Mycroft.

"They probably won't even care," Balthassar scoffed. "Just think of the logistics of shipping their army three thousand miles for a battle, especially when we control the ports. No, there will be a few years of diplomatic bleating, of course, but we will control Canada."

"With you as president?" Sherlock asked. "A man in a china mask?"

Balthassar's head jerked to one side. Sherlock's words had hit home.

"John Wilkes Booth, perhaps," he answered tersely. "With the proper guidance and medication, of course. Or perhaps even General Robert E. Lee. There are plenty of candidates. But I will be the power behind the throne."

The sudden motion disturbed one of the smaller leeches. It fell from his face and hit the table with a quiet *plop.* Balthassar glanced at it. "Old," he said, "one of my longest-serving partners. I think it's time to retire you, my friend."

He picked it up from the tablecloth and popped it into his mouth, then swallowed like a man eating an oyster.

Sherlock noticed that the leech had left a red smear on

the tablecloth. He kept his gaze fixed on that red smear. He had a feeling he might throw up if he didn't fixate on something. Anything.

"I must say," Balthassar murmured in his fragile, whispery voice, delicately replacing the porcelain mask on his scarred and leech-infested face, "you have demonstrated an uncanny ability to predict my plans from a few scattered facts. Either that, or my plans are considerably more obvious than I had thought. Either way, I cannot afford to delay. If you—a mere child—can work them out, then surely the Unionist government can work them out too. I think that our advance into Canada needs to start within the next few days. Thank you for your assistance."

"And what about us?" Virginia asked. Sherlock was proud of how level she kept her voice.

"Oh, I have no need of you now," Balthassar said. There was no trace of anger or vengeance in his voice. There was barely a trace of anything at all. He might just as easily have been discussing the price of tea leaves. "You will be disposed of."

"How?" Sherlock asked.

"Ah." Balthassar's porcelain face was impassive. "There, I confess, I may have misled you. I have a fate in mind for you which will solve three separate problems I have, but it does involve quite a lot of pain and suffering." He gestured to the brutal Rubinek. "Captain, please take our guests to the new enclosure. My latest acquisitions need to be fed." He turned back to Sherlock. "My collectors of rare and unusual creatures made sure they had eaten before they were captured," he said conversationally, "and it takes them several weeks to digest their food, during which time they are almost comatose, but they have had a long journey from Borneo and their current behaviour suggests they are hungry again." He paused, and Sherlock suspected that he was smiling beneath the mask. "I anticipate that they will draw huge crowds when I display them. By feeding you to them I get rid of you, I dispose of your bodies, and I also make sure my pets have a decent source of good quality meat to keep them satisfied for a while." He paused for a moment. "I am told they take their food underwater and store it beneath rocks until it becomes . . . tender. We will all enjoy watching that process."

Before Sherlock could say anything, two more men had moved from the shadows at a gesture from Rubinek. The three men took Sherlock, Matty, and Virginia by the shoulders, pulled them roughly from their chairs, and started pushing them along the veranda.

Despair filled Sherlock. Despite everything, it looked as if they were going to die a particularly nasty and painful death. He didn't know what Balthassar's latest "acquisitions" were, but he doubted they were going to be anything as innocent as squirrels or parrots. Whatever they were, they were likely to be big and have sharp teeth. More cougars? No, he could get those locally, and would not have to hunt abroad for them.

He caught Matty's eye as they were pushed along the veranda. Matty was looking scared, but he smiled briefly at Sherlock.

The three of them were pushed off the edge of the veranda to the hard-packed earth, and then shoved towards the area of cages, paddocks, and fenced-off enclosures that Sherlock had seen from the train. They seemed to be aiming for a walled area off to one side. The wall looked freshly built. Adjoining one side was a balcony with a view down into whatever was enclosed by the walls. Steps led up to the balcony, and Sherlock found himself shivering when he saw a wooden plank that stuck out from the balcony and ended over whatever lay beneath.

Separate stairs led downward, into darkness. Sherlock wondered momentarily what was down there, but his speculations were broken when Rubinek pushed him up the stairs to the balcony. His two followers pushed Matty and Virginia after him.

Sherlock could see down into the enclosure. From that vantage point it looked more like a pit. The area inside the walls was rocky and uneven, with vegetation growing out of cracks between the rocks and a pool of brackish water taking up about a third of the space. There was no sign of anything living in there, but Sherlock didn't find himself particularly comforted.

Rubinek manoeuvred Sherlock to the start of the plank. The other two men herded Matty and Virginia together a few feet away.

"Go on," he said. "You know what to do."

"And if I don't?" Sherlock asked.

Rubinek raised his hand. He was holding a small pistol, barely larger than his palm, with two barrels, one above the other. "What's in there don't particularly mind whether you're dead or alive," Rubinek said. "And neither do I."

Sherlock looked back towards the house. He had expected Balthassar to follow them and watch from the balcony, but the tall man in the white suit was still on his veranda. He had spread a map across the table and was consulting it. He appeared to have already forgotten about Sherlock and his friends.

Reluctantly Sherlock walked out to the end of the plank. It dipped beneath his weight. The drop to the rocky floor of the enclosure was about ten feet.

"Jump," Rubinek ordered. Now that Sherlock was following orders, Rubinek slipped his tiny revolver back into his jacket pocket.

"I'll break my legs!" Sherlock protested. "That's hard rock down there!"

"So?" The man patted his jacket pocket. The threat was clear.

Sherlock glanced into the enclosure, looked across at Virginia, then took two steps back before running towards the end of the plank and jumping into the enclosure.

He used the springiness of the plank to push himself out as well as up, angling himself so that he arced towards the pool of water. He hit, sending a massive splash up into the air. The water had been warmed by the bright sun, and Sherlock struck out for the edge before anything that might be living in the water could get him. He scrambled out quickly onto the rocks, dripping wet, and looked around. Nothing was coming for him yet.

He looked up at the balcony. Virginia was at the end of the plank, looking scared. Matty was just stepping onto the plank, but he stumbled and fell back against Captain Rubinek, who pushed him roughly back onto it.

Sherlock quickly glanced around in case something was sneaking up on him. There was a splash from the pool, and then another, as Virginia and Matty joined him. He reached out and pulled them both to the rocks when they surfaced, spluttering.

"What's in here with us?" Matty asked, breathless.

"I'm not sure," Sherlock replied, looking around. Up on the balcony, Rubinek and his men were leaving. Whatever was going to happen in the enclosure, it wasn't classified as a spectator sport.

"They're not watching us," Virginia pointed out. "We've got a chance to escape."

"The walls are too high to climb," Matty said dubiously.

Sherlock looked around. "There are loose rocks around. Maybe we can pile them up and climb up so we can reach the top of the wall." He thought for a moment. "No good. They could see us from the house as we climb over the wall. We need to find a way out where they can't spot us."

A scrabbling noise from the far side of the enclosure caught his attention. He glanced that way, heart pounding in his chest. What was in there with them?

For a moment he couldn't see anything, but then a nightmare head appeared from a dark gap between two rocks. It was long and narrow, with small eyes set on either side. The creature's skin was a dirty grey-green, and folds of it hung down from that long jaw. The mouth opened as Sherlock watched to let a forked red tongue flicker out, tasting the air, but inside he could see a row of vicious teeth the size of his little finger, curved backwards so that any prey caught by them would not be able to tear itself free.

Matty gasped, and Virginia let out a stifled moan.

"What *is* it?" Matty whispered.

The creature moved further out into the open. Its body was as long as Sherlock's, half of it made up of a long, muscular tail. It walked on four legs that splayed out sideways from its body. Its feet terminated in hooked claws that skittered on the rocks as it moved. The grey-green skin seemed like a baggy fit, hanging loose beneath it and swaying as it moved.

Even at that range, Sherlock could see that there was no emotion in those eyes: just a cold and hungry intelligence.

"Some kind of reptile," he said, "but it's huge. I've never seen anything like it before."

"It's the same size as *us*," Virginia whispered. "I thought it might be an alligator—they have them down in Florida, I've heard, but this is something else. Alligators are slow and stupid, and they don't like being out of water, but that thing looks quick and intelligent, and it's walking on the rocks with no problems."

Sherlock gazed at the thing's feet. "Those claws look like they could climb trees," he pointed out. "Not that there are any trees here to climb anyway."

The creature moved out onto a flat rock and stared at them, flicking its tongue towards them. It knew there was food around.

Something moved off to one side. Sherlock glanced that way. A second creature was emerging from another gap in the rocks. This one was even bigger than the first.

"Look!" Virginia warned. For a moment Sherlock assumed she'd seen the second creature as well, but when he looked over at her he saw she was facing the other way. He followed the line of her pointing finger. A third lizard was moving towards them along the line of the wall. Its head was swinging from side to side as it watched them.

The first creature that he'd seen moved in the other direction while the second one began to head towards them, its body swinging from side to side as its claws got purchase on the ground.

The three creatures appeared to be working together, like dogs. They were pinning Sherlock, Matty, and Virginia down, giving them nowhere to escape.

Sherlock's mind was racing. Given the size of the

creatures and their massive and sharp teeth, they were obviously carnivores, and they were moving as if they were hungry and they knew there was food in the enclosure. They didn't seem wary or cautious, the way dogs might have been. They seemed deliberate in their movements. Sherlock had a feeling that reptiles couldn't be scared. Their brains just weren't made that way. They would keep coming, no matter what Sherlock and the others did. Noises wouldn't stop them, nor would sudden gestures. Thrown rocks probably wouldn't work either. They were like calculating machines with teeth.

The monstrous creatures were edging closer and closer now, from all directions. Sherlock, Matty, and Virginia edged backwards, towards the nearest wall. Their options were progressively being closed off by these freakishly intelligent reptiles.

"What's that *smell*?" Matty asked, his face wrinkling up. Sherlock could smell it too: something like rotted meat. If those creatures really did swallow their prey whole and then spend weeks digesting it then the smell was probably part of them.

"Sherlock," Virginia said in a too-controlled voice, "what do we do?"

"Thinking," Sherlock said, and he was. He was thinking as fast as he'd ever thought in his life.

The creature on their right took a few steps closer. Matty bent down and picked a stone up from the ground. He lobbed it at the creature. It didn't move as the stone hit the wall beside it and bounced off. No fear, no caution, nothing. It just didn't care. After a few seconds it took another two steps, legs splayed out to either side of its body.

The creature to their left hissed, head held up as it sampled the air. The other two hissed as well. Sherlock wasn't sure if they were communicating with each other, or just making noises designed to cause their prey to freeze in terror.

The distance between the reptiles and the three of them had almost halved now, taken up gradually by the reptiles in small steps. No rush, no sudden attack, just a progressive and intelligent process of backing their prey into a corner where they could be eaten at leisure.

And Sherlock couldn't think of any way of stopping them.

FIFTEEN

"What about the water?" Matty whispered, as if the reptiles might hear and understand him. "Couldn't we get in the pond and wait them out?"

"I think they're partly amphibious," Sherlock said. "Look at those feet. They're webbed. They can probably swim better than we can."

Sherlock looked around desperately, hoping there might be something lying about that might help, but apart from rocks and bushes there was nothing.

The reptiles were getting closer now, and the stench of rotting meat was becoming almost too much to bear.

"Oh, I dunno if it helps," Matty said, "but I got this from that bloke's jacket pocket."

Sherlock turned to see that Matty was holding the small, two-barrelled pistol.

"It's a Remington derringer," Virginia said. "Pa got me one, once, but I lost it."

"How the hell did you get that off him?" Sherlock demanded.

Matty shrugged. "I live off my own resources," he pointed out. "Pickpocketing is one of them."

Sherlock looked from the gun to the advancing reptiles and back again. "Two lead balls, three creatures," he said. "Not good odds."

"It increases our chances," Virginia said.

"It just means that one of us gets killed and eaten rather than all three of us, and that's not an acceptable solution."

"You got a better idea?" Matty asked.

"Actually," Sherlock said, "I have." His gaze scanned the walls. "How did they get these things in here? I doubt they walked them along the plank. Too much chance of them getting hurt when they fell."

"You think there's a gate or door or something?" Matty demanded.

"It seems logical. All we need to do is look for it."

Sherlock considered the approaching reptiles more closely. "They're slower than us," he said, "but they'll wear us out eventually." His gaze skipped over the rocks. "Look, if we're fast we can climb above them, then jump over their heads and get behind them. Then we can look for the way in. They can't move fast."

Before Matty or Virginia could stop him, he ran towards the reptiles. Three mouths full of sharp teeth opened, and the sudden hissing nearly deafened him. Without stopping to think, he leaped onto one of the rocks and from there to a larger boulder. It shifted beneath his feet, and he knew that if he slipped the creatures would be on him in a flash. He jumped, off balance, and saw the reptiles climbing on their hind legs beneath him as he flew through the air, stretching up with their long jaws, hoping to snag his heels.

He landed safely on a patch of open ground. He turned, to find Virginia hurtling towards him. He caught her as she landed and pulled her to one side so that Matty had a clear area. The reptiles snapped at him as he jumped, one of them using its muscular tail to propel it into the air, but its teeth snapped shut a split second after he passed. He hit the ground and stumbled, rolling before he could get to his feet.

Without any show of emotion, the three reptiles turned around and started advancing again, their beady black eyes fixed on Sherlock, Matty, and Virginia.

"Quick!" Sherlock shouted, and led the way to the wall that separated the enclosure from the outside world. To his right the wall was unbroken all the way down to the ground, but to his left piles of rocks hid its base. He ran along the side of the wall, checking in the space behind the rocks. Nothing! Another patch of open ground, and then a large bush that hid the wall. He pushed it to one side, and his heart leaped when he saw a metal grille, rising from the ground to waist height, hinged on the left, and the simple sliding bolt that secured it.

Then he saw the huge padlock that held the secured bolt in place on the other side of the grille.

Matty came up alongside him. "Can you blow it apart with the gun?" he asked, holding the derringer out.

Sherlock considered for a moment. "Unlikely," he said. "That padlock is massive. The lead balls will probably just bounce off."

"What about the hinges?"

"Three hinges, two bullets. Same problem."

Virginia joined them, looking worriedly over her shoulder. "I'm not sure we have much of a choice," she pointed out.

Matty kicked against the grille. It barely moved under the force of his foot.

Sherlock's mind was a whirl of conflicting thoughts. Two choices: shoot the reptiles, and leave one still alive, or shoot the padlock and probably waste two bullets. Which choice should he make?

A small voice in the storm of his thoughts asked: "What would Mycroft say? What would Amyus Crowe say?" And, just like back on the train, a voice answered: "When you've only got two choices, and you don't like either of them, make a third choice."

His gaze wandered across the pool that the three of them had jumped into, and he suddenly remembered the stairs that had led *downward*, next to the steps that had led up to the balcony. They hadn't been leading to the grille, because that opened out onto flat ground. They had to lead somewhere else. The pool was on that side of the enclosure, and Balthassar had spoken of watching the reptiles storing their food beneath stones underwater. Maybe the steps led to an underground viewing gallery;

a subterranean room with a glass window looking out into the depths of the pool, so that Balthassar and his guests could watch the reptiles swimming.

But how to break through the glass—if there was glass? It would be thick, to withstand the pressure of the water.

So what he had to do was cause more pressure than the window could stand.

He snatched the derringer from Matty's hand. Two triggers, of course, which made sense with two barrels. You'd want to be able to fire them separately. He stared down the barrels. "You used to have one of these," he said to Virginia. "How did you load it?"

"You pour some black powder down the barrel, then you ram a patched lead ball down onto the powder," she explained, "being careful not to leave any air gaps between the patched ball and the powder. You then put a percussion cap on the other end of the barrel. Then the gun is loaded and ready to fire."

"Patched lead ball?" he asked, staring more closely down the barrels. "Ah, yes, the ball is wrapped in paper. That must form a seal."

"Waxed paper. Why is that important?"

"Because it means it's airtight," he said. "At least, for a short time. And if it's airtight, it's watertight."

Before Virginia could say anything, Sherlock turned and ran towards the pond, cocking the twin hammers at the back end of the derringer as he did so. When he got to the edge he dived, hands held out in front of him, derringer held in his right hand. The water closed over his head: warm and filled with floating motes of dust and vegetation. Sound was suddenly muffled. He kicked with his feet to take him towards the far wall, beneath the balcony.

And there, where he knew it had to be, where deduction had told him it was, was a glass window set into a metal frame. Before any water could leak into the derringer he placed it flat against the glass.

And pulled both triggers at once.

Somewhere in the back of his mind was the fact, read once and never forgotten, that water was incompressible. No matter how much you squeeze it, water never gets any denser. All that happens is that the pressure you exert gets transferred elsewhere. Such as to whatever the water is touching.

And so when the hammers at the base of the barrels hit the two percussion caps, the fulminate of mercury inside ignited. This caused the sulphur, charcoal, and potassium nitrate in the black powder to burn rapidly, producing a huge volume of hot gas. The gas pushed the lead balls along the barrels, burning the paper patches away as it did so. The bullets pushed against the water in the barrels, and the water pushed against the window.

Which cracked and shattered.

The entire contents of the pond poured into the underground room, taking Sherlock with it. He struck out blindly for the corner of the room where the stairs had to be, hoping desperately that Virginia and Matty would realize what he'd done and follow him. Should he have warned them in advance? It hadn't occurred to him. He'd just followed through on his deductions without considering that the other two might not understand.

His lungs were burning with the effort of holding his breath, and his heart was thudding within the cage of his ribs. He pulled himself through the murky water with desperate movements of his arms. Suddenly he felt his knuckles brush against the stone edge of a step. He aimed upward and swam as hard as he could.

When his head emerged from the water, level with the bottom of the doorway that led outside, into the sunlight, he took huge gulps of breath one after the other, waiting for his racing heart to slow.

Matty's head popped out of the water beside him. Virginia was moments behind.

"You," Matty said, breathing hard, "are some kind of genius. I don't know what you did, but you saved us."

"Not quite," Virginia pointed out breathlessly.

"What do you mean?" Matty asked.

"Sherlock said those things were amphibious."

The three of them looked at each other for a long moment, then scrambled rapidly out of the water.

The steps to the underground observation room and to the balcony were out of sight of the house. The three of them sat down for a moment to catch their breath.

"What now?" Matty asked. "What do we do?"

"Only thing I can think is that we follow the train tracks back to the last town," Sherlock replied. "There'll be a telegraph office there. We can send a message to Virginia's father. We have to tell him about Balthassar's army and the invasion of Canada."

"Ah," Matty said, "walking."

"We could try stealing horses," Sherlock said, "but we'll probably be caught. I suspect these people look after their horses, especially if they're planning an invasion."

Matty sighed. "All right," he said, "let's go. We can dry out while we're walking."

Staying out of sight of the house, the three of them made their way through Balthassar's collection of animal pens and cages. Many of them were empty, but Sherlock saw some things in the occupied ones that he would remember for the rest of his life—animals he had only ever seen in illustrations, which in the flesh looked like the creatures of dreams or nightmares. Animals with elongated legs and elongated necks whose skin was covered in large brown patches; a massive creature with a square head that hung low in front of it, two horns on top, between its eyes, and a skin as thick as armour; and things that looked like pigs but that were covered with wiry hair and had tusks sticking out of their jaws. A bestiary of fabulous animals.

When they got to the edge of the enclosures and cages, Sherlock looked around carefully. The grass-covered ground ahead of them was clear, and far away, over to their right, he could see Balthassar's house. The orientation of the house indicated where the train line had to run, although it was hidden by the high grass. Somewhere out there was the boundary fence, and past that, along the rail lines, was the town called Perseverance. Across at least one wooden bridge that spanned a deep ravine, as far as he remembered.

Not that they had a choice.

"Come on," he said wearily. "Let's get this over with."

And so they set out, walking across the grasslands. It only took ten minutes to find the twin metal rails of the train line, laid across parallel rows of wooden sleepers, and another half-hour to get to the boundary fence, and the point where their train had diverted off the main line towards Balthassar's house. Once they discovered the train line, Matty had spent a few minutes walking between the rails, stepping from sleeper to sleeper, but the gap was slightly larger than his stride and his legs started aching quickly, so he joined Sherlock and Virginia walking alongside the rails.

Within another half-hour the fence and the house had vanished into a heat haze that made the horizon shimmer. All that was left was the rails, leading away from them in either direction, and the grasslands. Off in the distance to his left Sherlock thought he could see the dim shapes of mountains, but the haze made it difficult to judge.

Birds circled above them. Matty thought they might

be vultures, but Virginia said they were chicken hawks. Sherlock reserved his judgement. He didn't know what either a vulture or a chicken hawk looked like, so he wasn't prepared to speculate.

While they walked, he found himself turning over and over in his mind the plans that Duke Balthassar had explained to them. It all sounded so preposterous—a revived Confederate Army seeking to invade a neighbouring British colony in order to set up a new nation where they would be allowed to run things the way they wanted rather than the way that the winning Unionists wanted. Sherlock didn't approve of slavery, but he wasn't sure that he approved of one group of people using force to tell another group how to live their lives. But what was the alternative? Should everyone simply be allowed to live according to their own moral codes? And if that was the case, what happened if your neighbour believed that theft was allowed, but you didn't, and he stole your pigs, or your sheep, or your horses? The alternative was allowing someone to impose a moral code on you that you didn't yourself believe in, but had to follow.

Strangely, all this led Sherlock's thoughts back to the copy of Plato's *Republic* that Mycroft had given him before he left Southampton. Plato had anticipated all of these questions, over two thousand years ago. And in the intervening time, nobody had managed to create a society that everybody could agree on and that actually worked properly.

Was that what Mycroft himself, in his quiet way, was trying to do—make Great Britain into a society that worked about as well as it could?

Sherlock found that he was developing a stronger and stronger understanding of his brother as he got older.

The sun slipped inexorably closer to the horizon behind them as they walked, casting giant shadows ahead of them across the undulating grassland. For a while Sherlock thought he could see a dark slash against the sunset-tinged grass, and as time went on and the sun slid closer and closer to vanishing, the slash turned out to be the ravine that the train had crossed earlier, on its way to Balthassar's house. The dying rays illuminated the bridge from a strange angle, making it look more like a child's model than something real.

"We've got to cross *that*?" Matty asked in a hushed voice as the three of them stopped at the edge of the ravine and gazed at the bridge.

Sherlock indicated the depths of the ravine with a wave of his hand. "I don't think we're in a position to climb down, cross, and then climb up again."

"I think," Virginia said, "that he means 'We've got to cross that *tonight*?' and I think I agree with him."

"We can't afford to stop and sleep," Sherlock pointed out. "For a start, we don't know what's out here. Cougars, bears . . ."

"Raccoons," Virginia murmured.

"There could be anything," he continued. "And we

need food. Apart from orange juice and a bread roll, I've not had anything since this morning."

"Food . . ." Matty moaned. "I'm *starving*. Do you think there's anything out here we could, you know, *hunt*?"

"More likely to be the other way around," Sherlock said. He took a deep breath and started out over the ravine, stepping from sleeper to sleeper.

"What happens if a train comes along?" Matty called.

"They don't run at night," Virginia said. "Too much chance of hitting a cow, or a landslide, or something else. They stop in the nearest town and let people off. There's hotels for people to stay at until the train leaves, next morning."

"Oh," said Matty. He sounded as if he'd been hoping for a reason not to cross.

Sherlock found, like Matty before him, that stepping from sleeper to sleeper was exhausting. Although he had long legs he still had to stretch for each step. He could see down between the sleepers, but because the last rays of the sun were shining horizontally across the landscape, the ravine was in darkness, and all he could see between his feet was an empty void. If he stared too hard, he started to lose track of where his feet were. Twice he stumbled and almost lost his footing. Eventually he decided that he had to just look ahead, and trust his instincts to let him find the sleepers. Each one was the same distance apart, and he found that if he didn't look he could still work it out.

He glanced back over his shoulder every now and then to see Virginia and Matty, silhouetted by the red disc of the sun, following him. They seemed to be managing all right. There was, he told himself, nothing he could do to help them. Each of them was in a universe of their own on that long walk over the ravine.

He heard a sound behind him. He stopped and glanced over his shoulder. Virginia was sprawled across the tracks. She looked exhausted. She raised her head and gazed at him with weary eyes. "Sorry," she muttered. "I tripped."

"I can't come back to help," Sherlock said desperately. "I can't turn round without risking a fall, and if I bend down to help you up I might fall anyway!"

"I know," she said quietly. "I know."

From behind her, Matty called, "Virginia, you've got to get up!"

"Oh, yeh, thanks," she hissed, pushing herself up. "I would never have thought of that!"

They started off again, one after the other. Time seemed to melt away, each second, each minute blending into the next, so that when Sherlock realized that there was solid ground between the tracks they were already a hundred yards or so past the edge of the ravine.

"Let's take a break," he said. "Just ten minutes."

Matty groaned. "I need to sleep."

"My brother says that a man can go without sleep for days on end, if what he's doing is important and interesting enough."

"Walking to the nearest town might be important," Matty responded, "but it's certainly not interesting."

Sherlock allowed them what seemed like ten minutes, but might have been anywhere from thirty seconds to an hour judging by the way time was stretching and blurring, before he got them to their feet and started them walking again. They continued to walk in silence along the side of the tracks. Twice, in the distance, Sherlock heard a howling noise. For a terrified moment he thought that Balthassar had spotted their absence and had sent his cougars after them, but Virginia said quietly, "Coyotes."

"What's a coyote?" Matty called from the back.

"It's like a wolf," Virginia replied.

"Oh." A pause. "I wonder what they taste like."

"Funnily enough," Virginia said, "that howl probably means they're wonderin' the same about you."

The moon rose above the horizon: a bloated white disc, seemingly much larger than Sherlock remembered from England. Surely America wasn't any nearer the moon? The world was round, after all. Every point on its surface had to be the same distance from the moon. The only explanation he could come up with was that there was something about the atmosphere, some trick of the heated air, that magnified the image and made the moon *look* larger.

After a while he realized Matty was talking to himself. Sherlock had assumed that he was talking to Virginia, but Matty was leaving gaps that Virginia wasn't filling. It was as if Matty could hear a voice that nobody else could. A hallucination? Maybe the tiredness and the lack of food were getting to him. He'd had a stressful couple of weeks, after all.

Even though he was thinking about Matty hallucinating, it didn't seem odd to Sherlock that Mrs. Eglantine, the housekeeper from his aunt and uncle's house, was walking alongside him for some of the journey. She didn't say anything. She just looked at him with disapproving eyes, her mouth pursed into a tight little bud, her head shaking from side to side. He didn't know when she had appeared and he didn't know when she vanished. All he knew was that for at least part of the journey she had been there, a silent companion keeping pace with him. Odd, he thought—of all the people he might have imagined walking beside him, why her? Why not Mycroft, or Amyus Crowe? Come to that, if his mind was disturbed, why not any of the people whose lives he had been responsible for—Mr. Surd, Ives, or Grivens? Even Plato would have been a better travelling companion than Mrs. Eglantine.

If Virginia saw anyone who wasn't there, then she never said anything about it, either then or later.

By the light of the moon, Sherlock saw the occasional barn or farmhouse silhouetted on the horizon. He thought about diverting from their path and stopping to ask for help, or at least food and drink, but something kept him going along the line of the tracks. Explanations would take time and might just land them in more trouble. And besides, the one thing they needed was a telegraph office, and that would only be found at a train station in a town.

After a while the few scattered barns and farmhouses turned into a handful, and then what looked like a scattered community. They were on the outskirts of something. If they were lucky, it would be the town. Sherlock didn't remember the train passing through any other large collections of buildings after leaving the station at Perseverance, but he hadn't been looking out of the window all the time. Other things had been happening to distract his attention. It was possible this was a different town, one without a station or a telegraph office, in which case he decided that they *would* stop anyway, if only for a short while. Maybe they could hire a carriage to drive them to Perseverance.

A flush of rose-hued colour spread across the horizon as they walked. The sun was coming up. Had they really been walking all night? Judging by the stiffness of his muscles and the dryness of his throat, Sherlock suspected they had.

Or was it just another hallucination, like Mrs. Eglantine?

After hours of travelling in a straight line across the landscape, the train lines curved now, leading into the centre of the town. And finally, there ahead of them was the cluster of buildings that Sherlock remembered from when the three of them had briefly got off the train—the station and the outhouses. They had arrived. Against the odds, they had arrived.

A train was drawn up on the sidings beside the station. It was shorter than Sherlock remembered from the day before. It was also deserted and dark.

There was nobody around when they staggered onto the raised station platform. Even the telegraph office was locked up. Sherlock banged on the door, in case anyone was sleeping inside, but nobody answered. The whole town seemed to still be asleep, despite the daylight blue that was spreading across the sky.

"Come on," he said, the words catching in his dry throat, "let's find a hotel and get something to eat. The telegraph office probably won't open until later."

"Food," Matty said, his voice cracked. "Sleep."

Virginia just nodded. Her face was chalk white, the freckles standing out like spots of ink, and she looked like she was at the end of her tether.

The hotel was across the street from the station. The street was dry earth rutted by the wheels of countless carts, and strangely Sherlock found it harder going than the grasslands.

The doors weren't locked, which felt like the first piece of good luck they'd had in a while.

And standing over a table in the centre of the open main room, looking down at a map spread out in front of him, was Amyus Crowe.

He glanced up at the sound of the three of them entering, and his face registered so many different emotions within the space of a second that Sherlock felt he was looking at several different men at the same time.

Virginia ran to her father and threw her arms around him. Matty just sank into a chair and closed his eyes.

"You tracked us," Sherlock said. He couldn't hear any emotion in his voice. Maybe the night-long walk had burned it out of him. He just felt very tired.

"I talked to the newspaper boys," Crowe said. He was obviously struggling to keep his voice level. "There's not much happens in the city that they don't know about, and they manage to get by largely ignored by the rest of the population. They told me about you bein' followed, an' managin' to reverse the process. Neat trick with the cap, the jacket, an' the papers, by the way. One of them saw you at the boardin'house, an' another saw the two of you at the ferry. I managed to piece the rest of it together myself." He took a deep, shuddering breath. "I think I can work out what got you from there to here. If I thought you'd done it deliberately, son, I'd put you on the first boat back to England an' make sure you an' I were never on the same continent again, but I reckon what happened was a series of small accidents, at the end of which you were far away from where I was an' where I could help."

"That," said Sherlock, "is about the size of it. Not intentional. Not in the slightest."

"It's true," Virginia said, voice muffled by her father's

chest. "We were following the men who had Matty, and the train started to move before we could get off."

"But they did rescue me," Matty added, eyes still closed.

"That they did," Crowe admitted. He glanced at the three of them. "I think you need food and drink and rest, but I think I need to find out what happened to you while you're eatin' an' drinkin'." He turned his head towards the rear of the room, where a doorway led out. "Mrs. Dimmock! Four breakfasts, with all the orange juice an' coffee you can muster!" He glanced at Sherlock and Matty. "Make that *eight* breakfasts," he shouted. "There's hungry people here!"

The next hour was a blur. Food arrived while the three of them were telling Amyus Crowe everything that had happened to them, and they ended up talking while they were stuffing their faces with ham, fried potatoes, eggs of various sorts, and juice.

"He's planning to invade Canada," Sherlock said to Crowe when they got to the end. "He's got an army built up, and he's planning to set up a new country within Canada and declare it the New Confederacy."

"That's pretty much what the Pinkertons had already worked out," Crowe said, nodding. "They've had their eye on this Duke Balthassar for some time now. The fact that he's usin' John Wilkes Booth as a figurehead to give his troops some backbone an' give this new nation some legitimacy in the eyes of the Southern states was news to them, but it served to explain what he was waitin' for."

"What are they going to do about it?" Sherlock asked. "They can't be letting it go ahead, surely? It'll poison relationships between America and England for generations."

Crowe shook his massive, craggy head. "They got a plan," he rumbled. "Can't say I think much of it, but Secretary of War Stanton has personally endorsed it, so that's about all a man can say."

"They're going to attack?" Matty asked, mouth still full of fried potatoes.

"The Army's been mobilized, an' they're forming a cordon somewhere 'tween here and the border," Crowe said. "But there's somethin' else afoot. The government wants to resolve this without hand-to-hand fightin', if at all possible." He sighed and glanced away, towards the front door to the hotel. "Secretary of War Stanton was quite taken with the use of balloons for reconnaissance durin' the War Between the States. He reckons that balloons are the future for warfare. He's directed that the Army Corps of Engineers deploy with as many hot air balloons as it has. Come evening, he intends floatin' the balloons over Balthassar's encampment an' droppin' explosive devices."

"But—" Sherlock started, then stopped, appalled. "But that would be a massacre! I know these men are about to invade another country, but to drop *bombs* on them! Can't he at least give them a chance to surrender?"

Crowe shook his head. "It don't work that way.

Secretary of War Stanton wants to send a message. He wants everyone to know that the war is over an' the Union won, an' any attempt to revive Confederate fortunes will be met with overwhelmin' force."

"But hundreds, maybe thousands of men will be killed!" Sherlock protested. "And not even in a battle, where they might defend themselves. They're going to die when fire rains down on them from above! That's just *wrong*!"

"It may be wrong," Crowe said quietly, "but it's goin' to happen that way. Welcome to the real world, Sherlock."

SIXTEEN

Sherlock's dreams were full of fire falling from the sky and the screaming of charred and stick-thin figures running around in chaos. He woke up after a few hours, still tired but unable to sleep anymore.

The bedroom was one of three spare ones the hotel manager had found for them to sleep in. Sherlock had wondered if the empty train in the station had meant that the hotel would be full of travellers, but in fact the train had been hired as a special by Amyus Crowe and a small group of Pinkerton agents who were monitoring the situation.

As he lay there, his mind kept coming back to what was going to happen in a few hours. It wasn't as if the men in Balthassar's army were necessarily *evil*—they just had a different idea of how they wanted to be governed. Invading another country was wrong, obviously, but did that mean they deserved to be wiped out like ants?

Mycroft would have found a way to stop it. Sherlock was sure about that. Mycroft was a cog in the machinery of the British government, of course, but he had beliefs, and morals, and convictions. The same beliefs, morals, and convictions that had been inculcated into Sherlock by their father, Major Siger Holmes of the King's Dragoons.

They were both Siger's sons, and they had inherited his values in the same way that they had inherited his blue eyes.

He had to do something. But what? What could he do to stop the Army Corps of Engineers?

Maybe he could send a telegraph message to Mycroft in England. He didn't know how much that might cost, although he suspected it would be expensive, but he still had some money left from earlier. Mycroft could call in the American ambassador, or something, and get it stopped.

Or could he? *Would* he? And, more to the point, did Mycroft have enough time? He was several thousand miles away, after all, and perhaps his superiors in the Foreign Office would be more concerned with preventing an invasion of a British territory than in saving the lives of men they had never even met.

Sherlock knew that he needed to get out there, to see Balthassar's army and the Army Corps of Engineers balloon force. Maybe he *couldn't* do anything, certainly not if he stayed here at the hotel. There, out in the grasslands, maybe something would occur to him.

But how to get there?

He could rent a horse here in town, he guessed. He could ride out to where the balloons were being launched from. He'd seen the location, marked on the map that Amyus Crowe had been consulting a few hours before. He hadn't consciously memorized it, but, like so many things that he read, it had just lodged in his brain.

Should he take Virginia and Matty? Their presence would be comforting, but he had a feeling that this was *his* battle. They cared about it less than he did, and he had no right to drag them into it.

He got up and got dressed in fresh clothes that Amyus Crowe had managed to find somewhere in town. They were still new and made him itch, but the thought of putting on the same clothes he'd been wearing for so many hours filled him with horror.

Crowe was in the dining room, talking with two other men in suits. They had guns on belts slung on their hips. Sherlock assumed they were from the Pinkerton Agency. He slipped past them while they were distracted and headed out into the open air.

The boardwalks along the edges of the street were filled with people wandering back and forth or just standing and talking. Sherlock walked along with the flow until he saw something that looked like a stable. He went inside.

"Can I help you, son?" a voice said. Sherlock looked around. An elderly man came out of the darkness—bald, apart from a fringe of white hair around the back of his head, with a bushy white moustache.

"I need a horse, just for the day," Sherlock said.

"That's convenient," the man said. "I got a horse that ain't had any exercise for a while. Looks like we got ourselves a perfect match."

"How much?" Sherlock asked.

"Let's call it a ten-dollar deposit, an' nine dollars back when you return."

Sherlock passed the money across, and the man led him to a stall where a brown mare stood patiently. She eyed him speculatively as the elderly man saddled her.

Sherlock glanced around the stable. Apart from the general tack—saddles, reins, stirrups—that was hanging from hooks, there was also a whole load of stuff that he didn't recognize. They looked like weapons—bows, spears, axes—but they were decorated with feathers and leather thongs.

"Mementoes of the natives we've traded with over the years," the man said, noticing the direction of Sherlock's gaze. "Mainly the Delaware tribe."

Sherlock thought about what he was heading into—a hostile army, an attacking force, and a wilderness where coyotes prowled. He didn't want to take a gun, and he was pretty sure nobody would give him one, but some kind of weapon might be a good thing. "For another dollar," he said, "could I borrow a bow, a quiver of arrows, and a knife?"

"No," the man said. He cocked his head to one side. "But five dollars would do it."

Ten minutes later, Sherlock was riding out of the stable with a knife in his belt, a quiver full of arrows on his back, and a bow strapped to his saddle. He thought he saw Matty and Virginia outside the hotel, but he rode past too quickly to tell for sure, and he wasn't going to stop.

Remembering Amyus Crowe's map, Sherlock struck out across-country, at an angle to the train line. The landscape he was heading into was more hilly than the plains that the train line had been built across. He cantered along the edge of the foothills that emerged from the grasslands, rising up to a series of low, rounded peaks.

After an hour of riding through a landscape of bushes and small copses he crossed a wide, shallow stream that flowed like a blue, sparkling ribbon from up in the hills. As his horse's hoofs splashed the water and kicked up small pebbles he wondered if somewhere downstream the water had managed to cut its way through the soft rock to form the ravine that he, Matty, and Virginia had crossed over the night before. The terrain in America was very different from what he was used to back in England: younger and more raw.

He had thought to pick up a leather water bottle from the stable before he left, and he stopped briefly to refill it and to let his horse drink.

Judging by the sun it was now mid-afternoon, and judging by the map in his mind he was getting close to where the Army Corps of Engineers was setting up its camp. They would almost certainly post sentries, and he didn't want to run into any of them. Chances were they would shoot first and ask questions afterwards.

Rather than keep skirting the foothills, Sherlock pulled his horse's head around and headed up into the hills. If he was right, if he was where he thought he was, then he could get a good view down onto the camp from somewhere up there.

It took him another couple of hours of climbing up shallow slopes and crossing rocky patches before his horse came around the edge of a steeper section of hillside and Sherlock found himself gazing down on what it was he had come looking for.

Leaving his horse out of sight he crept forward, moving on hands and knees, until he could lie in the shelter of a large rock and stare down on the plain below.

The sun was dipping towards the horizon now, and the scene was illuminated partly by its red rays and partly by scattered campfires. By that mixed light he could see the Army Corps of Engineers' camp spread out beneath him: a series of tents grouped in the centre surrounded by a cleared area of ground. Perhaps a hundred men were moving purposefully back and forth. On one side of the camp the horses had been corralled together in a makeshift stockade. On the other side were the balloons.

The sight took Sherlock's breath away. There were perhaps ten or twelve of the things spread across an area the size of a rugby pitch. Some of them looked like massive versions of the kind of baggy jellyfish that Sherlock remembered seeing from trips to the coast when he was younger, while others had been fully inflated into glossy spheres that gleamed in the waning light of the sun. Ropes and swathes of the same material as the balloons themselves—varnished silk, Sherlock recalled from his meeting with the Count von Zeppelin on the SS *Scotia*—attached them to baskets beneath, and they were being inflated by pipes that led away from them to carts filled with gleaming copper tanks. The tanks were producing hydrogen, Sherlock remembered, from a combination of sulphuric acid and iron filings.

Thinking of the Count von Zeppelin, Sherlock scanned the camp looking for his upright, Germanic figure. He had come across to America to talk about the military applications of balloons. It would be unusual if he *wasn't* here.

The figures moving around were too small for Sherlock to make out faces, but he thought he saw a bearded man in a different uniform from the rest standing near the balloons, watching with fascination as they were being filled.

The campfires were being kept well away from the balloons, Sherlock noticed. That was a good idea—hydrogen was highly inflammable, he remembered from school. On the other hand, hundreds of metal spheres that looked like cannonballs but were almost certainly explosive devices were piled up near them. And in an hour or two, if the wind was still in the right direction, the balloons would be released, each with its own aeronaut, and they would drift silently across the desolate landscape towards the place where Duke Balthassar's army was encamped. And then there would be death and devastation on a scale that made Sherlock feel sick.

He had to stop it. He *had* to. He'd seen too much

death in his life already. If he could stop people from dying, then he would.

Hydrogen. Inflammable. The answer was there, but how was he going to do anything about it? If he tried to sneak down and set fire to the balloons, then he would be caught and probably shot as a Confederate spy. There were guards placed in a circle around the balloons.

But there were no guards around the campfires on the other side of the camp, and from where he lay he could see that most of the tents had oil lamps in front of them, hanging from poles that had been thrust into the ground.

His mind raced as he began making connections between things that he'd previously seen as being separate. The solution was there in front of him. He had some of the things he needed, and the rest were down there, in the camp.

And the sooner he started, the sooner he would finish.

He made sure that the ends of his horse's reins were secure beneath a rock and began the slow descent to the plain. There was only a thin sliver of sun above the horizon now, and the shadows cast by the scattered rocks were long and black. He found he could manage to keep to them most of the time, scooting across open ground only when he had to.

By the time he got down to the plain the sun had vanished below the horizon and the sky was the colour of a fresh bruise. Most of the balloons were fully inflated, and there was increased activity around them.

Sherlock moved away from the balloons, towards the area where the campfires were clustered. Most of the Army engineers in the camp were over near the balloons, standing just the other side of the cordon of guards, watching and waiting for the launch. Sherlock crept through the tents until he could see out onto the campfires. Meat was roasting, stews were simmering, and nobody was looking his way. He glanced around, straightened himself up, brushed the dirt from his clothes, and then walked over to an unattended tent and unhooked an oil lamp from the pole outside. For good measure, he took a second one from a pole nearby. Not from the tent next door—that would probably be noticed—but from one a little way away. Nobody called out to stop him or ask what he was doing. His heart was beating twice as fast as normal, but he kept his face impassive, and when he turned to walk back he walked slowly, keeping the oil lamps upright but wrapped in his jacket so nobody would see the lights moving.

Once in the safety of the tents he sped up, heading back to the base of the hills. He glanced over towards the balloons as he went. They were all fully inflated now, and he could see activity as the Army aeronauts checked their maps and made their final preparations.

He climbed the hill as fast as he could, aware that he was carrying hot oil and flame, and that if he fell he might set himself alight. The wind was picking up now that the sun had gone down, and without his jacket he was feeling cold.

His horse made a quiet whickering sound, welcoming him back to the flat area where he had left it. He put the oil lamps down, then crossed over to the horse and retrieved the bow and the quiver of arrows that he'd borrowed—well, rented—from the stable keeper.

He was going to need something to keep the flame going while the arrows flew through the air.

Wadding. Some kind of wadding.

He looked around, cursing himself for not having picked something up in the camp. The only things he had up there in the hills were his clothes. He began to rip strips of material off his own jacket, then tied them around the arrowheads. It wasn't as if he was going to be trying to get them to stick in anything, after all.

Once he had ten arrows with their heads wrapped in material, he crossed back over to where he'd left the oil lamps and brought them over to the arrows. He thought for a moment, then snuffed out the flame on one of the lamps and opened it up so that he could dip the wrapped arrowheads in the oil, one by one.

A single lit lamp should be enough. He opened it up so that the flame was exposed. It flickered in the breeze.

He took the bow and stood upright. It was dark enough now that he couldn't be seen, and the flame on the remaining lamp was shielded by the rocks.

He flexed the bow experimentally. The principle seemed obvious. A notch in the base of the arrow slotted onto the cord, and he could pull the cord back with the fingers of his right hand, holding the bow in his left hand and flexing it as far as it could go. Then he would aim—high, because the arrow would follow a ballistic trajectory—and release the cord.

Time to try. Time for action.

He touched the tied-up strip of jacket at the head of the first arrow to the flame inside the oil lamp. The oil-soaked material caught fire instantly. He raised the arrow up and fitted the cord into the notch, then took up the tension, pulling the cord back while holding his left hand straight out in front of him, grasping the bow. He aimed towards the balloon that seemed to have fewest people around it, but he aimed over it so that the arrow would fall down onto it.

The cord bit into the fingers of his right hand. He could feel the bow trembling under the tension. The glowing material caused a bright spot in his vision that almost blanked out everything else.

Was he doing the right thing?

Too late to wonder about that now.

He released the cord. The arrow arced high in the air, reaching a peak and seeming to hang there for a moment before falling like a tiny meteor straight down onto the top surface of the balloon.

Nothing happened for several heartbeats; long enough

that Sherlock was convinced that the burning material had somehow extinguished itself, or the arrowhead had failed to connect with the varnished silk, or that the gas in the balloon wasn't hydrogen at all but something else, something non-flammable, but then the material around the top of the balloon seemed to peel back like the petals of a flower, and Sherlock's vision was blinded by a ball of flame that leaped up from the balloon and reached towards the sky.

A tremendous shout welled up from the area of the camp. People were running around, throwing buckets of water and trying to douse whatever burning material was raining down on them, but the inferno was rising *up*, not falling down. Hydrogen was lighter than air, after all.

Sherlock grabbed another arrow and lit it, then quickly aimed at another balloon and fired. The tiny spark of the flaming arrowhead described a glowing line in the air as it flew, first up into the darkness and then down onto the sloping side of the second balloon.

This time he couldn't see the material peel back, but the resulting fireball was equally as impressive as the first.

As chaos reigned in the camp below, Sherlock fired arrow after arrow at the remaining balloons. By the time he had run out, the air was filled with smoke and the ground was littered with the smouldering remnants of the varnished silk. And nobody had been hurt! He marvelled at the thought, but he couldn't see a single person injured. Frantic and frightened, yes, but not hurt. The incandescent hydrogen had risen into the air, and whatever burning fragments of material had fallen to earth had been easily avoided.

He took a deep breath. The balloons would not be flying tonight, and it would take days, perhaps weeks, to get more balloons to the area. By that time, Balthassar's army would either have dispersed or marched on Canada and been intercepted by the Unionist army. He had succeeded.

Part of him wanted to do something about the pile of explosive devices that sat at one side of the camp. They had survived unscathed. Sherlock had been worried that scraps of burning material might have fallen on them, setting them off and causing general carnage, but either they were more difficult to ignite than he thought or they were sufficiently far way from any falling sparks or flaming cloth. He supposed he could creep back down and pull their fuses out, or something, but what would be the point? They were useless, now there was no means of delivering them.

A shout went up from below. He glanced down, towards the camp. A man was pointing at him. The light from the burning hydrogen had revealed his presence. More people stared up at him. Some of them started running towards the slope that led up to his hiding place. Most of them were holding guns.

Ah. He was holding the bow.

Time to leave.

He turned and ran across to where his horse was tethered. It was nervous and skittish—the reins to its bridle were pulled tight as it had tried to back away—but it wasn't panicking yet. Quickly he retrieved the ends of the reins from underneath the rock that held them and pulled himself up into the saddle.

With luck, he could get back to town and pretend that he'd been there all the time. Nobody need know what he'd done.

He pulled the horse's head around and headed away.

The journey down out of the hills was easier than the way up. The horse seemed more sure-footed now, and it was glad to be getting away from the fire and the smoke.

The horse could see its way by the light of the stars, now the sun had set, and Sherlock let it choose its own path down. Once they got to the flat grasslands he could work out a course back to town.

As the horse picked its way through the rock-strewn landscape of the foothills, Sherlock found that the gentle rocking motion was causing him to nod off. The tension was draining away from him, leaving him empty and melancholic. He wasn't looking forward to the long trek back to Perseverance.

Doubts began to set in as he rode. What if the Unionist army failed to intercept the Confederate invasion force? What if the invasion went ahead and he'd facilitated it?

No, Amyus Crowe had told him that the Unionist forces were already preparing to stop the Confederates if they advanced, but that Secretary of War Stanton had personally decided that he wanted the Confederates slaughtered. Unless something went badly wrong, Sherlock's actions had only saved lives. They wouldn't lead to a diplomatic incident.

Somewhere in the darkness an animal screamed. The sound startled him. It sounded too much like a person screaming. It didn't sound like a coyote. More like a big cat of some kind.

The horse was picking its way along the bottom of a gully between two steep slopes now. Sherlock thought they were close to the bottom of the hills, nearly ready to make their way across the open grasslands towards the town. The sides of the gully were just black shapes, with only the stars shining in the sky above marking where their jagged edges cut the night sky.

One of the jagged edges moved.

Sherlock jerked awake. Part of what he'd thought was the top of the gully had suddenly shifted sideways and pulled back.

Something was up there. Something was tracking him.

Nerves stretched and quivering, Sherlock looked around. Nothing. Just darkness, thrown into sharp relief by the starlight filtering down from above.

A pebble skittered down the steep slope, bouncing off the floor of the gully.

Sherlock's horse was looking around now. It knew

there was something else out there. Its ears were pricked up, and Sherlock could feel its muscles quivering beneath his legs.

The gully began to broaden out ahead of them, opening onto a flat section of rock with a sheer drop down to the grasslands at the far side. In the light from the low moon that cut across from one side like a spotlight, Sherlock recognized where they were. Despite the appearance of a sheer drop straight ahead, he remembered there was a path off to one side, sloping down to the grasslands, that he and the horse had come up earlier.

Another pebble fell, bouncing from rock to rock. Sherlock's horse edged sideways and sped up. It wanted to be out on the plains as badly as he did.

Something above Sherlock's head screamed and leaped down on them from the blackness.

SEVENTEEN

The horse leaped sideways in shock, saving both of them. Whatever it was that had jumped towards them fell past and hit the ground off balance in a flash of slashing claws, stumbling to one side but immediately springing back up to its feet. Sherlock had a momentary confused impression of eyes reflecting moonlight and pointed fangs wet with saliva gleaming in a slavering mouth.

He ripped the knife from his belt and held it out. It wasn't much consolation, but it was all he had.

A voice from up ahead said something guttural in a language Sherlock didn't recognize, and the animal retreated towards it, hissing in frustration at Sherlock and the horse.

He recognized it now. It was one of Duke Balthassar's cougars. That meant the other one was probably out there somewhere. And that meant Duke Balthassar was out there too.

His horse was paralysed with shock: eyes wide and lips pulled back over exposed teeth. It wasn't going anywhere; not with the cougars around. Sherlock slipped from the saddle, heart pounding in his chest. He was tired, he was hungry, and he was thirsty. He didn't want this. Not now. Not here.

But he didn't think he had a choice.

He walked forward, into the moonlight at the mouth of the rocky gully.

Duke Balthassar stood a few feet to one side. He was still wearing his white suit, white hat, and white porcelain mask, but he had a revolver strapped to his thigh. Behind his right ear Sherlock could see the red leech gleaming wetly in the moonlight, the only spot of colour in the entire scene. It seemed to pulse slightly as Sherlock watched.

The cougar that had leaped for Sherlock and his horse was by Balthassar's side, tail flicking restlessly. Sherlock noticed how it kept casting glances up at the red leech. It seemed nervous, frightened even. The other cougar wasn't in sight.

"Sherlock Scott Holmes," Balthassar said, his voice barely perceptible over the sound of the wind. "I fear we are fated to keep meeting, like Shakespeare's star-crossed lovers."

"What are you doing here?" Sherlock asked simply.

"I was looking for you," Balthassar replied. "When I found my dear reptiles still hungry and my observation gallery flooded, I could only assume you and your plucky friends had escaped. You know too much: I had to track you down and deal with you. My cougars picked up your scent just outside the town and we followed you here, to the hills." He paused, head cocked to one side. "I must admit, I had expected you to go into the town, but instead you came out here. Why?"

Sherlock thought for a moment. Balthassar must have confused two different trails: the one that Sherlock, Matty, and Virginia had left as they went *towards* Perseverance and the one Sherlock and his horse had left as they went *away* from the town. That meant Balthassar didn't yet know that his plans had been exposed. Should Sherlock tell him?

If Balthassar knew that it was too late, that his army had already been discovered, then he would have no reason for killing Sherlock. In theory, at least.

"The Union Army already know about the invasion of Canada," Sherlock told him. "There's no point in going ahead now. Just call it off, Balthassar. You can save a lot of lives."

Silence, as Balthassar considered what Sherlock had said. It wasn't possible to tell what he was thinking behind the white mask.

"How long have they known for?" he asked eventually.

"Long enough that there's no chance your army will ever get to the border."

"In that case, what are you doing out here?" Balthassar asked.

"The Unionists were preparing to drop explosives on your men. I couldn't let that happen. I had to stop it."

"I presume that was due to some form of misguided nobility, rather than agreement with the Confederate way of life?"

"I just don't want to see any more people die," Sherlock replied wearily.

Balthassar shook his head. "Do you expect me to be grateful?" he asked, and suddenly there was a grating tone of anger in his voice.

Sherlock felt tiredness weighing him down like a lead weight on his shoulders. "I don't expect anything," he said. "I'm not doing this for you, or for anyone else. I'm doing it for *me*. For what *I* believe."

"Then you've wasted your time," Balthassar snapped. "The invasion goes ahead, despite everything you have told me."

"Then your people will be rounded up, and if they choose to fight there will be a battle."

"And people will die anyway," Balthassar snarled. "So you have failed."

"I can't control the world," Sherlock pointed out. "Just the bits I can reach. At least I've done what I can to stop a massacre. The rest is up to you, and Amyus Crowe, and the government."

"Your problem," Balthassar said, porcelain face impassive and glowing in the moonlight, but voice bitter, "is that you let your emotions get in the way of logic. If I had any advice to offer you, it would be for you to suppress your emotions. Keep them in check. They can only lead you astray. They can only hurt you."

Sherlock's mind flashed with memories of his mother

and his sister, and the memories were coloured with emotions, and those emotions hurt. But then there were memories of Virginia too, and those memories didn't hurt. They made him happy.

"I appreciate the advice," he said, "but I think I'll hang on to my emotions, if you don't mind. I like them, for better or for worse."

"I would say you'll live to regret it," Balthassar said, "but you won't." He snapped his fingers. The cougar at his side advanced towards Sherlock, teeth exposed and eyes narrowed.

Sherlock brought his hand around in front of him. The blade of the knife caught the moonlight in a liquid gleam.

The cougar didn't even hesitate. It just kept on coming.

Feet padded on rock behind him. Sherlock turned his head, slowly.

The second cougar was behind him.

His thoughts raced through possibilities, none of which helped. How could he fight two wild animals with only a knife?

But they weren't wild, were they? They were partially tamed—or, at least, they obeyed Balthassar. They *feared* him, and that gave Sherlock a chance.

A sudden acceleration in the padding of feet behind him made him drop to the ground and roll sideways. Something dark flashed over his head. He jumped to his feet, but the cougars were quicker. They were side by side now, snarling at him.

Cats could climb trees, but they couldn't climb rock.

As fast as he could, Sherlock scrambled up the sheer side of the gully; fingers scrabbling for gaps in the rock, feet trying to find small ridges and shelves that would take his weight without crumbling.

Below him, the cougars leaped.

His fingers closed over a flat area of rock and he hauled himself up desperately, just as a clawed paw caught at his boot and pulled him backwards. He put all of his strength into one tremendous heave, and pulled himself to safety on a ledge that ran along the side of the gully, heading upward in one direction and downward in the other.

He looked down, checking that his feet had survived unscathed. The heel of his boot had been pulled off by the big cat, but other than that he was intact.

From below, the gleam of the cougars' eyes vanished as they headed off in different directions, looking for a way up to him. And this was their territory, not his. They would find a way.

"Entertaining as this is," Balthassar's voice called, "you are merely postponing the inevitable. That isn't a logical course of action. Just give in; it'll be easier and less painful."

"You promised me that before," Sherlock panted, "and you lied."

The ledge was barely wider than his body, and he sprinted along it trying to get to somewhere relatively safe. He could hear the click of claws on stone from somewhere off to one side, and the deep rasping of breath echoing throughout the gully.

If he didn't do something soon, he was dead.

Pressed against the side of the gully, he glanced downward. He could just make out Balthassar's white hat below.

With a fleeting prayer that his deduction about the cougars and their relationship with Balthassar was correct, he jumped.

He crashed down onto Balthassar, knocking the man to the ground and sending his revolver skittering away into the darkness. Sherlock's left shoulder hit the rock of the gully floor as he tried to roll away, sending a spike of red-hot agony through his body. By the time he climbed to his feet, Balthassar was already standing. He was cradling his left arm with his right. It looked malformed, as if his thin bones had snapped in the fall.

His porcelain mask had been knocked off. It lay on the ground a few feet away, broken into three pieces. His face, bereft of the mask, was twisted into an expression of pure hatred.

"Southern courtesy aside," Balthassar snarled, "I will see my pets strip the flesh from your bones while you are still alive and screaming." The smaller, black leeches on his face looked like holes through to the darkness of the night sky behind him. Balthassar looked past Sherlock. "And here they are," he said, and barked three words in the guttural language that he used to communicate with the animals.

Expecting at any moment to feel the weight of a cougar on his back and the agony of its claws ripping through his flesh, Sherlock stepped forward, towards Balthassar.

The thin man wasn't expecting that. He flinched backwards, still cradling his left arm, but Sherlock reached out with his throbbing left hand and ripped the red leech from behind Balthassar's ear. It tore free with some resistance. Blood spattered on the shoulder of Balthassar's white suit, black in the moonlight.

Balthassar screamed: a high, thin noise of distilled rage and shock.

The giant red leech was squishy and wet in Sherlock's hand. Before Balthassar could do anything, before the cougars could spring, Sherlock brought his knife up and sliced it in half. It writhed and twisted, leaking Balthassar's blood into his palm. He turned, each hand holding a part of the leech, and threw them at the two cougars that were advancing towards him.

Given their reaction earlier on Balthassar's veranda, he had thought they might turn and run in terror, but they surprised him. The cougars snapped the halves of the leech out of the air as if they were tidbits thrown as treats and swallowed them whole.

They continued to advance on him.

No, not on him. Their eyes were fixed on Balthassar.

Sherlock moved slowly to one side. The cougars ignored him and continued moving towards Balthassar.

It made a strange kind of sense. The man who had

dominated them was injured, weakened, and the leech that they feared was gone. Whatever power Balthassar had over them appeared to have been broken. They had the power now. He couldn't hurt them.

Balthassar backed away. The rocky edge was behind him. He said something in the language he used to control the cats, but they ignored it.

Sherlock watched, his mouth dry and his heart pounding. Balthassar took another step back, hands raised to ward off the cougars, but his right foot ended up past the edge of the rocky overhang, over empty air, and he fell, screaming, into the darkness.

The cougars stood there for a moment, looking over the edge, and then, without looking at each other or at Sherlock, they padded away, into the hills.

Sherlock stood there for a while, getting his breath back and letting the pain in his shoulder subside. It didn't seem broken. At least that was something.

The cougars didn't come back.

Eventually he went over to where his horse was cowering and calmed it down, stroking its flanks until it stopped shivering. Then he pulled himself up into the saddle and continued his journey, down the slope that led to the grasslands.

At the bottom of the slope he found Balthassar's body. It lay, twisted and broken, in a flattened area of grass. The leeches had vanished from his face. Presumably they had left to seek other prey the minute his blood had stopped pumping through his veins. Not necessarily a logical decision, but an instinctive one.

Sherlock must have fallen asleep on the ride back, because the next thing he knew the horse was trotting through the outskirts of town and there was a blue blush on the horizon. He left the horse tied up outside the stable and headed for the hotel. He could pick up his deposit later.

There was nobody in the dining room when he walked in. He headed up to his room. Nobody tried to stop him. He almost expected someone to leap out and attack him, or something to leap onto his shoulders when his back was turned, but there was nothing. Everything was peaceful and calm. He let himself into his room, washed quickly, and slipped beneath the covers. It was as if nothing had happened. It was as if he'd not left the room since he'd first entered that morning, after the long trek across the grasslands from Balthassar's house with Matty and Virginia.

He slept without dreaming, or if he dreamed then he did not remember the dreams when he woke up, and that was probably a good thing.

The sun was shining through his bedroom window when he awoke. He lay there for a while, cataloguing what had happened and consigning it to his memories. Then he got dressed and went downstairs.

Amyus Crowe was in the dining room, talking with two of the Pinkerton agents. He said something to them, then crossed over to Sherlock as they left.

"Ain't seen much of you since yesterday morning," he said. "I've been busy with the Pinkertons, but Matty and Virginia said you never left your room. You must have needed your sleep."

"I did," Sherlock said.

"There's scratches on your hands that I don't recall from yesterday."

"I think they came up overnight," Sherlock said.

"Maybe they did." Crowe gazed levelly at Sherlock for a few moments.

"What's been happening?" Sherlock asked. "What's the news on Balthassar and the invasion of Canada?"

"The balloon attack on the Confederate Army was called off," Crowe replied. "Someone set fire to the balloons. Probably one of Balthassar's agents. That's the general theory, anyway, and who am I to disagree?"

"At least a massacre was avoided," Sherlock pointed out.

"It was," Crowe agreed. "The Secretary of War was all for a big confrontation between his troops and Balthassar's, but his orders got held up somehow, an' I took the opportunity to put a plan of my own into effect. We used John Wilkes Booth to tell Balthassar's army to disperse. He can be very persuasive when he's given the proper medication an' when he's offered an alternative to the gallows. I don't think many of the troops had the stomach for a real fight. They were glad to be told to go home."

"And John Wilkes Booth?"

"As far as history is concerned, he's already dead. A man named John St. Helen will be committed to a lunatic asylum in Baltimore. If he's given the correct medication at the right dose, he should be manageable. Until his death, at least."

"Incarceration," Sherlock said.

"He's an assassin, when all's said an' done. It's better than he deserves."

Sherlock nodded, not so much in agreement but more because he didn't particularly want to argue. "And what about us? What happens next?"

"Next," Crowe said, "we return to New York and get tickets for England. That'll probably take a day or two. I think we've spent more than enough time here. Much as I love the country of my birth, I do enjoy England. Overcooked vegetables and steamed puddings excepted."

"You're not . . . staying?" Sherlock asked tentatively.

Crowe shook his massive head. "Too much to do elsewhere," he said. "There's lots of us here, but only me in England. I got a job to do. An' I promised your brother I'd teach you to think logically an' use evidence, an' I suspect I've not done as much on that front as I should've done."

Later that day the four of them—Crowe, Virginia,

Sherlock, and Matty—took a train back to New York, and Crowe found them tickets on a ship leaving in a few days for England. They even managed to eat at the famed Niblo's Garden on their last night—oysters, of course, and huge steaks—but Sherlock found himself distanced from it all, watching it go past with little emotion. It was as if he'd been through so much over the past few days that something had been burned out in him. He hoped it would come back sometime soon. He didn't like the feeling of being separate from the rest of the world.

Virginia was worried about him, he could tell. She kept glancing across at him while they were eating, and once or twice she would just rest her hand on his arm for a moment, then take it away when he didn't react.

The next day, on the ship, watching from the rail as New York harbour slipped away in the distance, Sherlock found himself shivering despite the warmth of the sun and the lack of wind. He felt ill, out of sorts, but he didn't know how to make himself better.

"So," a familiar voice said from beside him, "how was the great metropolis of New York? Did you do whatever it was that you needed to do?"

He turned his head. Rufus Stone, the violinist he'd met on the journey out, was standing nearby, leaning on the rail. His violin case was slung across his back and his long black hair was loose across his collar.

"I thought you were staying in America," Sherlock said, surprised.

"Ah, about that," Rufus said ruefully. "I may not have mentioned, but I was in a bit of trouble back in the old country, and I was hoping that seeking the fabled pot of gold at this end of the rainbow would be a good move, but it turns out that people have been sending messages along that very same rainbow, and someone was waiting for me when I got here." He sighed. "Who would have thought that the Irish would have the whole criminal underworld in New York sewn up like a corpse in a shroud?"

"So what happens now?" Sherlock asked. "Where do you go?"

"That depends," Rufus said, gazing out across the water. "Do you know of anyone who is in desperate need of a violin tutor?"

"Funnily enough," said Sherlock, "I think I do."

AUTHOR'S NOTE

And so here we are, at the end of teenage Sherlock Holmes's second adventure. I hope you enjoyed reading it as much as I enjoyed writing it.

In the first book Sherlock had started to pick up his logical way of thinking and his eye for evidence from the genial but rather mysterious Amyus Crowe. I also showed him starting to become interested in bees and in boxing, setting the scene for the skills and interests he later displays in the stories by Arthur Conan Doyle (in "The Sign of Four," for instance, a bare-knuckle fighter compliments Sherlock by saying, "You're one that has wasted your gifts. You might have aimed high, if you had joined the fancy"—"the fancy" being a slang term for the boxing fraternity).

In this book I have tried to imagine how and where Sherlock first learned to play the violin, as well as the events that provoked him to take an interest in tattoos (again, in the Conan Doyle stories, he can work out where a tattoo was done just by the pigments in the ink). In a more general sense I've laid some of the groundwork for the sympathy that Sherlock later shows towards America and Americans (Sherlock says in one of Conan Doyle's stories that he expects there to be a day when people in

Great Britain and America will be "citizens of the same world-wide country under a flag which shall be a quartering of the Union Jack with the Stars and Stripes").

I've tried to make sure that the things that happen in this book are as historically accurate as possible. The SS *Scotia* did indeed go back and forth across the Atlantic, for instance, taking passengers from Liverpool to New York, as did the SS *Great Eastern*. I'm not sure whether it ever sailed from Southampton, but for the purposes of this book I'm assuming that it did at least once. The *Scotia* made its first voyage as a passenger ship in 1862 under Captain Judkins and its last in 1875, and for a while it held the record for the fastest transatlantic crossing, but its consumption of coal made it uneconomical and it did not make the Cunard Company, who built it, the profits they expected. After spending some years laying undersea cables for transatlantic telegraph messages, the *Scotia* ended up sinking off the island of Guam in the Pacific Ocean in 1904. For details on the SS *Scotia*, and other ships that plied the Atlantic passenger trade, I am indebted to the following books:

Transatlantic Paddle Steamers by H. Philip Spratt. Brown, Son & Ferguson, 1951.

Transatlantic—Samuel Cunard, Isambard Brunel, and the Great Atlantic Steamships by Stephen Fox. HarperCollins, 2003.

The story told aboard the SS *Scotia* by Captain Judkins, the one about the strange earwig-like creature found holding on to the undersea telegraph cable when it was brought up from the depths of the ocean, is a fabrication of mine, but such creatures do actually exist. Scary, but true. Check out the following Web site if you don't believe me:

http://news.ninemsn.com.au/national/1034874/monster-bug-attaches-itself-to-submarine

On the other hand, the giant red leech of Borneo that is known to science is not actually a bloodsucker, but instead eats the giant Borneo earthworm. The leech that Duke Balthassar uses for medical purposes here is, I suggest, a currently unknown species, but given the number of previously unknown species of animals discovered every year, from insects up to mammals, it's entirely possible that there *is* a giant red bloodsucking leech out there somewhere. The substance secreted in leech saliva to suppress the clotting of blood is factual: the substance is called hirudin, and leeches are increasingly being used in hospitals to stop potentially dangerous blood clots from forming in surgery patients. You can't yet get them on prescription, though.

The large reptiles that chase Sherlock, Matty, and Virginia in Duke Balthassar's animal enclosure are monitor lizards. Monitor lizards can grow up to several metres in length, have a high metabolic rate compared with most other reptiles, and can be as intelligent as a small dog (experiments have shown that monitor lizards can count up to six, although no scientist has yet shown what use this is to them).

The laying of the first undersea cables between Ireland and America is one of the nineteenth century's most incredible stories. I can recommend the following book as a great account:

A Thread Across the Ocean: The Heroic Story of the Transatlantic Cable by John Steele Gordon. Simon and Schuster, 2002.

Ferdinand Graf von Zeppelin, who meets with Sherlock on the SS *Scotia*, took leave from the German army in 1863 and travelled to America, where he acted as an observer for the Northern Potomac army in the American Civil War against the Confederates. Crucially, while there he also met Professor Thaddeus Lowe, who was using tethered balloons as reconnaissance platforms in the Civil War, observing Confederate troop movements on behalf of the Union. All balloon rides had been made off-limits to civilians, so instead Professor Lowe sent Zeppelin to visit his German assistant John Steiner, who could talk to Zeppelin in German, rather than using Zeppelin's halting English. Zeppelin made his first ascent with Steiner's tethered balloon. Fascinated with the possibilities of balloons, Zeppelin returned to America in the 1870s to talk to Lowe again (although I have moved the date of this trip slightly to make it fit in with the time line of this book). Later, back in Germany, he would design the rigid balloon—the Zeppelin—that would make him famous.

Detail on New York, and the rest of America, in the 1860s was provided by:

Transatlantic Crossing: American Visitors to Britain and British Visitors to America in the Nineteenth Century selected and edited by Walter Allen. William Heinemann, 1971.

The Sun and the Moon: The Remarkable True Account of Hoaxers, Showmen, Dueling Journalists and Lunar Man-Bats in Nineteenth-Century New York by Matthew Goodman. Basic Books, 2008.

Material on the assassination of Abraham Lincoln and the historical aftermath was gleaned from:

"They Have Killed Papa Dead!": The Road to Ford's Theatre, Abraham Lincoln's Murder, and the Rage for Vengeance by Anthony S. Pitch. Steerforth Press, 2008.

It proved strangely difficult to find out very much about American railroads in the 1860s. A map would have been nice, or at the very least a timetable to show me how many changes of train a man would need to make to get from New York to Pennsylvania, but if such books exist I couldn't find them. What little detail I did glean came from:

The American Railroad Network, 1861–1890 by George Rogers Taylor and Irene D. Neu. University of Illinois Press, 2003.

Guide Book for Tourists and Travellers over the Valley Railway from Cleveland to Canton (facsimile of the 1880 edition) by John S. Reese. The Kent State Press, 2002.

Bizarrely, there have been several plans by Americans, some associated with the U.S. government and some not, to take parts of Canada off Great Britain's hands by force of arms over the years. In 1864, during the American Civil War (or the War Between the States as it was known at the time), a group of Confederate soldiers went through Quebec to get to the U.S. state of Vermont, which was in Union hands. In 1866, two years before this book is set, a group of Irish Americans advocated invading Quebec and Ontario in order to use them as a base from which to strike against Britain in retaliation for what they saw as the British occupation of Ireland. Three times they sent an armed force into Canada—on the second and third attempts they had about a thousand men—but the first attempt just fizzled out and the later two were beaten back by force of arms. Years later, in 1896, Secretary of the Navy H. A. Herbert ordered the U.S. military to construct a plan to seize control of the Great Lakes and St. Lawrence when it looked as if a border dispute between Venezuela and the British territory of British Guiana might escalate into war between the United States and Great Britain. Tensions fortunately subsided. Amongst other sources, I consulted the Straight Dope (www.straightdope.com) for the above information.

As before, I am indebted both to the descendants of Arthur Conan Doyle for giving their permission for me to write these books and to my agent and my editor, Rob Kirby and Rebecca McNally respectively, for giving me the space to do so.

By the time you read these words I should have finished writing the third Young Sherlock Holmes novel. I'm not going to reveal anything about it here, except the fact that it may well take Sherlock and his brother, Mycroft, to the depths of Siberia. Or it might involve the mysterious Giant Rat of Sumatra (a tale, Conan Doyle later tells us, for which the world is unprepared). Or both. I haven't decided yet. Keep reading, and you'll find out.

QUESTIONS FOR THE AUTHOR

ANDREW LANE

Helen Stirling

In Sherlock Holmes: The Legend Begins, we meet Sherlock at age fourteen. What made you want to write about Sherlock at this age and at this time in his life?

I've always been fascinated by the character of Sherlock Holmes, as created by Sir Arthur Conan Doyle. He's such a conflicted man—probably borderline autistic, almost certainly manic-depressive, hugely talented (expert chemist, violin player, boxer, sword-fighter, and practitioner of martial arts, as well as highly theatrical and an expert in disguise). For a long while I wanted to write about him as a grown-up character, but more and more I found myself wondering how he became that way. Where did he learn all these things that he can do? What had to have happened to a relatively normal teenager to turn him into the adult we all know about? Obviously borderline autism and manic depression aren't necessarily caused by life's events, but they can probably be made worse by them, be triggered by them. So, over the course of however many books I end up writing, things aren't necessarily going to go well for Sherlock.

So have you always been a Sherlock Holmes fan? How did you discover him?

I was ten years old, and the first two books I ever bought with my own money (from a church jumble sale in East London, U.K., where I lived at the time) were *A Study in Scarlet* by Arthur Conan Doyle and *Three to Conquer* by Eric Frank Russell. One was the first-ever Sherlock Holmes story, and the other was a cheap science-fiction novel. Ever since then I've been strangely obsessed with Sherlock Holmes and cheap science fiction. In the intervening years I've collected lots of Sherlock Holmes material—not just the Conan Doyle stories but all the pastiches and parodies I could lay my hands on (that's basically stories by other people where they either try to do something serious with Sherlock Holmes to continue his adventures or try and do something that makes fun of his bizarre eccentricities). I've also got a fair collection of films and TV programs where Sherlock Holmes turns up as a character.

You've said you wanted to avoid the "Sherlock clichés" of foggy streets and gaslight streetlamps, but that you also sought to create an appropriately authentic setting and mood. What kind of research did you do to ensure historical accuracy? What were some of the things that were most fascinating or surprising to you during your research?

I already had a number of reference books on Victorian England, including a couple on the various underground tunnels and buried rivers in London, which is a particular interest of mine. For the rest of the research I was driven specifically by things I needed to know. For instance, in *Death Cloud* I had Sherlock and his mentor, Amyus Crowe, taking a train from the town of Farnham to London. I had to do quite a lot of digging to find out what the train line was like between those two points in those days, and it was a good thing I did because I discovered that the lines have been moved in the intervening years, and their positions now are not the positions then. I could, I suppose, have just written something like "Sherlock and Amyus Crowe took a train from Farnham to London," but by mentioning the stations along the way I think I'm adding a layer of historical accuracy that's important. That's what I keep telling myself, anyway. As to the most surprising thing I discovered, it was that the journey from the port of Southampton in the U.K. to New York only took a week by ship. I would have expected it to be a month, at least. The Victorians were amazingly ingenious when it came to engineering.

Why do you think Sherlock remains such a popular fictional figure? What is it about him that is so enduring and seemingly timeless?

I'm becoming more and more convinced that it comes down to the complex, contradictory character of Sherlock Holmes himself. There were other Victorian detectives, but they were all rather stereotypical policemen or investigators with no depth to them. In Sherlock Holmes, Arthur Conan Doyle created a character who is flawed and difficult to deal with but doesn't know it, and who has made a success of his chosen profession despite, or perhaps even because of, his character flaws. I think it's difficult to put ourselves in the position of, say, James Bond, who is good at everything he does, but much easier to put ourselves in the position of Sherlock Holmes, whose good qualities are balanced by his bad ones.

Your series is the first with a teenage version of Sherlock to be endorsed by the Conan Doyle Estate. What is it like to receive such support from the actual family of Sir Arthur Conan Doyle?

I'm massively honored to have the backing of the descendants of Arthur Conan Doyle. A lot of writers have taken liberties with the character of Sherlock Holmes over the years, and the family is rightly protective of the legacy left to them by their illustrious ancestor. The fact that what I have done has pleased them is, to my mind, one of the greatest compliments I could have received as a writer.

You've also penned novelizations of some enormously well-known pop-culture creations, such as *Doctor Who*. Can you tell us a little bit more about your writing background? And how was writing this book different from your past creative enterprises?

I've written something like twenty-three books over the past twenty-five years, most of which have been in the field of film and TV—either fictional, using characters that someone else has established but putting them in original situations, or factual, talking about the process of making films or TV episodes. In a sense, writing for Sherlock Holmes as a character is not that much different from writing for Doctor Who as a character—there's an established fan base with vociferous opinions on how "their" character should be treated, but also there's a wonderfully rich universe that you can set them against. The only two ways in which writing this book was different was (a) in the knowledge that I was writing for the young adult market, which meant (paradoxically) that I had to work harder in making sure that the pacing of the book was correct, because while adults will excuse bits where the action slows down, or people talk for too long, teenagers won't, and (b) in the knowledge that I was writing for (hopefully) a considerably larger audience than I had been before. Fortunately I managed to forget most of that while I was actually doing the writing.

Rebel Fire has Sherlock coming to America and crossing paths with John Wilkes Booth. To the best of your knowledge, did Conan Doyle's Sherlock stories ever stray to a United States setting? And what inspired you to bring Sherlock to the American South?

Conan Doyle wrote two Sherlock Holmes books that had sections set in the United States—*A Study in Scarlet* (set partly in Utah) and *The Valley of Fear* (set partly in Pennsylvania)—but Sherlock himself never went to America in Conan Doyle's stories. A fair number of American characters turn up, however, and Sherlock Holmes is typically very sympathetic to them (in one story Doyle has Holmes say to an American visitor: "I am one of those who believe that the folly of a monarch and the blundering of a minister in far-gone years will not prevent our children from being some day citizens of the same worldwide country under a flag which shall be a quartering of the Union Jack with the Stars and Stripes."). Sherlock's sympathy seems to be based on some close experience of either Americans or America itself, so I decided to make it clear that he had direct experience in America during his formative years. I chose the East Coast because it was considerably easier to get to from England in 1868, and Virginia in particular because I've traveled there on a number of occasions. For the same reason I had Sherlock's mentor, Amyus Crowe, coming from Albuquerque, which is one of my favorite places in the world. I'd love to live there if I could.

For the Sherlock Holmes fans out there, how about answering a few "speed round" highly subjective questions:

Do you have a favorite actor who portrayed Sherlock?

Robert Stephens in the Billy Wilder film *The Private Life of Sherlock Holmes*. He makes Sherlock into a complex, sensitive character who gives the impression that his brusque exterior is protective armor that prevents him from getting hurt. I think it's a marvelous performance, and I can imagine my version of the fourteen-year-old Sherlock growing up into him as an adult.

A favorite line from a story?
I'm going to list a couple:

1. "It is of the first importance," he cried, "not to allow your judgment to be biased by personal qualities. A client is to me a mere unit, a factor in a problem. The emotional qualities are antagonistic to clear reasoning. I assure you that the most winning woman I ever knew was hanged for poisoning three little children for their insurance-money, and the most repellent man of my acquaintance is a philanthropist who has spent nearly a quarter of a million upon the London poor." (*The Complete Sherlock Holmes*)

2. "Matilda Briggs was not the name of a young woman, Watson," said Holmes in a reminiscent voice. "It was a ship which is associated with the giant rat of Sumatra, a story for which the world is not yet prepared." (*The Case-Book of Sherlock Holmes*)

And

3. "It is, of course, a trifle, but there is nothing so important as trifles." (*The Treasury of Sherlock Holmes*)

Is there a common misconception in Sherlock lore (or two!) that you'd like to debunk?

There's a general opinion, I think, that Sherlock Holmes is an unemotional, calculating machine. He is not. He has clear views on morality and justice. He can frequently be seen to be angry or depressed or ecstatic. What he does do is suppress his emotions, not let them get in the way of his logical reasoning. What I have to do is find out what it is that made him that way.

When Sherlock and Amyus Crowe visit Mycroft in London, they find a locked room, a dead body, and Mycroft holding a knife. The police are convinced Mycroft is guilty—only Sherlock can save his brother from the gallows.

Follow Sherlock on his next adventure in

BLACK ICE

ONE

Sunlight sparkled on the surface of the water, sending daggers of light flashing towards Sherlock's eyes. He blinked repeatedly, and tried to keep his eyelids half-closed to minimize the glare.

The tiny rowing boat rocked gently in the middle of the lake. Around it, just past the shoreline, the grassy ground rose in all directions, covered in a smattering of bushes and trees. It was as if it were located in the middle of a green bowl, with the cloudless blue of the sky forming a lid across the top.

Crowe took the oars and rowed the boat back to the shore. After tying it to a post that had been set into the ground, he and Sherlock set off back to his cottage.

Their path led up the steep side of the bowl containing the lake. Crowe pushed on ahead, carrying the wicker basket. His large body made surprisingly little noise as he moved. Sherlock followed, tired now as well as bored.

They got to the ridge at the top of the slope, where the ground fell away steeply behind them and levelled out in front, and Crowe stopped to let Sherlock catch up.

"A point to note," he said, gesturing down at the blue surface of the lake. "If you're ever out huntin', don't be tempted to stop at a place like this, either to take in the view or to get a better look at the surroundin' terrain.

Imagine what we look like to any animal in the forest, silhouetted here on the ridge. We can be seen for miles."

Before Sherlock could say anything, Crowe started off again, pushing through the undergrowth. Sherlock wondered briefly how the man knew which way to go without a compass. He was about to ask, but instead tried to work it out himself. All Crowe had to go on was their surroundings. The sun rose in the east and set in the west, but that wasn't much help at lunchtime when the sun would be directly overhead. Or would it? A moment's thought and Sherlock realized that the sun would only be truly overhead at noon for places actually on the equator. For a country in the northern hemisphere, like England, the nearest point on the equator would be located directly south, and so the sun at noon would be south of a point directly overhead. That was probably how Crowe was doing it.

"And moss tends to grow better on the northern side of trees," Crowe called over his shoulder. "It's more shaded there, and so it's damper."

"How do you do that?" Sherlock shouted.

"Do what?"

"Tell what people are thinking, and interrupt them just at the right moment?"

"Ah." Crowe laughed. "That's a trick I'll explain some other time."

Sherlock lost track of time as they walked on through the forest, but at one point Crowe stopped and crouched down putting the basket down.

"What do you deduce?" he asked.

Sherlock crouched beside him. In the soft ground beneath a tree he saw a hoofprint, small and heart-shaped.

"A deer went this way?" he ventured, trying to jump from what he saw to what he could work out based on what he saw.

"Indeed, but which way did it go and how old was it?"

Sherlock examined the print more closely, trying to picture a deer's hoof and failing.

"That way?" he said, pointing in the direction of the rounded part of the print.

"Other direction," Crowe corrected. "You're thinking of a horse's hoof, where the round bit is at the front. The sharp bit of a deer's hoof always points in the direction it is heading. And this one's a young 'un. You can tell by the small oval shapes behind the print. Those are made by the dewclaws."

He looked around. "See over there," he said, nodding his head to one side. "Can you make out a straight trail through the bushes and grass?"

Sherlock looked, and Crowe was right—there *was* a trail, very faint, marked by the bushes and grasses pushed to either side. It was about five inches across, he estimated.

"Deer move all day between the area they bed down in and their favourite watering hole, trying to find food," Crowe said, still crouching. "Once they find a safe route they keep usin' it until they get spooked by somethin'. And what does that tell you?"

"Prey tends to stick to the same habits unless disturbed?" Sherlock replied cautiously.

"Quite right. Remember that. If you're lookin' for a man who likes a drink, check the taverns. If you're lookin' for a man who likes a bet, check the racin' tracks. And everyone has to travel around somehow, so talk to cabbies and ticket inspectors—see if they remember your man."

He straightened, picking the basket up again, and started off through the trees. Sherlock followed, glancing around. Now that Crowe had pointed out what to look for, he could see sets of different tracks on the ground: some deer, of various sizes, and some obviously something else—maybe wild boar, maybe badgers, maybe foxes. He could also see trails through the underbrush, where the bushes and grasses had been pushed to the side by moving bodies. What had previously been invisible was suddenly obvious to him. The same scene now had so much more in it to look at.

It took another half an hour to reach the gates of Holmes Manor.

"I'll take my leave of you here," Crowe said. "Let's pick up again tomorrow. I've got some more to teach you about trackin' and huntin'."

"Do you want to come in for a time?" Sherlock asked. "I could get Cook to make a pot of tea, and one of the maids could gut and bone those fish for you."

"Mighty accomodatin' of you," Crowe rumbled. "I believe I will take advantage of that offer."

Together they walked up the gravelled drive towards the impressive frontage of Holmes Manor. This time Sherlock was in the lead.

Without knocking, he pushed open the front door.

"Mrs. Eglantine!" he called boldly.

A black shape detached itself from the shadows at the base of the stairs and slid forward.

"Young Master Sherlock," the housekeeper answered in her dry-as-autumn-leaves voice. "You seem to treat this house more like a hotel than the residence of your family."

"And you seem to treat it as if you are a member of that family rather than a servant," he retorted, voice cold but heart trembling. "Mr. Crowe will be taking afternoon tea with me. Please arrange it." He stood waiting, uncertain whether she would take his orders or dismiss him with a cutting word. He had a feeling that she wasn't sure either, but after a moment she turned and moved towards the kitchens without saying anything.

He felt a sudden and irresistible urge to push things a bit, to needle the woman who had done so much to make his life uncomfortable over the past year.

"Oh," he added, gesturing towards the wicker basket at Amyus Crowe's feet, "and Mr. Crowe has caught some fish. Be so good as to have someone gut them and bone them for him."

Mrs. Eglantine turned back, and the expression on

her face could have curdled milk and caused sheep to give birth prematurely. Her lips twisted as she attempted to force back something she was going to say. "Of course," she said finally, through gritted teeth. "I will send someone up for the basket. Perhaps you would be so good as to leave it here and repair to the reception room."

She seemed to melt back into the shadows.

"You should watch that woman," Amyus Crowe said quietly. "When she looks at you there is violence in her eyes."

"I don't understand why my aunt and uncle tolerate her presence," Sherlock replied. "It's not as if she's a particularly good housekeeper. The other staff are so terrified by her that they can barely do their jobs properly. The scullery maids keep dropping dishes when she's around, their hands shake so much."

"The subject would benefit from some further investigation," Crowe mused. "If, as you say, she's not a particularly good housekeeper then there must be some other compellin' reason why she's kept on, despite her vinegary personality. Perhaps your aunt and uncle are indebted to her, or to her family, in some manner, and this is a way of repayin' a debt. Or perhaps she's privy to some fact that your family would rather keep secret, and is blackmailin' herself into a cosy job."

"I think Mycroft knows," Sherlock said, remembering the letter his brother had sent him when he first arrived at Holmes Manor. "I think he warned me about her."

"Your brother knows a lot of things," Crowe said with a smile. "And the things he don't know generally ain't worth knowin' anyway."

"You taught him once, didn't you?" Sherlock asked.

Crowe nodded.

"Did you take him out fishing as well?"

A laugh burst through Crowe's usually calm expression. "Only the once," he admitted through chuckles. "Your brother an' the great outdoors ain't exactly on speakin' terms. It's the first time and the last time I've seen a man try to catch a fish by chasin' it into its natural environment."

"He dived in after a fish?" Sherlock said, trying to imagine the scene.

"He fell in, tryin' to reel it in. He told me, as I was haulin' him out, that he would never leave the safety of dry ground again, and if that dry ground was a paved city street then so much the better." He paused. "But if you ask him, he can still tell you the feedin' an' swimmin' habits of all the fish in Europe. He may have a dim view of physical exertion, but his mind is as sharp as a seamstress's bag of pins."

Sherlock laughed. "Let's go into the reception room," he said. "Tea will be on its way."

The reception room was just off the main hall, at the front of the house. Sherlock threw himself into a comfortable chair while Crowe settled himself on a sofa large enough to take his considerable bulk. It creaked beneath his weight. Amyus Crowe was, Sherlock estimated, probably as heavy as Mycroft Holmes, but in Crowe's case it was solid bone and muscle.

A soft knock on the door heralded the appearance of a maid carrying a silver tray. On the tray were a pot of tea, two cups and saucers, a small jug of milk, and a plate of cakes. Either Mrs. Eglantine was being unusually generous or one of the staff had decided to make the guest feel welcome.

There was also an envelope, white and narrow.

"A letter for you, sir," the maid said without making eye contact with Sherlock. She set the tray down on a table. "Will there be anything else?"

"No, thank you."

As she left he reached out eagerly to take the envelope. He didn't get many letters at Holmes Manor, and when he did they were almost always from—

"Mycroft!"

"Is that a fact or a deduction?" Crowe asked.

Sherlock waved the envelope at him. "I recognize the handwriting, and the postmark is Westminster, where he has his office, his lodgings, and his club."

He ripped the envelope open, pulling the flap from the grip of the blob of wax that held it firm.

"Look!" he said, holding the paper up. "The letter is written on the headed stationery of the Diogenes Club."

"Check the postmark on the envelope," Crowe murmured. "What time does it show?"

"Three-thirty yesterday afternoon," Sherlock said, puzzled. "Why?"

Crowe gazed imperturbably at Sherlock. "Mid-afternoon on a weekday, and he's at his club, writing letters, rather than at his office? Does that strike you as unusual behaviour for your brother?"

Sherlock thought for a moment. "He once told me that he often walks across to his club for lunch," he said after a moment. "He must have written the letter over lunch and got the footman to post it for him. The post would have been collected in the early afternoon, and the letter would have gotten to the sorting office for around three o'clock, then been stamped half an hour later. That's not suspicious, is it?"

Crowe smiled. "Not in the slightest. I was merely tryin' to indicate that there's a whole lot of facts that can be deduced from a simple letter. If the postmark had been Salisbury rather than Westminster it would have been unusual, and would have prompted further questions. If we knew your brother never left his desk durin' the day, not even for lunch—an unlikely occurrence, I have to admit—and yet the letterheaded stationery was from his club then that would have been unusual as well. You might have surmised that your brother had lost his job, or was sufficiently disturbed that he had not gone into work, or left early."

"Or maybe he'd just taken some stationery from the Diogenes Club and was using it in his office," Sherlock pointed out.

Crowe looked discomfited. "I guess there's always an alternative explanation," he growled.

Sherlock scanned the letter quickly, excitement growing as he read the words until he was almost at fever pitch.

My dear Sherlock,
I write in haste, as I am awaiting the arrival of a steak and kidney pudding and I wish to do it full justice before I return to my office.

I trust you are well, and that the various scars from your recent adventures have healed. I trust also that our aunt and uncle are well, and that our Mrs. Eglantine is not proving too unpleasant.

You will be pleased to hear, I am sure, that arrangements have been satisfactorily concluded to allow your education to continue at Holmes Manor. The news that you will never have to return to Deepdene School will, I presume, not come as too much of a shock.

Amyus Crowe will continue to school you in the more practical and sporting aspects of life and Uncle Sherrinford has agreed to become responsible for your religious and literary education, which only leaves mathematics. I will ponder on that, and let you know when I have reached a decision. The aim, of course, will be to prepare you for university in a few years' time. We can discuss at some stage whether you have a preference for Oxford or Cambridge.

This morning, by the way, a letter arrived from our father. He must have posted it in India the moment he arrived, as it summarizes everything that happened to him on the voyage. I am sure that you would rather read the letter than have me tell you about it, and so I invite you to dine with me (at my club, naturally) tomorrow.

Please pass the invitation on to Mr. Crowe: I have some details I wish to discuss with him about your education. The 9:30 a.m. train from Farnham will bring you to Waterloo in good time to meet me at 12 sharp.

I look forward to seeing you tomorrow, and to hearing all about the events that have befallen you since we last met.

Your loving brother,
Mycroft

"Anything interestin'?" Amyus Crowe asked.

"We're going to London," Sherlock replied, grinning.